THE ONE
WHO SHOWS
THE WAY

THE ONE WHO SHOWS THE WAY

Evolving Humanity From Psycho-logical To Psycho-spiritual Living

BILLY GRANT

Print information available on the last page.

Rev. date: 06/01/2017

To order additional copies of this book, contact:
Xlibris
800-056-3182
www.Xlibrispublishing.co.uk
Orders@Xlibrispublishing.co.uk
755324

Acknowledgements

I just want to take this moment to acknowledge and say thank you to all of those that have been on this 12 year journey with me. My trainers and my colleagues, as well my clients; from whom I have learnt just as much. But mostly I want to acknowledge and thank my wife and family for enduring the different me's that I have been over the past years, and the ones that I have yet to become. And finally I want to acknowledge Vicki, a very special little girl who made a big impact and touched so many lives; setting an example to us all.

Introduction

I woke up this morning, 27 October; six weeks into writing this book, and as usual soon began formulating thoughts about how my day would unfold; it was a Thursday so I knew I would be able to spend most of the day working on the book. I was excited again after having lost my thread a couple of days ago, and I began to notice that something was wrong because I had lost the joy and enthusiasm, and because I was in my head, having to slog away at it to get it to work.

That last sentence reveals the disconnect of how most of us are living nowadays, and also reveals where humanity has ended up at, in its own collective developmental process. It is then also a microcosm for the rest of this book by demonstrating that life works best when we are in our joy and following the guidance that is there for us. Unfortunately we have become lost due to being disconnected from that guidance, but the good news is that we can find our way back, by realising what is happening and reconnecting to it.

As soon as I became present and noticed what I was doing, I dropped the whole thing and got back to what felt better and more joyful. I couldn't convince myself that the right thing to do was to continue, when it was all such a struggle, and I was not feeling inspired. It had become too teachy and heady and disconnected from the rest of me, and from what felt right. This is what I call being in my Tree of Knowledge, TOK, where life becomes a bit flat or dead or heady and I am only connected to what is going on in my own mind; I am not feeling anything, and there is no life or vitality in it.

Sometimes, it feels right to stay with a disturbance, and sometimes it doesn't, so learning to discern when to move and when to stay is a skill that develops with practice. In general, you get to know within your body which one feels like the right direction. An embodied joy and relief may come from leaving the disturbance, or it may not; you may still be curious and intrigued and just know that you are meant to stay with it. This is where we have the capacity to learn a way of discerning *truth* and *life* within our self. It is actually worth making any decision rather than none, because then your guidance can respond and give you more feedback.

So I was now back on track and ready to review the Psychosynthesis chapter before moving on. But that's not how it went. When I sat down and began merging back into the book, I could still feel something uncomfortable and unsettling within my body. It was nauseous and squirming around in me like when I am building up to being sick. The discomfort was quite disturbing, and so once again, I moved towards more joy by moving away from the discomfort and into a different chapter. When I checked it out within me, I didn't feel the need to stop doing the book; I just needed to do something different. The feelings in my inner body were steering me somewhere, and I was able to follow by remaining present to them. As a Heart Intelligence practitioner we work with two basic questions: 'What's moving?' and then Given that, 'what do we want?' seeing that our disturbances are part of the holistic guidance of life.

Heart intelligence (or Heart IQ, as a brand name,) is the method of approach developed by Christian Pankhurst to serve the same thing that this book is about: understanding and assisting our journey through life, so as to serve us all individually and serve humanity and the world collectively. This disturbance was validated by the small relief that I felt when I came out of the Psychosynthesis chapter and ended up back at the Contents page. I sat there, half-vacant, looking at the Contents page and feeling into my body, wondering what this was all about? Why had I ended up back here, but nonetheless feeling better? Then suddenly, I received the pop-up, (as we say in Heart Intelligence when we get out of the way and let the guidance get through); this pop-up was an intuitive knowing from somewhere that I needed to restructure things yet again. The Contents page was no longer in resonance with where most of the latest writing had gone and with how things had evolved. Something separate from my normal everyday consciousness knew that I was at a point in the formulation of the book where I now needed to be getting a more solid overarching context of what the book was eventually trying to be about and what it was trying to do. There was a miss-truth within the collective being of the book. Something was now incongruent with another part of itself, and there was defilement in me, alerting me to this reality. It was communicating with me through how I felt in my body. It was like some kind of higher knowing of truth that has this way of guiding me when I align with it, and it was alive and vital. I was in a relationship with it, as I followed the subtleties of what was moving within me. This had been an ongoing process as the book was evolving and I was back here again after a couple of days of moving forward.

So staying in the discomfort this time, now that I was sensing that my truth of being was to stay with this discomfort rather than leave, it spat out this and that and the other offerings as it groped its way towards what felt right and what clunked into gear. That clunk was a set of chapter headings that revealed the broader story all on their own and could inform readers of exactly what the book was about right from the start, so readers now had a container to hold them throughout the book's further differentiation. This is actually similar to human development, in that we have a body right from the start and then begin filling out the other aspects of who and what we are within it, as we gradually awaken unto ourselves. The chapter headings could now show a common theme of breakdown as a precursor to breakthrough and reformation and could demonstrate how this is happening at every level in ourselves and in society.

Now I felt much better. I could feel such a relief and joy again. Something had facilitated me into what felt better than where I was at. Something that seemed outside of me, yet could also guide me through how I felt on the inside when I paid enough attention and followed its lead.

Heart intelligence is about following our joy, and this is what I was doing; did I feel immediately better with the first decision to move? Yes, and then with the second? Yes, and then with the third decision of not moving? Yes, even though there was something missing, and it was a bit uncomfortable to stay there, my feel or read for the space was to stay, because I could sense that it was wrong to move and that something was trying to happen here.

Now I had what I needed in order to reshuffle things around: a body, a container, something to hold me again in joy and allow more growth to unfold and awaken unto itself. I felt great and re-energised and started changing the Contents page to suit. Then I suddenly realised that I had to break things down even further; I now had to separate my initial moment of starting to write the book from my midlife crisis stuff, and give them their own chapters. That meant changing the Prelude to an Introduction, for some reason. Everything was taking off at speed again now that it was pointing in the right direction, and it was restructuring itself to find its new place in this new level of development. I realised that I still hadn't restructured the second half of the books chapters, so off I went and did that so that they could demonstrate my chronological journey so far in my own ongoing breakdown and reformation journey through life; my ongoing psychosynthesis.

The reformed Contents page now didn't just show the microcosmic and macrocosmic nature of reality, by showing the common theme between all these levels of breakdown, breakthrough, and reformation. It also showed the constant psychosynthesis, or constant self-adaptive process going on, a constantly ongoing fluxing which functions holistically to serve our survival as well as our constant aim of awakening and evolution towards self-fulfilment.

But there was even more. This reformed Contents page could now also show the path of guidance that I unconsciously followed in my journey back out of breakdown, with the intention of demonstrating how that same path could be required for the church and humanity to follow in this present time of breakdown and Reformation, (the word *church* being used here to mean a body of people connected to the abundant source of life and following their higher holistic guidance as I have just demonstrated, rather than be unconsciously and ignorantly squabbling and fighting, due to being in disconnect from it).

This above opening paragraph is an example of how we can live a life that is guided by spirit, rather than live a life in disconnect from source and spiritual guidance. This is also then an example of what this book aims to demonstrate: One, that our lives are constantly being holistically guided at a level beyond our everyday consciousness. Two, that we have become conditioned into following our own minds and what they tell us, instead of being in the flow of that guidance where life feels more real, alive, and vibrant. Three, that this is essentially what God was saying to Adam in the Garden of Eden when he told Adam to eat of the tree of life, TOL, and not of the tree of knowledge, TOK.

So in general, the book aims to demonstrate how we are constantly being facilitated in every moment between self-survival and self-fulfilment by something beyond our general level of realisation and consciousness; this being the ongoing fluxing or psychosynthesis of life. One of the main offerings of this book, is that we have the ability to realise that this is happening and let ourselves be led by it. In addition to this, and more generally, the book is essentially evidencing this same thing happening to me as I attempt to synthesise conflicting perceptions of Christianity within myself and also get it to integrate with my Psychosynthesis and Heart Intelligence training. At an even larger level above and beyond that, the book is also showing through my own ongoing life story, a constant journey of awakening, at the same time as revealing the same dynamics and objective at play in our society and religious institutions, as well as other systems such as education, law, health services, and politics etc.

In fact, we can take the same dynamics right down to the atomic level and show them at play in nuclear fission and nuclear fusion. Nuclear fission is the division of one atom into two, and nuclear fusion is the combination of two lighter atoms into one larger one; so even nuclear fission and nuclear fusion can be seen to be about breakdown and reformation, with great amounts of energy being released in the process. Then jumping back to the opposite end of the scale again, nuclear fusion is what brings stars into existence and keeps them alive; gravity always wrestling with nuclear fusion.

My hope for this book is that it can keep going and that I don't get in its way too much, so that this Holy Spirit or holistic guidance can evidence itself to the reader. In fact, as I write that, I wonder what the difference is between that and a prayer. After all, what is a prayer if it is not an authentic longing and calling from our truth to a higher power or dimension for something holistic to happen in service of all? I also hope that the readers of this book are then encouraged to read further into all I introduce in this book. For instance, I urge you to take up practicing Heart Intelligence, because Heart Intelligence is all about learning to discern and follow your heart's truth, rather than continue to be run by your unconscious childhood conditioning. Heart intelligence is mostly done in group settings, or circles as we call them, so that we can actually practice it for real and change back from the psychological way we had become to survive childhood. This group approach makes it easier for us all to progress as we advance the whole group society at the same time and don't have to struggle so hard on our own against our usual environment. I encourage you to read Watchman Nee, as it was his writings that gave me further insight into the teachings of Jesus and opened me to seeing Christianity completely differently from what I see going on in the world. Psychosynthesis will give you an excellent way to understand the psychology of how we function and the psychospiritual dynamics of life and human development. This helps us to understand how we are caught up in a space of seeking both self-survival and self-fulfilment and how we initially take the form required to manage childhood, before adapting back towards our true form as we become more secure in later life. This in my opinion is the real religious process that we go through in life whether we call ourselves religious or not. Celtic Christianity is then also very important because it brings the abundance and celebration of life back into Christianity, seeing us as essentially pure and good and simply disconnected from both our divine higher spirit and sacred earthly nature (quite a different picture from the regular scriptural everyday Roman Christianity that is active in our churches, offering us only a partial view).

Part 1 of the book introduces you to the fact that our lives, families, communities, businesses, society, and even humanity are always in constant breakdown and reformation, always seeking to survive whilst also seeking to function at their highest form, but even more urgently evidencing that we are in a great breakdown phase at this time in the evolution of humanity. Showing you this will hopefully help you to see the psychospiritual dynamics of life at play.

Part 2 of the book starts by introducing you to the writings of the great but little-known Christian seer, Watchman Nee. Watchman's teachings offer us a fresh and profound understanding of Jesus and the Bible; helping us to understand the guidance of Spirit. This is followed by a broader and deeper look at the teachings of Jesus, before introducing you to Celtic Christianity; a more alive and vibrant, creation-based Christianity that sees the divine in all of life and sees us as all equally begotten of God or the great source of creation. This is a side of Christianity that was outcast seventeen hundred years ago in favour of our present-day Roman Christianity, a Christianity that is more preoccupied with scripture and sin and salvation. These three chapters will perhaps reveal something as new to you as it was to me, so that you can get a sense of my dilemma and also consider the difference between how life is and how it is meant to be.

Part 3 of the book then offers you an introduction to Psychosynthesis and Heart Intelligence to add to what was given in Part 1 and 2, so as to reveal what can help us progress from the disconnected way that we are living, to the connected way that we are supposed to be living. Psychosynthesis and Heart Intelligence being the two main trainings that changed my life, and I believe can change yours too.

Part 4 of the book will then be my conclusion of where I am at after writing the book, with particular regard to my Christianity clash and looking at what I may have resolved or learned along the way. This may then give me a chance to understand why I am trying to resolve my disturbance by writing a book, as this has never happened to me before, and was not planned.

This has been a difficult and long journey for me, but it can be shortened greatly for others, especially at a time when everything is in breakdown and needs to move forward into the new, rather than regress back to the old. This being what frequently happens in crisis, and is what our so-called leaders are ignorantly trying to do.

At this point and before going into any of the specific chapters, I just want to make it clear that I do not speak for any of these organisations or businesses etc. or represent any of them. Some are very new to me, and I simply offer whatever comes out of me in the moment, whether it is accurate in anyone else's eyes or not. The essential point of this book being that it is the spirit of our actions that matters most, not the right and wrong of it. I mostly want to stay present to whatever comes out of me, trusting that it is guided and in the form that serves me at this time. I am also sure that all of the chapters will overlap with all of the teachings that I have received, and so we will have them all interwoven throughout every chapter, just as they are mixed throughout this introduction. You will probably find some spelling and sentences a bit odd, but that is deliberate.

In joy and suffering, we become transformed.
Enjoy and be transformed.

Today is 27 November, and here we are yet again. It is always the same pattern; two steps forward and one step back again. Every time I complete a new chapter, the book reconsiders itself and updates its sense of who it is in its self-identity and purpose.

Now that I have started to write the Celtic Christianity chapter, I am back upgrading the Contents page once again. This has been happening continually and always brings the container back into line with the most recent developments. It always releases a new and higher realisation of self-awareness and greater purpose. It is almost like a building checking out and restructuring its own foundations every time it gets a little taller. This of course also self-evidences what I am writing about. At this current moment of reorganising, the book is breaking itself down and reforming itself into four main parts. These parts have then reordered themselves through using how I feel in my body, to firstly show you the common theme of breakdown and reformation at every level in our lives and society, particularly in relation to the critically difficult position that humanity finds itself in at this present time.

Part 3, now also includes the knowledge, tools, and skills that show my twelve-year journey out of my own midlife crisis and that could assist us to make the transition that is trying to happen at a larger level. This is followed finally by a summary of where I am now within myself and with my particular Christianity dilemma, as I conclude the book. The difficulty that this higher order reframe brings me, is that I now have to go through the whole book again and adjust it to refit this new revelation; and on and on it goes until the book has fully self-realised itself, just as we are doing in life.

My invitation, as you read the book, is to stay present to your self and what you are feeling as you read it.

PART 1

How it Works and Where We Are At

What if you were suddenly given a deeper insight
into the awe and wonder of life to see and feel how
amazing life really is?

B ecause that is what happened to me twelve years ago, and is
what I want to do for you over the course of this book. I want to
show you something amazing that's changed my life, something that
makes life come alive and feel exciting again. I want to show you
a way of living that invites us to function consciously from guidance
rather than unconsciously in disconnect, because that is what we are
meant to be doing. All the materials are just sitting there waiting for
us to pick them up. Our world and humanity is in crisis in all sorts of
ways because we are disconnected from our source, and that source
is trying to communicate with us all of the time. All we have to do is
learn how it works.

Since the start of my midlife crisis twelve years ago, I have slowly but
surely been progressing my way forward by following a guidance
that has led me to study this and learn about that. And during all of
that time, I was gradually filling out a fuller understanding of what I

was initially introduced to and overwhelmed by during the best and worst moments of my initial breakdown.

This first part of the book aims to help you see how life works from a psychospiritual context, and let you see what is going on at present from a developmental perspective. It reveals experiences encountered by myself over the past twelve years and how I have been guided to the point of writing this book.

More specifically, Part 1 is about introducing you to the nature of our organic and spiritual reality, in the context of breakdown, breakthrough, and reformation. It is about how everything is always in a constant state of psychosynthesis or fluxing between self-survival and self-fulfilment. It shows this in several ways through several chapters, including, present moment demonstrations and revelations, my example of this process over the course of a day, and my ongoing midlife crisis. I also then go on to show how I see the church in breakdown, seeking breakthrough and reformation, and how our society and its sub-components, as well as our collective humanity, is in the same state due to being out of touch with its source and holistic guidance. Humanity is now left with no vision or sense of any greater or collective purpose by having been unconsciously guided to abandon a religion that was immature and corrupt and functioning at more of an egoic level than a spiritual one, leaving us in a present-day birth canal waiting for the new womb to reveal itself. This part of the book also looks at society and education and the masculine suppression of the feminine, as well as the more recent rise of the feminine and softening of the masculine, and the chaotic effect that that is having in today's more recent society.

CHAPTER 1

Today's Breakdown and Reformation

I just want to start by saying that this was actually the very first moments of this book starting to come into existence.

Spontaneous Manifestation

Today, 20 September 2016, I woke up and just started writing. My youngest daughter is up from London for a few days, and my two eldest granddaughters are here for the week as their mum and dad have finally managed to take their overdue honeymoon. Between them and my wife and our foster daughter all vying for space in the kitchen, I've slipped off to the office to check my e-mails, and suddenly started writing some ramblings of what could gradually turn into a book. The book, or outpouring, as it feels, seems to be starting from some place deep within me, a place that seems to feel relieved as it manifests itself out into the world because I have no resistance or need to stop it. I am really just escaping the noise of the kitchen and not really that bothered about what happens in this time. There has been lots of busy activity within me though, about life and what it's all about, and especially a clashing of two different experiences of Christianity.

The thought crosses my mind. *Perhaps this is how creation happens and continues to happen, something just comes into form out of pressure on one side of reality and little resistance on the other.*

After that initial outpouring, all the stuff that I have been learning about began to differentiate itself into chapters, which then randomly began to gain subsections and sporadic bits of content. It created for itself several chapter headings in seconds and jumped all over the place back and forwards, filing bits of ideas into each. It occasionally shuffled things around that didn't quite land in the right place until an embodied knowing within me felt better when it was in the right place.

During all of this, a centre of conscious awareness seemed to be watching and was still wondering what was happening, as it reflected that it still hadn't checked its e-mails and had no intention of writing a book. Now as all this happened, yet a third level of conscious awareness could track that this prior observer was amused and curious about what was going on. It became aware of my face taking on the expression of a curious dog trying to figure something out. It was trying to understand something, and it was just watching to see what happened till the energy and ideas dried up. *After all, the kitchen was still busy anyway,* seemed to be its attitude.

Self-Survival versus Self-Expression: The Price of Being Your Truth

21 September. Later yesterday afternoon, I was visiting St Salvator's chapel on North Street in St Andrews with my daughter and wife, as my daughter and her fiancé are considering it for their wedding. St Salvator's, I later discovered, was named such after Jesus, the Holy Saviour. It was the middle of the afternoon as we casually exited the university's beautiful quadrangle at the North Street entrance, and for one of those weird, time-stands-still moments, we stood looking at the initials PH formed into the pavement in cobbles

beneath the square bell tower, beside the fifteenth-century chapel. The initials stand for Patrick Hamilton, a twenty-four-year-old Protestant who was burned at the stake right there. He was burned in 1528 for promoting Protestantism. As I stood there subconsciously feeling into the reality of his ordeal, I dissolved into myself, and as St Andrews and life disappeared, I was inside a part of me that was fearfully contemplating how best to pitch this book, especially given the message that I feared it may be seeking to express, a message about my own difficulties with Christianity, and especially in light of what I learned through Watchman Nee, a Chinese Christian seer of divine revelation from the last century. Then, just as spontaneously and as if in contrast, I felt myself being taken over by a sudden empowerment and strength of conviction, confirming and empowering me to be my own truth and stand fast in what I want to say (Stand fast being my surname's coat of arms motto). So firstly, I had felt something trying to protect me, and then secondly, I felt something was trying to empower me to be my truth.

Our Lost Connection to Source

A few minutes ago I got up from the laptop and wandered through the living room for a break and to see what the others were up to. I began a random conversation with my daughter about what she was watching on TV, and in the empty vastness of mind, a realisation popped up, informing me that I seem to be writing this book implicitly rather than from a conscious explicit desire to write about something. After yesterday's download about this unusual inner event within me; of how I just started writing a book and then about what happened at St Andrews, I thought that I had a sense of what the book was going to be about and what form it would take. I sensed that it would be about different approaches to the same thing; how humanity has become lost and directionless because we are so disconnected from our source energy: love. I would explain how we did this when we threw the baby out with the bathwater, in other words, when we threw out our spiritual connection to the divine source when we threw out God and Christianity. I would explain how this throwing out happened because we felt angry and hurt and betrayed by the behaviours of those who claim to be closest to that source, and in whom we trusted to lead us. But then in fairness to them, I would also go on to explain how through my own recent learning, I could now see that these leaders were unconsciously up against their own distorted development, and that they had also been given a limited understanding of life and religion and what Jesus and Christianity was actually teaching.

My Psychosynthesis chapter would show the whole thing from a psychospiritual context, both our investment into following a distorted leadership, and then our abandonment situation due to being let down and betrayed by it. To add to this; I would show the same psychospiritual dynamics being at play by other leaders and organisations in our societies. I would go on to share my recent learning about the suppression of Celtic Christianity and show the negative effect that that has had as we removed the feminine from playing its role. And then finally how all of this knowledge, brought together with the addition of what Heart Intelligence can offer us, can be used to set us back on the right track. I would go on to explain how most of us are now running around unconsciously provoking each other to get our love needs met, or alternatively being kind to each other to get the same love needs met. Both of these are unconscious compensations due to that disconnect from source, and both are a less healthy and pure way of trying to get to a place in ourselves that feels good.

Yet curiously, I seem to be writing a live account of what's happening to me, as something else uses me to covertly work something out; this covert composer makes full use of my conscious awareness and willingness to just write what's happening. It's like being taken over by some higher being and watching it write a book through me, an allowing of life to unfold and happen in its own way through me, rather than it be unconsciously inhibited by my resistances such as thoughts, opinions, needs, fears, and desires. As I pause right now, I realise that it actually feels okay, weird and unfamiliar, but okay. Life feels free and easy this way, compared to thinking about everything all the time.

As I look back at what I have just written, I suddenly realise that perhaps Christianity is actually going through its own religious developmental process, just the same as we do: its own midlife crisis. This would imply that it started out pure before having to adapt into a psychological functioning organism in its earlier life, before its realignment and religious return in adulthood. Perhaps this demise and falling apart of Christianity is the early breakdown phase before its twenty-first-century reformation and the second coming of Jesus: not Jesus as an individual person, as many believe or hope, but as an understanding of how to live. A second coming of more divine wisdom being amongst us as we awaken to this next level of human development. Perhaps the church should stop trying to get itself back to where it was (just as we see happening with people in midlife crisis, as well as in politics), in an act of unconscious resistance and ignorance and with this insight, help itself to evolve into its new form. *Did I really just write that?* Flashes through my mind as I feel the weight and significance of what I have just written.

From Chaos to Order

Nonetheless, this is definitely beginning to solidify and feel like what this book is going to be about: my struggle to integrate everyday Christianity with what I have learned from Watchman Nee about the Bible and Jesus, whilst trying to get it to fit with everything else I have learned. I can now anticipate myself using what I have learned from my Psychosynthesis and Heart Intelligence training, and my recent discovery of the differences between Celtic and Roman Christianity, to move forward from here. Suddenly, I can see how they have all played their part in getting me to this point, by meeting my different developmental needs along the way. For the past twelve years, I have wondered when I was going to feel like I used to feel, before this disturbance and questioning all began. This was back when I felt focussed and centred and on my purpose, building up my joiner and builder business before it all started to change. *This could be it. This could be what it was all for; for me to write a book.* excitedly flashes across my mind in excitement.

Something Save Me from Myself

Actually, as I wrote that, my heart sank at everything I had been through over the past twelve years. Was it only for a book? *You must be joking,* is reverberating around in my head right now, and I feel quite deflated. I was just getting excited about having figured out what was happening, but now, I feel flat as a pancake. In fact, there is now actually a part of me that is beginning to get angry at the thought of all of this. *All of this for a bloody book,* it's screaming. *You must be having a bleeping laugh.* But as I sit with this simmering away inside me and slowly get used to it in my body, I shake my head and move towards resentful, surrendering acceptance. Then, as I gradually get used to the idea and adapt to this new realisation, I begin to feel thankful, because I have made the mistake of getting too inflated in my ego before. This happened when my ego was taking the credit for something that was not of its doing. On that occasion, I came crashing back to earth massively, when my nemesis caught up with me. In fact, this was the straw that finally broke the camel's back and slammed me to the ground in pieces, twelve years ago.

What on earth am I supposed to do with this now? I just got to a point where I thought I knew what I was going to write about, and now this! Straight back in the soup bowl; this is too hard. More stuff to muddy the waters. No sooner do I get to my knees, and I am pushed back down again. *So what do you want me to do now? Write a book about my breakdown, or write a book about where I am at right now? I can't do both,* I internally call out in desperation.

The answer that slowly arises from an embodied place of knowing and truth within me, is that this other stuff was for another day, and in that moment of being present to myself and my body, my body relaxes, and I experienced relief. The offering feels right; it doesn't feel like avoidance. It feels clean and true within me and doesn't leave me disturbed, just relieved.

So back to where I was before all that. In fact!, that little derailment was another example of the same thing, some energy that's still trapped in disturbing memories, wrestling to get back to its natural peaceful and uncompressed state: a part of me that wants to express its self (express its self meaning that this part wants to reveal its trapped truth about how painful and difficult my midlife crisis was for it; the turning point in my life that has led me to here). So now I can at least feel love and compassion for that part, as these were very difficult times. I could even go into coaching it by asking it what it wants right now. In fact, just in writing that, I can feel it wanting recognition and acceptance for what it went through. I can feel it just wanting to be acknowledged and felt, wanting to be held and feel understood. Like a distressed child, it just wants five minutes of my time, and it will be okay.

As I sit with it, allowing it to be felt in the present moment by my conscious self, I notice I am picking at my thumbnail with my finger; another part of me wants to mentally move away, but I stay with it and continue to feel it like a hunger pain in my solar plexus. As I stay here with it, holding it gently in love and understanding, it begins to ease and release some trapped energy, and I know that I can move on again, this part having gained some therapy and love and also having now realised that it is a vital part in what this book has to offer and how its suffering was for a higher purpose. As is always the case once we understand how life works.

So now as I write from a slightly tired and more soulful place, I think I was about to say. If I can bring twelve years of learning together and continue to be led by the higher guidance that is here, then hopefully I can reach some resolution in myself whilst also demonstrating to you the higher guidance that is at work in our lives. In Psychosynthesis, we call it the higher Self, but is that actually the same thing as the Holy Spirit in Christianity? If I can manage to integrate all of this stuff that I have been learning for all these years, then hopefully I can reveal the great picture of what I see going on as our souls, individually, and humanity, collectively, journey through our sacred and purposeful life.

Everything Is an Act of Love

This great picture that I refer to is that I now see love being ultimately at the centre of every act. It is either pushing its way back from some suppressed place within our psyche, trying to get back to its natural state. Or alternatively, when it is not being suppressed, it is graciously being given from an open heart that feels safe and abundant enough to give it away, knowing that it is its own divine and sacred source. The love that we essentially are, then, endlessly replenishes itself by reconnecting in presence and grace to the beauty and splendour of its own existence. We do this by consciously connecting straight to the awe and wonder of life itself or by consciously connecting to it through the knowing that children, song, dance, nature, food, animals, or other people are love in another form. It doesn't really matter, as long as we are doing it from love and not lack of love. We can take from where there is plenty and give to where it is lacking. Everything is essentially love, either feeling safe enough to express itself or feeling inhibited from doing and being that, due to psychological insecurity.

This is the kingdom of heaven; being connected to source instead of being disconnected from it and living in ignorance and fear and compression, fighting to get back to abundant expression. I believe that all of our behaviour comes from our unconscious need to express that joyous abundance that is love and life and beauty and truth; it is our essential nature. Perhaps this is what Jesus meant when He said, I am the way and the truth, and the life, and nobody comes to the father but by me. In other words he was saying that He was love. Our heart's intelligence, wisdom, and truth is always guiding us towards feeling joy by feeling safe enough to express our truth.

Unfortunately, however, due to the lack of psychospiritual wisdom in our society, and the lack of any sense of higher purpose or vision, we are left with no impetus to help us work at being able to be our purer self. This is where my understandings of Jesus' teachings adds to my other skills, tools, and learning because that is what I believe Jesus stands to give us most: loving masculine direction and guidance. I can often see love coming forward tainted by our mental and emotional and psychological baggage, due to our pathology, lack of education, and disconnection from source.

The Reason Why We Need to Move the
Whole Environment Together

This disconnect from source and lack of wisdom that I talk about is what leaves us all squabbling around, unconsciously taking whatever energy or lift we can get from each other. Alternatively, we get some relief and temporary joy through less healthy relationships such as drugs or alcohol, or perhaps it's work, or losing ourselves into a good book: anything that brings us some joy through escape, relief, avoidance, or unconsciousness. For many people these days, that relationship comes through their mobile phones or iPad's or television. So as you can see, we are always finding our way back to joy by one means or another, either by healthy connection to source or by getting one over on each other, or perhaps by exploding back out of compression at someone, or by using some other means. In many cases, we get our need to feel better, met through our attachment to our material goods, such as our house or our car or feeling wealthy or having high status among our peers or society.

So if we take all of this into consideration and can see that it is actually the effect of our environment on us, good and bad, then we can begin to see the need to move the whole environment at the same time. I can also see the same need to move the whole environment at once when I look at what often goes on in schools, teachers doing emotional development with children that gets undone because the parents are emotionally immature. Energy always tends to fall to the level that it can sustain if the vibration being asked of it is too high.

The Tree of Life and the Tree of Knowledge

I suddenly remember (or am reminded of) Watchman Nee's explanation of God's instruction to Adam in the Garden of Eden. God said something like, you may eat of any tree in the garden but not of the tree of knowledge of good and evil, for on that day you shall die, a teaching that I have learned is very true. I feel alive when I am talking with some people but numb and disconnected with others, with no real life in the space, no juice as Christian Pankhurst calls it. It doesn't matter whether we are in joy and happiness, or in pain and suffering as we chat; I still feel the connection of life and living waters between us. But when we engage in meaningless conversation or whinge on about what's wrong in the world, I feel dead, disconnected, and see the same in others too. In the tree of life, TOL, I can feel my connection to people and feel my spirit amen them, enjoying the gift of their existence. I can feel my defences relaxing and my heart opening to them as my sense of safety increases in their presence. But in the tree of knowledge, TOK, I can only feel the spirit of life becoming defiled inside me or feel heavy, untouched, and flat. We need to track ourselves to feel if we come alive in each other's presence, or fall into death in each moment that we chat?

Summary

So it now looks like I'm going to write some kind of autobiography involving some present moment realisations as I go along, as well as including bits of my journey and training to date. This is in an effort to help me integrate my conflicting perceptions of Christianity as well as integrate that with my other learning and realisations. It looks like this is going to show that there is a source of, and purpose to, our existence. Its interactive guidance facilitates us along that path despite our disconnect from it, because we threw it out with a flawed version of truth. This guidance that is nurturing and guiding this book into manifestation also wants to show us how poorly we are living as a consequence of that partially flawed act and how we can turn it around again.

As an end to this chapter, I invite you to reflect back and evidence for yourself that you can actually witness the guidance that has functioned within this chapter, a guidance that has been exposed within my moment-by-moment examples as well as by my collective example over the full day of disturbance, breakdown, and breakthrough.

I am love, and I am alive; and all I need is safety to express myself.

I think that the words to "I Will Survive," written by Dino Fekaris and Frederick J. Perren, speak to all of this quite well; the song is about how we get our love needs met in less pure ways and suffer the consequence. Yet somehow, we find the inner resource to carry on from somewhere, dealing with betrayal and loss and abandonment and blame and all sorts of psychological stuff because we haven't quite got it right.

As long as I know how to love, I know I'll stay alive.
I've got all my life to live,
and I've got all my love to give, and I'll survive.
I will survive, hey, hey.

CHAPTER 2

My Midlife Crisis Seen as a Breakdown and Reformation

Different Paths Serving Different Needs at Different Times

Just over a year ago, I started going to church. I tried this one and that one in several different towns, but none of them really met whatever it was I was looking for. Something was still missing in my life, even after twelve years of study and growth and understanding of what goes on as we journey through life. I didn't really lack for much in a materialistic sense, but something more important was missing in some other way. Prior to that, I had spent a year or so attending St Andrews Quakers as well as going round other meeting houses, but that didn't seem to quite hit what I was looking for, either. Yes, I definitely gained something from it, but it wasn't fully hitting the bull's eye; some inner truth or knowing place in me wasn't being met. A few years prior to that, I had done the Alpha course, done levels 1 and 2 reiki, tried Buddhism (which I found a bit too removed), read bits of the Bhagavad Gita, and did several other things, such as a nine-day intensive esoteric retreat at Beshara in the Scottish borders.

This mostly involved studying poetry and teachings of Muhyiddin Ibn Arabi and Jalaluddin Rumi, both great spiritual teachers. As well as learning a little about Islamic spirituality and the Sufi path of love. I gained a lot from these nine days, especially one particular peak experience of dissolving into the oneness with everything as I stood outside in the garden. My psyche was very porous, and because we were spending so much time in connection to the divine love and awe and wonder of creation, I just dissolved in a solitary moment and blended into oneness with everything. I remember feeling this oneness and inwardly realising, *Oh my God, this is all mine; it's all me.* The voice didn't mean this to the exclusion of anyone else, but rather with the realisation that everyone else could do the exact same thing. Then I suddenly shifted and heard a distraught voice within myself saying, *Oh my God! Look what we're doing to it.* That was just one of many peak experiences that I had at this difficult time of disturbance and awakening, as I slowly progressed further into understanding how love was all that was really needed and all that was really going on. But somehow, I still had to go on a longer journey to get the rest of what I was looking for, particularly a return to being able to function in the world again.

I also took a little from reading the Bhagavad Gita in these early times of disturbance, but I actually gained a lot more after starting my Psychosynthesis training. I could then relate Arjuna's journey to the journey that we all take through life; coming into life as the pure non-conscious self and having to hand over our sovereignty to the ego so as to survive, before maturing and fighting to get it back with the help of our higher Self. For me, the Bhagavad Gita is easier to understand and more helpful in relation to life than trying to make sense of the Bible. The metaphor in Arjuna's case, is that his father dies when he is a child and so his uncle rules the empire until he becomes of age. But when he tries to reclaim what is rightfully his there is a great battle; this situation being a metaphor for the journey of our self through life. Arjuna wins this battle because he turns to his God to drive his chariot, (to steer his way) rather than choose the greater sized army.

The Difference that Confidence and Purpose Makes

Those few years of being lost and searching for something was a new experience to me, as I had always been quite a confident and focussed person. I had followed the typical route of the time: stick in at school, get a job, get a trade, get a career, get the wife, get the house, get the mortgage, get the kids, get the pension, get the life insurance, get a promotion, get my own business. There was always something else to get every time I looked up to see where I was at in life. I always had a sense of somewhere next that I was trying to get to, I always had some sense of direction and purpose. In my subconscious vision, it probably looked a bit like having the nice house in the country with the two cars in the drive, the kids, and the decent holidays with some money in the bank for a rainy day, with the pension in the background for future security. But then on this occasion of glancing up to see where I was at and see what was next, there was no obvious sign of what was next. I didn't want a bigger business because I had seen what it does to people as they become slaves to it; they suddenly end up working for a machine and are not so happy anymore. But I couldn't be finished! Surely there had to be something more to life that this?

This was the start of it: genuine seek and ye shall find, but not out of a light-hearted curiosity; it was more out of an existential need to make sense of why there wasn't just another thing to get. Why had the game just stopped and left me in limbo, wondering which direction to take next?

I was in a place that I had never been before. I was lost and having to find my own way forward from here. I had always been a fairly confident person, even from the age of about ten when we moved school, as we had moved to the country, and I could swing about in trees and hunt for bird's eggs and mess about with bicycles, creating all sorts of weird and wonderful contraptions. I put suspension on my bicycle years before it happened in the public domain. I was the oldest of the half a dozen kids that I played with in my hamlet. My dad would let me do alterations to the house from the time I could swing a hammer, and I built my own bedroom in the garage when I was about sixteen. I did all the trades from start to finish, and he just let me get on with it, electrocuting myself several times because I didn't turn the electricity off first. I didn't realise it at the time, but this was of major significance in my growing up at this time. I had been out working with him since I was about twelve, concreting house foundations and tiling roofs and installing drains. I was a teenager who could do almost any sport and had the body of a young man at an early age. We used to load three tonne of sand onto the lorry with shovels, without stopping even once for a rest. We could outwork anybody.

It is actually quite emotional writing this, as I can now see the value of what my father was able to give me, especially compared to the horror stories that I hear about other fathers. I can even remember a pivotal rite of passage when I was about fifteen. I had been converting an outbuilding to use for fixing motorbikes and was wiring up the lighting one winter night. I went into the house to ask my dad if he could come and hold the torch for me, just as I had done for him for many years. He came out with me, and after I explained where I was at, he reached for the screwdriver and said, "Okay, here, hold the torch."

I pulled the screwdriver back and said, "No, you hold the torch. I'm doing this."

After an awkward moment, he took the torch, and I wired up the switch. It was one of those moments in time where things change in an instant. It was like I became an equal in some ways. But how many teenagers get this opportunity, especially nowadays? How many fathers are able to do what he did for me in my young adulthood and in that moment? I also never realised until recently just how important working in the building trade was. That in itself is a rite of passage, leaving school at sixteen and being thrown into a man's world: "Up you go then," they said, with big smiles on their faces, waiting for me to chicken out as I was told to carry a chimney pot up a three-storey ladder on my first week of employment. But the smiles soon dropped; I had been going up and down ladders since I was twelve, building tree houses and tiling roofs with my dad.

I think I was being offered these memories to include in this chapter to show the mature masculine at play in our society and how it nurtures in its own firm, assertive way, and to fill out what made me quite a confident person, always willing to take the lead and give something a go.

But some of this went out the window when I got to this lost point in my life, where I had achieved the basics and was looking for whatever was next. I now sometimes explain it all as being a bit like a computer game. We work our way through the level we are on and then get invited into a whole new world at the next level.

Some Social Background Info about Who I Was Prior to Midlife Crisis

In a more social context, I had always been a fairly typical guy, part of the local pool team down the pub, messing about with cars, and racing motorbikes of some sort or other. As a parent, I also got involved in whatever my kids were doing, such as gymnastics, trampolining, and racing. But then after being reasonably successful in life, I suddenly found myself at this lost place of wondering what was next. Now when I say reasonably successful, I just mean not struggling or striving so hard. When I was at school, my parents always seemed to be happy enough with me if I got a C+, in other words, on the plus side of average, so it didn't take that much for me to be content enough in later life.

So as I found myself in this unfamiliar place of not knowing where to go next, I ended up with different interests, not the usual type. I read the Bible and the Bhagavad Gita and went to Beshara looking for answers. About this time, my sister-in-law mentioned that she was about to start a reiki course at our local evening college, and I said that I would give it a go. After doing the first evening, I came home and made myself a cup of tea, but I about jumped out of my skin at the sound the water made when I was pouring it from the kettle into the cup. I had forgotten to boil the kettle and could subconsciously tell the difference in the sound of cold water being poured into the cup from the sound that hot water makes. But it was the extremity of my reaction; I was even more hypersensitive.

Then quite foolishly, at about this same time, I decided to give yoga a go and jumped straight into Kundalini yoga, a very powerful self-transformation yoga that has been around for thousands of years. Kundalini evokes the very deep spiritual awakening energies in the body, and that was the last thing that I really needed to be doing. So as if all of this was not enough, my fourteen-year-old-son had been racing 125cc motorbikes in the British championships and had been going through a spell of crashing a lot, so we spent a bit of time in hospitals due to injuries. It was all taking its toll on me; I was overworked and worked hard at the racing, also worrying about whenever that red flag was going to come out again because he had crashed, as well as spending a fortune on transport vehicles and racing costs.

This eventually got to a point where I said enough is enough and I spent the rest of the money we had set aside on a cruise for the whole family. We headed off to the Med to enjoy a break, but I took a couple of books with me: Dan Brown's *The Da Vinci Code* and Deepak Chopra's *Synchrodestiny*. Reading these books threw me even deeper into a spin. I was angry at how my old belief system was being challenged by reading *The Da Vinci Code* and with what I was reading in *Synchrodestiny*. At one point on the cruise, I read about how something small at one place in the world could make incredible changes at another place in the world. It was about butterflies and a few minutes later, and completely in keeping with synchrodestiny,

I had an incredible experience with a butterfly. We were a full day at sea, heading away from Tunisia en route to North Italy, and I had decided to go on deck to check on the others; I opened the cabin door and immediately saw a red admiral-type butterfly coming down the passageway towards me. I watched it fly past all the bright pictures hung on the walls and past all the amused people in the passageway, knowing that it was coming to me. It flew the entire length of the passage and landed on my leg, sat there for a moment, and then as if to emphasise its point, flew all the way back in the direction it had come.

I almost couldn't cope; even birds and animals and insects had started interacting with me in a way that was peculiar, but affirming of some new reality that I was being introduced to. Everything I had known was falling apart, as some new version of reality was breaking through into my world, but I had no real answers to help me comprehend what was happening to my mind. Why was this happening? What was it that was happening? What was I meant to do with it when everyone else was just carrying on as normal, without a clue of what was going on or what I was going through? They were all in one world, and I was in some kind of birth canal between the old and new, trying to figure out if I was losing my mind. We returned from the cruise, and I carried on working, trying to hide the state I was in and run my business. I was now having psychotic episodes and constant peak experiences with nature and animals; I was lying in bed at night crying because I couldn't sleep for the constant stream of images that were flashing through my mind, as it tried to make sense of what was going on. I was hiding all of this from my wife and family out of fear for my sanity and out of the stigma of having to be the man. I also feared being locked up if anyone found out the state that I was really in.

During all of this, I carried on with the reiki and still could not figure out why all these women were letting me near them in this way. I began to be able to feel all sorts strange experiences in relation to other people's bodies and had to stop doing reiki because I realised that this was not just some new interest for a bit of curiosity and fun; there was something very real to this, and I shouldn't be messing with it. But this was not before I took another major fall; we had moved on to doing distance reiki, and I was doing distance healing on my mum. My mum had had psoriasis all over her legs for years and nothing seemed to help, but after one week of my doing distance reiki, her legs were spotless: not a blemish. And I had done that; I had made them clear up, or so my ego thought. I was taking the credit at my ego level and becoming inflated with my new-found abilities, when this is not of the ego's doing.

So here I was, a complete mess, yet full of myself in my ability to perform miracles and heal the sick; this is the hubris before the nemesis, the pride before the fall. Then came the slap back down to earth that took me years to recover from. I had also been doing distance reiki on a young girl, a friend of the family who was very ill and spending most of her time in hospital. I walked into the motorcycle garage that I was a partner in, and my younger brother told me the girl had died a couple of weeks before. He told me of how she had made the choice to leave this life rather than go on in a body that didn't work.

I actually can't remember how I felt in that moment because I probably shut down to manage it. I was numb for months; I had still been doing distance reiki even after she was gone. The arrogance of what I had been doing was absolutely horrendous; it was too much to bear. I couldn't believe it. I think the shock actually spared me from feeling what I could not have coped with. As families, we had been very close but had drifted apart in the past year; they had gone through all of that as I had played God with myself. I am even trembling and shaking my head as I write this, still in disbelief. I had fallen back down to earth with a massive crash, fallen from my great high. I never went back to reiki or Kundalini yoga after all of that, and to this day still fear and respect that there are energies at play that are not for our amusement.

Before writing this paragraph, I spoke face to face with the girl's mum for the first time since it happened; twelve years has passed, and only now could we manage to talk to each other about it. She truly was a special wee girl and the light of the world that touched so many people, never complaining through the years of her suffering and always tending to the needs of others instead. Despite horrendous situations like this and everything else that I was experiencing, I gradually came to see that this guidance at play was trying to serve me. I gradually became more able to tell when it was active and not, or perhaps it was more about when I was available to it or not.

How I Found Psychosynthesis (or It Found Me)

Eventually, however, it was by being guided to Psychosynthesis that I was really helped to make sense of it all and slowly get back to sanity and solid footing.

I had gone into town and was walking to the bank when I went past someone selling the *Big Issue*. "*Big Issue*, sir?" came a voice to my right, as I reflected and then said, "No, thank you," and kept walking.

At this same moment, however, I could feel some other dimension of myself, like my energetic body, stopping and staying with the man as I kept going and dragged it behind me. In fact; it was more like I stayed behind as my body took another couple of steps, and then I caught up with it again. Believe it or not, I actually forgot all about it, as I was having so many weird experiences at this time anyway.

After I came out of the bank again, the same voice, from my left this time, said, "*Big Issue*, sir!"

It was the same tone and energy really, but within me it felt emphasised, like I was being told to take the magazine. I took it and returned home, where I began to glance through it. On the back page, there was an advert about The Institute of Psychosynthesis coming up to Edinburgh to do a 4 day fundamentals training at the Salisbury Centre. It was the first time in about 20 years that they had done something in Scotland. I signed up immediately, went to the training session, and went into full training on the next intake in 2006.

I include this part of my life story to give you the fuller picture of my journey but also to evidence to you the guidance at play in our lives when we are open to it, or forced open to it in my case. Hopefully, this will help you see that this is something trying to go right in our lives rather than go wrong. I had many other experiences during this time that evidenced this other dimension to me. After three years of psychosynthesis training, an eagle flew straight into the front of my van, killing its self instantly. Immediately I knew that my friend's father had just died, and this later proved to be true once I had the chance to talk to her about it all. He died at exactly that moment and she was in another country, and I hadn't spoken to her for months.

That evening when I came home after the eagle incident I noticed a book sticking out of my bookshelf. It was *The Twenty-Nine Pages* by Ibn Arabi, a book that I had brought back from Beshara three years before. I randomly opened it and looked immediately at the line saying that birds of prey are about the heart. My friends dad actually died of a heart attack. I had noticed the book sticking out several times before that and ignored it, but now I knew why it was sticking out. All of these experiences were trying to introduce me to seeing and accepting another dimension to our reality, one that we don't generally see because we are so caught up in life, but I could not deny these few years of transition and the gift of where they have led me.

I could go on and tell you about a small lizard sitting on my doorstep one morning; lizards and butterflies represent major transformation, butterflies going from caterpillar to butterfly by turning into soup first, and reptiles symbolising transformation from water animals to land. Then there was the grasshopper on a doorbell in Kings Cross in London, a message that I interpreted as telling me that I was making too much noise about it all, and a few other stories, but hopefully you get the picture already. These types of experiences, however, are a bit more shamanic or Druidic in nature for me compared to the type of guidance that I am experiencing nowadays, but they still function to serve and guide us, as do dreams and many other things.

There have also been many other courses and teachings that I have been involved in over the years, such as quantum jumping by Burt Goldman, which is all about slowing our brain frequency down and accessing other dimensions of reality by stepping into subconscious visual scenarios, and then taking what is there to serve us in relation to what is emergent for us at the time. Then there was also the Love or Above CD course by Christie Marie Sheldon, where the focus once again is about frequencies and seeking to function at the higher frequency of love or above, and theta healing, which I did in Edinburgh with Jennifer Main. Theta healing is also about slowing our self down and accessing different dimensions of reality, inviting healing, clarity, and truth to emerge through being available to it instead of being our usual heady busy selves.

Fear of God

Having just gone for a tea break, I stood there, leaning on the kitchen worktop in mental emptiness, drinking my tea and gazing out of the window. Then suddenly I realised, or experienced a revelation, about why there can be a fear of God. I have never believed in a wrathful or punishing God. But perhaps the fear of God is not about being punished; perhaps it is about fearing for what may come our way. Because I do fear having such experiences again as the ones I just described, especially when I reconnect to how it was not of my conscious choosing or desire and how we don't understand what is happening to us at the time.

As I end this chapter, I invite you to see once again that something was at play behind all of this, something holistic or holy in spirit that was guiding me to transcend the level of development I was operating at.

An image has just popped into my mind, reminding me that something told me back in 2005 that I would ultimately end up working through the church. I was walking back to my bed and breakfast accommodation one evening after a day's training at the Salisbury centre, during the four-day Psychosynthesis fundamentals training. I walked down past the Commonwealth swimming pool, and as I began to turn right into the street where I was staying, I looked at the church on my left and just knew that this was where it was all going. We already had the body, in the form of the churches and mosques and other religious buildings all around the world, in which the awe and wonder of existence could awaken to itself at its highest level. All it needed to do was continue to synthesise its opposing parts that see things differently and come into interdependent unity at a higher level than its independent lower parts were operating at. But this would take either a collective insight into this new reality, as had happened for me, or a humanitarian crisis so that a new way and truth and life could be realised and initiate the will to make it happen.

Our Scottish national anthem, written by Roy Williamson of the Corries, has always inspired me to carry on because I can see the more archetypal level of the song above and beyond the Scotland versus England level. I always think this incredible song is like a beautiful anthem of the soul, as it captures the story of its embodied earthly life, the soul's spiritual journey in flesh, from non-consciousness to full bloom against all the odds, the fighting, suffering, and dying that seems necessary to retain the beautiful and sacred.

For me, the first lines are always sung from the spirit of longing and calling back, from a place of love and loss but remembrance of what once was, the spirit of loss of connection to the wonder and the divine, like the loss of the innocence and freedom of childhood. The spirit singing the song knows that the greater war is not over and that this was just one battle; at the end of the last verse; singing, we can still rise and be that nation again. The spirit of freedom, abundance, love, truth, and beauty lying dormant in the dark, until sunlight comes so that it can rise again and fight the oppressive resistance to bloom. The will to fight for what is pure and true still burns, knowing that the battle that was just won, was just a microcosm of humanity's greater battle; a battle that involves learning to fight differently, learning to fight from love rather than hate and resentment.

O flower of Scotland
When will we see your like again
That fought and died for
Your wee bit hill and glen
And stood against him
Proud Edward's army
And sent him homeward Tae think again.

CHAPTER 3

The Church in Breakdown and Reformation

Searching for a Church and Finding a Minister

As I mentioned in the previous chapter, just over a year ago, I started investigating what the church may have to offer me. I had done the Alpha course several years before and didn't get much out of it, but there was something comforting about coming together with others who were seeking higher guidance and soulful community. I had never been involved with any form of religion and just felt this curiosity to see if it had anything further to offer as part of my ongoing awakening. In fact, I had spent several lunch breaks with my work colleagues, arguing my case about the irrationality of it. But I was also aware that we all have unconscious mindsets about all sorts of things in life. I decided to go and see rather than deprive myself of something out of some mindset about how religion causes all the trouble in the world.

As I write this in this moment, from where I am now, I realise that although I hadn't taken much from the Alpha course itself, I had taken something more subtle and unspoken from the nature of the people I met. The majority who were not Bible bashers were very nice people to be around, very kind and considerate and caring. Perhaps this was what had unconsciously met a need in me and was drawing me to take a second look. Perhaps my head had gone looking for something from the Alpha course and didn't get it, so I walked away again. But it now looked like I hadn't fully realised that another part of me had actually got something less obvious. Perhaps that was what I had been guided there to get, and it had taken this long for the penny to drop.

So I started where I had left off and spent a few weeks in the same church before an elderly lady told me to go and meet a particular minister in town called Jan. She had a sense of what I was about and pointed me to him as she felt he may serve my need. I did as she suggested, and it went okay, but after a few weeks, he suggested I continue experimenting and get an even broader feel for what was out there. So once again, I followed the advice that I was given and spent several weeks roaming round lots of different churches looking to get my needs met, but something didn't quite click with any of them, so I returned to where felt right. But it was due to trying this and trying that and listening to a knowing within myself that I found what was right for me.

This also allowed me to notice the lack of attendance in churches; sometimes, less than 10 percent of a church's capacity was filled. Even more alarming was the lack of young and middle-aged people. That was when I realised that the minister had a lot to do with whether a church worked or not. They could be the key for someone to stay or leave a church, or even stay or leave Christianity. There was some need in me that Jan and his ministry were meeting, and I could see the same thing happening for other people, with their respective ministers at other churches.

Suddenly, I realised that my life and development wasn't always being facilitated relative to what I thought I wanted or was looking for; it was often being facilitated around what I unconsciously needed.

So what was this role that Jan was playing for me? What awakening part of myself was he able to be and hold for himself, so that I could feed on it and introject it, to get that piece of growth for me? Only now as I write and with this realisation, I see that the gap between the me I was at the time, and a possible Christian me was too wide; but this particular minister was able to hold that tension and bridge that gap. I could however, see now, that it was about the minister, not God or Jesus or the Bible or the church. It was about whether the minister, as a minister and normal man at the same time, was convincing or not; could he hold them both? Did I believe him and believe in him? Was this man able to help me move into whatever it was that was trying to establish in me? Perhaps the gap between me and Jesus or me and Christianity was too big for something productive to happen. But the gap between myself and the minister was a manageable and serving stepping stone.

Watchman Nee and the Problem with Awakening

In addition to this search for a church, which turned out to be a search for a minister, I have spent the past year or so engrossed in Watchman Nee's ministry and writings about the Bible and the teachings of Jesus. During that time, he has given me a much deeper understanding of the spirit of Jesus and what I think He was really teaching (and is still teaching) when we embody Him through it. This learning was quite a contrast to what I had previously gleaned from the Bible or the church or life. With this enlightenment, however, I now have a sense of what I am looking for, but the difficulty is that it seems to come and go like some flickering light bulb trying to stay on. It flickers between what I have just learned and what I see in day-to-day society and Christianity.

Once again, as I write, I have a sudden realisation that in a similar way to how the minister is holding something for me to grow into, I can also suddenly see that Watchman Nee's teaching is doing the same thing in acting as a further bridge to this gap, as well as the fact that he is teaching about Jesus. I am also intrigued by the fact that it is all males: my father, the minister, Watchman Nee, Jesus, and God, who is also generally seen as masculine. But then in writing this book, I am also affirming something that we teach in Heart Intelligence work: that a healthy, mature masculine energy holds and gives form and shape and containment to the feminine outpouring and divine abundance that is essentially love.

I now realise that it is due to this polarity between Watchman Nee's teaching and what I see as mainstream Christianity that I am struggling and suddenly find myself writing in an effort to work something out, something that will hopefully help me to find peace and move back into contentment again. As I write the above paragraph, I notice that from some higher nurturing place, I am comforted by the reminder that this is usually the case as we journey through life. We stand in our existing paradigms, searching for the next one, only to find that by the time the new one can hold us, we can see the problems with the old one. In most developmental progressions in life, there are always others already operating at the new level that we have just attained, and so we move into relationships with those at that level, gradually letting go of those old relationships and beliefs that no longer serve. In this way, we continue to awaken whilst also continue getting our belonging needs met.

On this occasion, however, this doesn't seem to be the case. I have arrived at a new facilitating environment that seems polarised. So perhaps I am writing this book in an effort to get my old environment to catch up with me, or perhaps it is to get this new one to adjust to meet my needs. This new part of me is holding fast in what I have learned from somewhere above my present location and is offering this book so as to get something to happen, so I can feel normal again and feel like part of the tribe once more, rather than isolated and doubtful in my lonely new level of perception.

A Moment of Presence with Source Is Enough to Reawaken Us

I pause and glance out of the office window, probably to unconsciously disconnect from the disturbance of what I was writing. My instant reconnection to life and the sky and garden sweep me up and reawaken me in this new relationship that exists to replace the old one. It immediately comforts and reassures me about what is true and good and what I am doing, by the instant cellular reaction in my body, by reconnecting to the awe and wonder of life, by sensing the energy of pure existence and being, and by sensing my embodied connection and its connection to life and everything that is. I immediately feel plugged back into life and feel its replenishment within me. This is Celtic Christianity, our connection to life and its abundance, and I feel myself come alive again as I become present to life and the moment and step back into the tree of life and out of the tree of knowledge. My body comes alive again, and I feel the ease of being able to see this abundantly available nurturing relationship, as something holistic or wholly in spirit that ministers to my need and that I could call God rather than the image I have been resistant to for such a long time.

Suddenly, I feel that belonging need being met again as it answers my call, and I am swept up in its motherly loving embrace. Instantly replenished by this reconnection to source, I am once again empowered to continue, knowing that a different reality and truth exists that is trying to awaken us to it.

The Suppression and Re-Emergence of the Feminine

Then once I have replenished my self, I am swept off into a polarised experience as I am reminded of the differences between this sublime reality and where we are at in society with our tree of knowledge way of seeing it all. Squabbling and arguing due to disconnect, about this religion or that religion or whatever else being correct. Then just as suddenly I am guided back to seeing the contrast between today's mostly Roman Christianity (the Christianity that has ruled for the past seventeen hundred years) and the more nature-al, less scriptural Celtic Christianity, which was suppressed along with the feminine in the past. This Celtic Christianity is mostly unknown nowadays and barely survives on the fringes of society; but her roots are well anchored on the Scottish island of Iona awaiting return, as well as in parts of Ireland and England such as Glendalough and Lindisfarne. This divine feminine cannot be stopped and continues to flower itself in subtle ways, such as in the church service I attended on Sunday, which felt more Celtic than usual. It was a harvest thanksgiving service, and the church was full of flowers and food donations, and the service included singing along with Louis Armstrong to "What a Wonderful World" as a beautiful video played on the screen at the front of the church. The hearts, spirits, and souls of the whole congregation could be felt as we all sang in union and resonance, reunited with the divine. What a difference to the usual service.

But there are lots of other unseen good things going on in churches that often don't get full recognition for being an aspect of Christianity; such as Messy church and various seasonal events, again showing that Celtic connection in our hearts. There are also frequent coffee mornings that bring people together and raise money for good causes. There are house groups and Bible studies and gardening groups and elderly groups and parent groups. There are those who give time to others who are housebound or in hospital or simply down in spirit. There is an endless list of events going on and people using churches and church halls; it's great to see the church being used for these things, given that they are the people of the community, and this is the spirit of community.

For me, this is often the unseen way in which churches are charitable and Christian and still play a central role in communities. But in saying all of that, Celtic Christianity and mysticism is not removed or averse to scripture; it is actually very tied up with the Bible and scripture in certain ways. Celtic Christianity is more associated with the Gospel of St John, whom many Celtic Christian teachers paid most attention to, seeing St John as the one who listens to the heartbeat of God. St John being seen to see that our transformation happens in relation to love. This is then perceived to be somewhat in contrast to our more traditional Christianity that follows St Peter and the way of God's law being handed down through tradition, in the interests of facilitating change; the former feels more feminine to me and the latter more masculine.

Roman and Celtic Christianity

So with that taken into consideration, what a difference there is between sitting in church connected to the spirit of life and creation, compared to listening to a long biblical scripture that is trying to teach us something through coded messages and unfamiliar words, using stories from two thousand years ago. These services just disconnect me from life, and yet they are still so common. They are actually what caused me to keep looking for something that felt better (not better as in making life easier for me, but better as in less heady and disconnecting, better as in being touched by something alive and joyous in its guidance).

But now, I'm in the tree of knowledge, judging what is good or bad, right or wrong. Or am I? Did I fall asleep and lose presence to feeling alive in the tree of life? Am I unconsciously rambling away to myself in disconnect, or am I still alive in the spirit and joy of life, simply feeling the contrasting life draining drop, back into the tree of knowledge? It doesn't feel like I am asleep, as I feel present to catching myself and feel energised. I am also still connected to the part of me that seeks to help bring that greater kingdom on earth; the spirit of my action feels holistic rather than condemning. So perhaps it is possible to be in the TOL while questioning right and wrong, with the thing to watch out for, being the spirit behind our action. Jesus says that we are not fit to judge by our self and

33

should judge only through Him. This is compared to being unconscious and judgmentally acting out of resentment or anger or any other symptom that we would be better to look into.

We need to pay attention to what we are feeling because that's where the life is; that is where my truth amen's me or defiles me. (As Christian Pankhurst say's, it's not what you think, it's what you feel). We can also watch for feeling numb or flat or disconnected, because then we are at least feeling again and have moved back to the tree of life. After having run out of oil in our lamps, we have refilled them again. This disconnection and not feeling is measurable against when we feel alive and in the abundance of life, or are even consciously alive in the numbness or suffering and struggle of life. Both of these are still being alive with energy to be consciously felt rather than simply behave from an unconscious symptom.

Getting back to these church services; I tend to see the main message being preached as being about trying to connect us to Jesus and how He is God made human, or God's only begotten son who died to pay for our sins. Dying and then coming back to life before going back to where He came from. I have to be honest and say that whilst I agree with so much of what I now see and understand Christianity is about; I still struggle with this bit of Christianity and my inner spiritual discernment doesn't resonate with it. I suppose that leaves me in a space somewhere between Christianity, Islam and Judaism, where Islam and Judaism have their own views about Jesus, views that are different from Christianity's. What it does do though, is remind us of how Jesus is guiding us to live together, by having Him within us as an inner compass, and that is definitely the fatherly guidance we need in the world today.

The thing I find fascinating about this feminine return is how it is emerging from the bottom up, like a long-dormant seed being given the little crack that it needed to emerge and grow towards full bloom. With the relaxing of masculine rules about Christianity and what is allowed and not allowed, the feminine is gently arising from the ground to show itself in the church. I don't see it so much being invited from the top down as being surrendered to, as the old system struggles to survive without it.

Disconnected Ministry

In some church services, I have often sat there conscious of my own disconnect during the minister's sermon but connected to the people who are fiddling with their phones and looking at their shoes, wondering where the sermon is going. After about fifteen minutes, I watch the gradual increase of people shuffling back and forward in their seats, waiting for the minister to get to the point and conclude, so they can sing again in hope of reconnection, or reconnect by feeling it through someone brave enough to do a reading, feeling that reconnection to life through the reader's anxiety or their longing to touch the other, because feeling anything can feel better than feeling disconnected. This is why we often unconsciously act out in relationships and society: anything to feel alive again. This can also be why people stay in abusive relationships; because they are alive.

Sometimes, that connection does return through the person doing the reading, or through the minister, when they come back out of what can often feel like dead letter and the tree of knowledge, back into presence and life by interacting with the people of the congregation again. I can often feel when some ministers are so connected to the material they are reading that they are not really present to the congregation. It feels like we become the thing they happen to be talking to. We are just what is there as they do their thing. Yes, they look up now and again to make some interaction, but I can feel they are not present to us. I don't feel them ministering, I just feel them identified with their own intended message. In spirit, they are identified with their own objective: teaching us something. They don't reconnect me back to source by connecting themselves to it as they interact with us. This is not all of the time and is not all ministers, but it is still fairly common in my experience from my travels. I just sense most of them are too identified with what they want to teach; too much in self-righteousness. They are often too much in relationship with that, not us (or not me, anyway); others tell me they don't feel it either, that the spirit of the message didn't touch them, even if the logic, emotion, psychology or metaphor did.

As I write this, I feel for my own spirit; from where within myself am I writing this? Is my spirit tainted by anger? *No.* Resentment? *No.* Disappointment? *Some;* longing? *Yes.* Pain? *Yes.* Dejection? *Yes.* Does it give me any pleasure to be writing this? *No, absolutely not; quite the opposite.*

So what's moving? I inwardly ask myself.

I am deflated by how it is, knowing how it could be. Is the reply from some part within me.

So what do you want, given that? I ask.

I want it to wake up and give itself a good shake. Church is like a funeral half of the time.

Then I stop and question whether or not I am being holy in spirit right here, or am I acting out of my own childish annoyance with not getting what I want, in seeing the polarity between what is and what could be?

The answer feels like both and says: *I am acting out of my truth. I am being real to myself, and I am inspired (en-spirited). I can feel that this isn't something that I self-righteously want for me or my glory but feels righteously for us all and for the coming of that greater kingdom.*

So can this still be holy in spirit? I ask myself with confusion and doubt.

I guess so, offers some half-hearted, unconvinced voice still groping within me to convince itself, *given that I mean no harm to anyone and no glory for my self, only good, and I am fully conscious.*

I return inwards, and then in a loving calm voice I hear the words, *How is it not holy in spirit?* The spirit of this voice is gentle, guiding and inviting, rather than challenging or argumentative in its energy. But it is also different; it is actually like hearing a voice internally rather than the usual internal experience. It seems like it is coming from somewhere outside of me.

Left in surprise at suddenly being questioned from somewhere, I try to get used to the idea, as another part within me decides to run this notion past some checks to see if it stands up:

So is this tender and compassionate and loving?

No, not in behaviour, but it is in the spirit of what it is seeking.

Is it seeking His kingdom come?

Yes.

Am I abiding in Him?

In intent, yes; in behaviour, perhaps not.

Am I loving my neighbour?

Yes.

Am I being self-righteous?

I don't think so.

So am I being the way and the truth and the life?

Well, I am certainly being some way and truth and life anyway, but maybe not the way and truth and life.

Then the Watchman Nee within me arises and asks, *Does my spirit feel defiled inside by what I am doing?*

And with a sense of truth and inner acknowledgement and embodiment, the argument feels finished with the realisation of, *No, I feel alive and real and clean and true.*

But then perhaps some of what we experience in church is our own failing. If we are identified in our own TOK trying to get it with our head instead of being in the TOL, present to the spirit of the message and the spirit of being in church, and even the spirit of the minister's struggle and longing to get something across to us, then is that the minister's fault? Well, actually, maybe it is. Watchman Nee teaches us that mind touches mind and emotion touches emotion and spirit touches spirit, so if the minister is in his mind, then that is likely to be where we will go: the TOK. Yes, we get the metaphors and sometimes get the point of the sermon, but to me, through Watchman Nee, Christianity is not about that; it is about creating life and bringing forward living waters, something more akin to Celtic Christianity. The metaphors and understandings are at the level of the outer man and in the TOK, but Watchman teaches us that the outer man needs to be broken so that the inner man can come forth and touch others in spirit. I sense that we often sit there waiting for the bridegroom to return in that moment of humour, when we touch each other in a moment of laughter or resonance rather than be in our minds or disconnect. But this is not the true bridegroom, even if it does get us out of the tree of knowledge and into the tree of life.

It is these alive and dead Sunday service fluctuations that emphasise to me what God's instruction to Adam was, right at the start of the Old Testament, almost his first piece of advice: eat from the tree of life, not from the tree of knowledge, because you will die. Not literally die because the Bible is not about the literal; die in spirit and connection to everything, because that is what I believe the Bible, Jesus, life, Watchman Nee, and probably several others are trying to teach us. It is the spirit that matters, and whether we are connected in spirit to source and living waters through other people or nature or whatever else, (including scripture when the gap can be bridged).

In these moments of feeling a ministry that's disconnected, I often sense that these ministers are unconsciously over identified with their desire or desperation for others to understand. Or they are caught up in wanting people to remember chapter and verse, because that will mean that they are better Christians. Perhaps these ministers are exhausted with all they do over the week and evenings, as they never seem to stop. I don't know; but I certainly feel their spirit's longing to make it work and touch people with the gospel, but then I also feel them trying so hard that they come out of the living waters and TOL and drop into the TOK. Isn't this a familiar pattern for us all: trying so hard to do something that doesn't quite turn out how we meant it to? I hope this book doesn't turn out to be another example of that. But then hopefully I can catch myself if I start trying too hard.

I wish that these ministers would connect with us more, so that we can really feel each other and feel felt by each other; people go to church seeking connection as much as anything else. Even if it is just emotion touching emotion and not the spirit touching spirit, I believe it would at least be a move in the right direction. I wish that more of them would really feel for where we are as they talk to us, instead of just trying to sell us something or talking at us. I wish that they didn't use us to affirm the answers that suit the agenda of their service, unconsciously affirming themselves that their message is right. But then like the rest of us when we are disconnected from source and doing what we do to compensate and get our own needs met, including my writing of this book, maybe they have unconsciously become ministers to get their own needs met. From a religious, relational, psychological or developmental perspective, it's not enough about me, the person in the pew, and them feeling for where my needs are.

Sometimes, it feels to be too much about them and what they want for me, just so I can see what they see and affirm to them that they are right. My point here is that these services don't seem to be alive and real to the moment; certainly some of it needs to be prepared, but none of it feels to be in the spirit of aliveness. None of it seems to be spirit-led by disconnecting from our minds and thoughts and feeling for what comes into the empty space, then follow its lead.

There is so much religious or realigning psychological material going on in all of us, all the time, from our childhood pathology, that we don't even realise, and neither do the ministers. We don't see it or know to look for it, never mind understand or try to transcend it. Writing this reminds me of the NHS development meetings that I used to go to, or some of the foster care meetings. They are usually much the same: someone trying to help others by telling them what research has shown to be needed, instead of simply being there for them and trusting that the spirit will guide them to unconsciously reveal what is emergent and seeking solution. These facilitators may very well be correct with the agenda that they bring, but they are similarly so caught up in telling what they want to offer that they mostly miss connecting in a more meaningful way. They miss the purpose of existence, the life that exists only in two way relationship. As I write and learn from these realisations, it also makes me question my own parenting approach, when I do exactly the same thing and will again a hundred times. This chapter is also helping me to see the pathological me that is still seeking good fathering and mothering from the minister and the church and anything else that will feed it, even at the age of fifty-four.

2 November. I have returned to this passage time and time and time again over the past couple of months to soften it, as I feel bad about my attacking energy. But my knowing is that I need to leave it. That actually feels difficult within me to hold, but truth is truth, and I need to walk my walk, or there is no point in writing this book. I am not writing the above in some unconscious outburst or childish rant because my needs are not being met. I am writing it because many people have the same experience, and I am calling for something to change. I keep wanting to go back and be more compassionate to ministers, who are sincerely doing their best and doing what they have been taught to do.

But that won't help the situation, says that guiding voice from somewhere, as I also feel love within me, wanting to let it go and say, It will be okay, we will still get there. Being pushy is not going to help; it will only cause resentment and reaction. Don't criticise! Nurture.

But the unconscious still needs to be made conscious and considered; it needs to be brought into the light to see if it stand or falls, difficult or not.

And how can anyone teach what they have not learned?

You didn't know either, until you were taught.

I suddenly resign my argument, as my truth knows that this is true, but this triggers my resistance to teaching. I have always had a problem with the thought of teaching and a resistance to being the teacher, even though I have taught motorcycle racing, trampolining, gymnastics, carpentry and joinery, and many other things.

I am reminded of how our shadow parts usually hold our greatest gifts to the world. Perhaps I should do a coaching session on this to see what my resistance is. The narrow gate is not an easy one at times, but if we wish to be truly led by Jesus' teachings, then we need to remember that He came not to bring peace but with a two edged sword, a sword to separate bone and marrow, spirit and soul. This is where we need to learn spiritual discernment and feel for which inner voice to follow. Do we unconsciously follow and worship the false idol of our own inner neurotic voice of fear for survival, based on childhood experiences, or stay awake and live in Him?

Life Only Exists in Meaningful Connection

At this moment, I notice myself disconnect from what I am writing and connect to you, wondering if you understand all of this and if it is of service to you at this time in your life. I wish that I could ask you; and notice how I long to be in a two-way relationship with you so I can move in a direction that would answer your questions. As I write the above sentence from some flash of intuition or higher connection,

I also notice the inner relationship I am in when I am writing much of this. In fact, perhaps that moment was an invitation to realise something. In Heart Intelligence, we talk about how energy flows best between clean positive and negative poles and how that can be seen more clearly in relationships that are working better. So perhaps this book seems to be working because there is a clean polarity between me calling up to the higher guidance and it reaching down, both longing for fruitful connection and intimacy, because life really only exists in that movement. Perhaps it was when I dropped out of that connection for a moment that I reached once again to connect with you, and perhaps it is when ministers are not connected to either that the water doesn't flow.

I am aware that it is only now that I can see that this was the difference with the other ministers and churches that I experienced in my search for a church. There was a lack of connection to them. In a collective and general sense, there was something that my own discerner of truth was not buying, and there was also something about not feeling felt or seen or accepted for who I am and where I am at, and just being told that I should be doing it differently. Then there were churches where the ministers felt too connected to the service or their message.

As I end this section, I feel defiled inside and want to find a more heart intelligent way to say the same words, but I am choosing to leave it as it is because many others have said the same; in fact, upon further enquiry within myself, I don't feel defiled at all about what I have written. I just feel sad and disappointed that this is how it is, that inner guidance always being ready to guide me when I seek its help.

The Price of Suppressing Celtic Christianity

I believe that we are now paying the price for having abandoned Celtic Christianity, in favour of only Roman Christianity, when both

42

should have remained alive and active after the Synod of Whitby in AD 664. This synod was convened by King Oswy of Northumbria because the two styles of Christianity were clashing, and this clash resulted in Roman Christianity emerging as the singular victor, with the loser being banished from society. What a massive loss to humanity that they couldn't see what was really trying to happen as these two archetypal energies struggled to come into harmonious relationship. But to me this suppression of the feminine is not just a present-day situation; I see it as being embedded in the archetypal psyche of humanity, as the masculine gives form to the feminine, but the immature masculine actually suppresses it in fear, disconnection, and ignorance. Nature can be watched to see them both harmoniously at work, but I think humanity has a way to go yet.

Historically, we can also look back to the first treaty of Nicaea, where the Roman emperor Constantine, the first Christian leader, gathered hundreds of bishops together. This was a previous attempt in AD 325 to establish a uniform observance in times of chaos, as once again different belief systems were clashing. What was not seen as Christian was lumped in with paganism, even though paganism was really more about the spiritual vitality of the natural organic world, and all of this was in contention with a new Roman Christianity that was in ascension. The main debate, however, was about Jesus' divinity; was Jesus (God) made man, or was He a great leader? The outcome was decided to be the former, and that continues to this day. But then surely that is no surprise, given the opportunity to put something in place that nobody could argue with, especially when everything is in chaos. Glorify someone who was truly great anyway and put Him to a level so out of reach that even debating it is almost a sin. It certainly makes leadership easier when we can say, It's not up to me. I'm not the boss, this book Is, and we have to do what it says or else. I suppose the modern-day equivalent is; the computer says no.

This arising Christianity wove and integrated its way into paganism and gradually squeezed it out. I don't, however, believe that this move away from Celtic and pagan belief and worship was done out of spite or bitterness or malice or manipulation. I am sure these were all good wise men with good intent. I believe it was done in good spirit, with the intent to make things less disruptive than they were at the time, to cope with the situation and move from chaos to order, to honour the position of responsibility and leadership. Perhaps it would have been wiser to add to the existing so as to evolve it somewhat, but not to the exclusion and total replacement of the former.

But unfortunately, like so often, we don't find a compromise or manage to blend together what seems like two polarised systems. We often don't take the higher qualities of both and use them to help us outgrow the lower level of development that is no longer felt to be acceptable. We don't attain a synthesis; we just accept one and outlaw the other. We make one right and one wrong, TOK again. This is similar to what I am up against in myself, as I work it out through writing this book. Will I find some form of synthesis and transcendent position to function from with all that is moving, or will I reject one thing and accept another?

In contrast to these outcomes from seventeen hundred years ago, I was on a Heart Intelligence Zoom call last Wednesday evening, 9 November, with Christian Pankhurst and many others. On the call, Christian was sharing how fluid and fast Heart Intelligence is evolving and changing; as he learns what makes the greatest transformation in others and then seeks to follow that realisation rather than stick to what he believed in and taught even a year ago.

This conversation in my words was along the lines of progressing from the TOK to the TOL, moving away from former set concepts and teachings and beliefs to feeling the space for what was alive and active, as well as feeling for where hearts were active rather than just heads. But the way he put it was that he saw it as a case of new ways being *added too and added to* the existing, rather than replacing or excluding the former. This is similar to Jesus when He says that He has not come to replace the Old Testament or law but to add to it.

I am not saying that what is going on in churches today is all bad or that Roman Christianity is wrong in contrast to Celtic Christianity. I am simply beginning to see what I believe is often missing, but gradually returning, so we can gain from having the grace of both. But as I have already said, the feminine cannot be totally suppressed anyway; it is the guiding spirit that is revealing her to us in those moments when we feel deeply touched.

The Beauty of What Can Happen When the Masculine Makes It Safe for the Feminine to Arise

I saw this yesterday in church, as a woman stepped up to the chancel to thank everyone for their help with the coffee morning. The way I saw it was that she was initially in her masculine self, her mind, and her ego, wanting to get it right, not wanting to slip up and end up feeling foolish in front of everyone and wanting to remain composed and in self control. So she bolstered herself and expressed her genuine gratitude, knowing what the money they raised will do for others in Africa. But as she shared, she relaxed a little and connected to her heart, becoming identified with how grateful she really feels and actually feeling that gratitude deep in her heart, the gratitude that her disconnected head had been talking about. Her true self came forward through her love and gratitude; her body and voice quivered for just an instant, as she let herself feel how much it really meant to her. Love overpowering will, the feminine archetype overpowering the masculine archetype, flowering for just a moment, and then it was gone. Almost immediately, she vanished from the chancel, her ego triggered back in fear of breaking down in front of everyone and feeling embarrassed. Yes, there was emotion in there, but there was also pure selfless love.

What a beautiful pure moment of grace, love, truth, vulnerability, gratitude and humanity, as she slipped from the TOK into the TOL and back again, evidencing the struggle between our need for self survival and our continuously being called into self-fulfilment. I saw her going from the closed way that our mind tells us that we need to be, to the pure childlike innocence that Jesus spoke of.

What a loss that I didn't just step up onto the chancel, trusting that I would be helped to reveal what had really just happened, to those who need help to see it and understand it for what it was. Instead, I went into my default coping mechanism of wanting to analyse it, due to uncertainty and because my head and neurosis were telling me it would be rude, and who am I to be so arrogant and presumptuous that nobody else got it? Fear ruling over love once again. This whole microcosmic explosion of fear to love to fear on her part and love to fear on mine, being a simpler way of seeing the divine at play, seeking both expression and survival moment by moment. We were both ministering unconsciously to the two primal objectives within us. Yet as I write this, I return to love, in acceptance of my own limitation against my own defence systems and survival instinct that seeks nothing more than to serve me.

Plato's famous words come to mind: 'We can easily forgive a child who is afraid of the dark; the real tragedy is when men are afraid of the light.'

Or Marianne Williamson's famous quote:

'Our deepest fear is not that we are inadequate. Our deepest fear is that we are powerful beyond measure. It is our light, not our darkness that most frightens us. We ask ourselves, who am I to be brilliant, gorgeous, talented, and fabulous? Actually, who are you not to be? You are a child of God. Your playing small does not serve the world.'

The Challenge ahead of Us, Even When
We Understand and Want It

But what could we do now with hindsight, or if we were to go back to that moment with this knowledge? Would either of us have the strength to do it any different? Could either of us step up to that chancel, like stepping up to the cross, ready to feel the pain of crucifixion in our psychological self, our ego, knowing that we do it for a greater good and to serve the coming of God's greater kingdom? Would either of us be able to break open our own alabaster box? Would we even be able to do it if we wanted to, given that our neurological defence system would be tearing itself apart trying to close us down, in fear of self survival.

For me, the answer is often yes, because I know that I do it on occasions. Especially when I have a vision or purpose to hold and empower me, but even when I can't, I usually show it up for what it is. This is what I call the real work of religion: freeing my true self by crucifying my psychological self. The existential shaming the neurotic so as to transcend it, whilst knowing that the neurotic is only trying to keep us safe as it has always done, so as to get us to this level of realisation and awakening. This work is very hard but worthwhile, and this is why we work in groups in psychosynthesis and heart intelligence work.

A Taste of Watchman Nee; Learning to
Use the Defilement of Our Spirit

In an attempt to redeem myself a little and avoid ministers banging on my door, this ministering from the tree of knowledge is in contrast to the moments when the minister is in the spirit of connection to the divine, really connected to the congregation.

In fact, it's not even the congregation because I can feel the defilement in my spirit as I write that; the word *congregation* feels like a thing, an object. I can actually feel disconnect within me by not seeing, feeling, and honouring the divinity of each and every person that makes up the congregation. My Heart Intelligence training shows me that when we connect deeply and meaningfully to just one person, even if we move from person to person, but take the time to go into them and feel them, we are with them in our spirit. That spiritual connection is then felt by everyone present, through their spirit.

As I started to write the above, I was also aware that I was acting out of some neuroses. I was writing out of guilt and fear and a shadow part of myself that tries to prevent me from showing up in the world as a nasty and spiteful person. Perhaps I don't want to appear immature, given that I keep talking about others being that way. The task in these situations is firstly to see them and then discern whether to follow them or stand firm in our existential self rather than be run by our neurotic self.

Calling the Change into Action

Hopefully, you can now begin to sense what I mean about the difference between the more frequent Roman Christian church service and the more Celtic Christian nature-of-the-harvest service I describe. Roman Christianity is more masculine, scriptural, heady, and analytic TOK, compared to the more feminine Celtic TOL Christianity that is more about doing the actual feeling and loving and expression, irrespective of any understanding. The Christianity that sneaks back in between the cracks and in my opinion is what keeps people coming back to church, even if they don't fully realise it. I think that the church will continue to decline as a more awakened society outgrows it and passes it by, especially if it doesn't evolve by awakening from its own infancy and psychological phase of development. Spiritually awaken and evolve from its limited understanding and over identification with the past.

But as I am saying here, I do see signs of change, as the church does become more truly Presbyterian, actually following the lead of the community and congregation out of need to survive, rather than to do what it thinks is Presbyterian in aspiring to teach what it perceives as the community's need. I can see that the church can lead from the top down, as long as it stays connected to source, but if and when it doesn't, as we have seen, it all falls apart. This is when I think it needs to be led from the bottom up by following what the divine has instilled into nature. In the past, the church was where people turned for knowledge and wisdom and guidance, but as the years have rolled along, it has been overtaken by increased literacy and technology and psychological understanding, and this has left the church in its dust.

In fairness, I do see churches trying lots of new things in an attempt to hang on, but I think they are not quite seeing what is happening. Just like in politics and banking, they are trying to get back what they had, when that is never what crises are about. They need to awaken to the next level so they can guide the people again. The kids have grown up and are now showing their parents the error of their ways. What I have seen through Watchman Nee's teaching is that there is a big gap between realising what Christianity is about and what we are actually doing, and it is in that direction the church should be focussing. It's like watching an outdated mindset of what church is about and how it works, trying to hang on when it's not able to reaffirm itself, slowly dying away in the background, instead of updating by breaking its own alabaster box. I see a church and religion that is actually in its own disconnection from source, simply going through the motions and rituals, waiting for the bridegroom to return. But in reality, they do not have any oil in their lamps to see with.

To me, the TOL that God tells Adam about is the feminine energy of feeling and connecting and suffering for the sake of full vibrant expression and outpouring, but the church is stuck in the dead letter of scripture and stuffy dusty old mindsets that are masculine and TOK and not even really what Christianity is about. The church actually needs the feminine to bring it back to life (not simply women, because women can be just as stuck in their masculine as the men are, but vibrant feminine energy, the feminine energy of life that can awaken the rigid and immature masculine in its constricting behaviour). It is there because I see it holding itself back all the time. Several women I know talk from wanting something more and I can feel their deep inner calling to act. In contrast to this, they can also feel their inner defilement (as Watchman Nee calls it) with some of what is. This is their feminine intuition and guidance that is embodied in them, and that should be followed; this is the way and the truth and the life. What it has needed is conscious awakening and watering, to help it come forward and take its place again. Just as Beatrice does in Dante's *Inferno*, once Virgil has done what he can. Following the spirit of life that brings us the struggle and suffering, as well as the joy and abundance of life, it is the job of the masculine to provide a container for that, not suppress it out of immaturity, ignorance, and fear.

Now if this is chapter is stirring you up, then please remember that that is how it works. Your disturbance is facilitated by your higher guidance empowering you into action: ask your self, What's moving? and What does your heart's truth want in relation to that?

As you have seen, I am trying to reveal a deeper understanding of life and scripture here, whilst also showing the wonder of what is beginning to happen as we unconsciously re-embrace the returning feminine or Celtic Christianity back into the church. But while I reveal this, I am calling for a more mature masculine or Roman Christianity to evolve from the dying ashes of the one that barely exists. Thank goodness (or the Holy Spirit) that church services are slowly changing from how they were in the not-so-distant past and that what I am calling feminine and Celtic Christianity is slowly creeping back in. Perhaps something is calling out for the return of a new updated level of Celtic feminine Christianity, along with a more enlightened Roman masculine Christianity. Perhaps it is because it is already happening that I can see it and am disturbed when it is not there. Surely it is because the divine masculine and the divine feminine are both equally precious, and their equal synthesis is required for our full awakening. With all that said, do I think I could do any better if I were to stand up there every Sunday, ministering His kingdom to come, as it is in heaven? No, I don't. Thank goodness for those who do get up there and try, week after week. But then maybe this is my ministering, right here in this book. Watchman Nee tells us that real ministry is about helping others from what we have truly learned at the hand of God and stored up in our spirit, not from what is in our mind or the knowledge acquired, and with there being no self in the mix.

Addressing the Immediate Need

My conclusion in looking back at this chapter is that whilst the church is definitely in demise, there are certainly many good things still being done by it. There is definitely a lot of true Christian behaviour going on that doesn't really get seen. Then there is the nature of churchgoing people: always pleasant and easy to be with. This is what I think is particularly unseen: the genuinely humble Christian behaviour that makes no claim to be anything. The Sunday services have definitely started moving in the right direction, as far as I am concerned. It is always great to have the children involved for some of the service. But I also think that we should be seeing and recognising the awe and wonder of the feminine aspect of God for what it is. In addition to this, we should also be seeing that the masculine aspect of God lies in using the teachings of Jesus to guide us in life and to keep us alive in the feminine, feeling the joy and suffering of life, knowing what it is that we suffer for. We need help to learn the difference between suffering for something greater and suffering in ignorance and avoidance. From the realisations and revelations that I have had in writing this, and the affirmation of being on the right track, it seems to me that what we need to focus on in the church and society is maturing and awakening the masculine in both women and men, because the divine feminine within both will naturally arise in the safety of that container. In addition to this and even more importantly, I think we need to reconnect to the TOL and stop doing the TOK. We need to feel the spirit of what we are doing and enjoy and celebrate that; even if it is difficult. In fact, especially because it is difficult.

Bringing Jesus Back down to Earth

As for the decisions of our predecessors in Nicaea, back in AD 325, and our having made Jesus the only begotten Son of God, when other writings translate as Jesus being the first begotten Son of God, I think we are back at that time of chaos again, seeking to reconsider their decision. To me, Jesus is of more use when he is also seen as a man who did incredible things and attained an incredible level of awakening and wisdom, transcending the limitations and needs of the body, emotions, and mind, and awakening into the more spiritual realms. If Jesus is the only begotten Son of God, then we can't succeed in aspiring to follow Him; we are just fallen sinners with no hope. We can even excuse ourselves and feel no responsibility. But if we bring Jesus back down to earth and also see Him as humanity's greatest human, then suddenly, we have something to aim for, something to follow. I can even feel the difference in my body as I write and feel into the two different perceptions. When I connect to the Jesus on high as the only begotten, my spirit arises out of me and engages with something out there and up there that is holy and above and beyond embodied experience, simply to be loved, worshiped, and appreciated.

But when I perceive Jesus in the second way, as a man who was in every cell of His being the same essence as the source itself, just as the rest of us are, then my spirit is suddenly brought back into my embodiment with a sense of realisation, accountability, and expectations about my behaviour and purpose of existence.

Try it for yourself: perceive Jesus one way and then the other, and see what happens within you. This is one of the things this book is trying to do: bring Jesus and the church and Christianity and the Holy Spirit all back down to earth a bit, not God or source, as I prefer to call it, because I believe that is more transcendent and independent in a panentheistic, that, God-in-all-things kind of way (or pantheistic, God-is-all-things kind of way).

But I think we need to bring the rest of it back down to earth a bit because we have put our love object on such a high pedestal to protect it and be able to look up to it that we can't reach it properly or follow it correctly. We have made it all into an alabaster box, where we stand back in some stupor and worshipfully gaze up at it all from afar, instead of living the fragrance and taking ownership of it all. We put the trinity on high, and in doing so put our self on low, subconsciously relieving our self of any responsibility. When we are awake enough to see what we have been unconsciously doing and are mature enough to take back what we once projected, we can take ownership and responsibility of ourselves again and engage with the reality of our self-created situation.

From here, we can then stop expecting some projection to resolve our problems for us like a child and approach the reality of our situation in a different way. To me, we are the church by what we do and how we are being with our self, each other, and everything else. The holy or holistic guiding spirit is here and alive amongst us in every instant, being unseen for what it is, because we call it all sorts of other things in our ignorance. We also don't look for it or expect to see it because we have placed it out of sight or told ourselves that we are unworthy sinners. As for Jesus, well, I think He is of more use to us when He is also seen in a more down-to-earth light, equally begotten and still leading the way two thousand years later. I think the opportunity that lies before us in these difficult times is to understand the meaning of church better. If a church is a place for us to come together in worship and celebration and align with the coming of a new kingdom, then the way we should be doing that includes the likes of Psychosynthesis and Heart Intelligence where we can practice being the way and the truth and the life.

CHAPTER 4

Our Society in Breakdown and Reformation

The Disconnected Oppressed

I sometimes wonder what most people are living for these days. What motivates or inspires them? What do they align with or believe in?

Many of us seem to have lost faith in religion, politics, education, and law; and are then left with little guidance or principles to stand by or hold us when making short- and long-term decisions. Some people seem to be living for the weekend or holidays or to buy a new car, whilst others are simply working to pay the bills or have food and shelter, never mind thinking about home improvements or trying to get on in life to somewhere better. Many are not working, and some are homeless, with some simply looking after number one, themselves and their kids, and if that is at the detriment of others, then so be it; it's up to them to fight for themselves. Many people have nothing to live for; no sense of purpose or hope of change; living a mundane existence, day after day after day, with their only stimulation or moments of joy being some unhealthy food that gives them a few minutes of pleasure. No wonder we are becoming more obese as a society, using food to give us something to do, to fill the void that is not about our stomach but about the emptiness of our lives. We have increasing mental health issues as more and more people become depressed and feel worthless, putting financial burden and stress on support systems that are barely hanging on.

On a national level, we are looking at another probable Scottish referendum. On a multinational level, we are in Brexit; Britain's actually leaving the European Union. Then there is the biblical-scale mass exodus that is going on as nations of people seek freedom from war, suppression and oppression.

This is obviously not the entire truth everywhere and for everyone, but collectively, I think it is the case for very many people at this time. It's like our old way of living is in breakdown and not working anymore; some people have given up hope. "What can you do about it?" They say, or, "You just have to get on with it. There's nothing else for it." But that's not true; this is simply stage 2, the victim stage in a 4 stage system of change. Stage 3 is when we begin to do something about it to get to stage 4, happiness again, but this happiness is at a different level from the former happiness of stage 1, before everything started to change and feel like our world was falling apart. Stage 2 is when we don't have any understanding of what's going on and why, and don't see any sign of the way out. Most people have no understanding of what is happening and no vision of what is realistically possible and therefore little impetus to be motivated. Perhaps we should really listen to our subconscious mumblings more often and realise that there is actually something trying to guide us within them.

There actually are productive things happening, such as lots of charities to be seen and lots of charitable work going on, as well as lots of community activity going on. In some cases, people with very little are still giving what little they can to others with even less. There is more voluntary work being done, and more food banks are being set up, as well as some of the wealthy trying to make a difference.

More people are taking up things like mindfulness and yoga and meditation; even schools are getting children involved in these things early on in life. These are all holistic practices that take us away from the heady manic world and into a calmer, more centred place within ourselves. Most of these things are about genuine service and giving rather than giving to subconsciously get our own love needs met. Then at the more multinational level, there is the humanitarian aid that goes on all the time and countries taking in thousands of refugees. So the beginnings of turnaround are there to be seen and have always been there, chipping away in the background. The will to good being the true nature of who and what we are is seen behind these actions. But surely this shouldn't have to be happening at all if we were all connected to the same understanding of reality and following the same vision for humanity. Yes, it is good to be charitable, but some of this is not about being charitable; some of it is out of desperation to help because we can see how difficult life is for others and sympathise with their situation. Some of it is coming from desperation to have something to do or self-righteousness of feeling better by giving. Then there is the situation that some of those who are in a very deprived state are milking the system for everything they can get, thinking the world or at least their local council, owes them a living. It really is in an incredible mess.

The Disconnected Oppressors

Then there are the big rich businesses and empires and the obscenely rich who have more money than they could ever spend; some admittedly give to those who have less and put back into society in varying ways, but many others probably don't, and others do it for vanity, self-righteousness and self-promotion. Yet are they really the ones at the top? Are they connected to the source of life, living in love and gratitude and the awe and wonder of all creation? Or are they the ones in most disconnect, getting their fix through attachment to material wealth and status, rather than the great source? In many cases, I would say yes, and that they have learned to do it out of their own childhood survival needs, learning to exploit the unconscious needs of others so as to get somewhere better themselves (this being the squabbling around in the mud that I spoke of earlier). When we are not getting our spiritual and developmental needs from the abundant source of all life, we end up manipulating it out of each other. We unconsciously get our love needs satisfied by praying on other people's unconscious needs, and we don't even realise that we are doing it. We just feel better by having more and by feeling safer in life due to wealth or status or fame; we sit there thinking, *It's their own fault if they don't have. I had to work hard for what I've got, and so should they.*

The Dynamics at Play in Politics

Not long after the Scottish referendum, there was a general election where the Liberal Democrats were annihilated. Shortly after that, I noticed thousands of people joining the Lib Dem's, as they were very much the beaten-down underdogs. Isn't it interesting how they didn't join the more victorious parties? Now we have the Labour party squabbling amongst its self and Ukip trying to implode on itself.

One day shortly after this situation, I sat down to apply a philosophy I was holding about life, to politics. I spent all day on the computer and came to the following conclusion: It seems like there are two types of political parties: masculine and feminine, although they do have their respective right and left wing components. Carl Jung would perhaps have said anima and animus: the feminine within the male and the masculine within the female. There seem to be parties that are mostly about growth and movement from the current position, and then there are parties that seem to be more about protecting and stabilising the current level of growth thus far attained, basically feminine and masculine, respectively.

The feminine ones are the likes of SNP, Labour, and Liberal, whereas the masculine are more like Conservative and Ukip. As I see it, the feminine is more preoccupied with the people and escaping poverty and oppression, such as the Scottish referendum scenario of seeking to escape from what is seen as the parental imago of the Westminster oppressor. Or Labour from the 1970s and 1980s doing a similar thing in seeking to empower the miners and car and ship building industries through the collective power of trade unions against the governing oppressor of the day.

The masculine parties alternatively seem to be more conserving such as Ukip wanting to protect what we have from being diminished by thousands of others coming into the country and taking what they haven't contributed too; both attitudes equally wise and necessary. But then is the SNP not also trying to protect its love object from what they see as the oppressing bad parent, and were Labour not doing the same thing for its union members? My point being that one side seems to be more masculine identified and the other more feminine, and we need a healthy balance of both. We don't want to be swinging from one to the other and back again every time there is another election. We need a leadership that is more balanced, more conscious, and operating from a higher context. I am not saying that I have a better answer or that I could do it any better, but it is easy to sit here and point the finger at what I see, hoping that some revelation will occur.

I think that schools and society are too far in the feminine at the moment, too soft and unstructured, but I will come back to that. So if this were to happen and any governing party was to take this approach to be the context they operated from, then perhaps we would see microcosms within that macrocosm, where certain areas such as NHS and construction were needing a feminine spell of growth, whilst education and public sector wages may need more of a containing masculine attitude for the time being. I think this does happen subconsciously, but maybe it would help if people could see the dynamics that are at play.

And then there is the extent of immaturity within politicians. Watching the House of Commons reveals more immaturity than watching a bunch of squabbling children. It's a disgrace. I think politicians should have to undergo five years of psychotherapy and psychospiritual training before they can even graduate. No wonder the country and the world is in the state it is in, with our leaders being as immature as they are.

A Humanity in Midlife Crisis

No wonder I find myself searching for something more. I too have lost faith in many of these systems in our society that are meant to parent and protect and serve and nurture, but they don't seem to be managing to do that as well as we would like. I still can't get my head around why banks are businesses and why profit is necessary. Profit is surely taking money that you don't really need, just out of greed for the sake of it or for the sake of extra financial safety and security. I am not talking about a cushion for a bad year that may come or the funding for new equipment in a couple of years' time. I am talking about completely unnecessary taking of something from others because you can, and because their need is exploitable. Thank goodness we are beginning to see the introduction of government policing organisations such as Ofcom. I ran my own business for twenty-one years and did okay, but I don't know if I really ever earned a profit. I sometimes earned what I could have earned doing the same job as an employee for someone else, but I often earned less. The human body to me is a system that seems to work quite well, and one part doesn't profit to the demise of another; it all stands or falls together. To me, this is also something that is being shown to us as a model of how an organism such as humanity or Gaia can actually work.

I am sure this is partly why I am looking for something more to hold me in life and help me to make sense of what's going on. At first, it seems like a bad situation to be in, but if these systems are failing, and I know there is a divine guidance at play, then perhaps it is not ultimately a bad thing at all, other than the unfair suffering. Perhaps I just need to have faith from having experienced this guidance several times and try to follow the guidance that comes my own way, such as writing this book.

In the Bible, there is something about God saying that He will bring down everything not built in His name; perhaps that is what we are seeing happening: big businesses, unions between countries, civilisations, all sorts of large and small systems. Even that which is supposed to be built in His name is in demise, resulting in churches being closed and sold and people being left with little to believe in, other than everyone for their self. But this is what happens in systems when they have no higher vision or alignment or guidance. This is all evidence of something not working, something not being right; we desperately need to see what that is, so we can find something to help us to begin moving in the right direction again, rather than do what those in power are trying to do and get back to where we were a few years ago: typical midlife crisis behaviour.

Most of what I am writing in this chapter will be nothing new to you, as there are plenty of people who can see what I have just described, but as a society, we don't have a psychospiritual understanding of what is really happening and why or how to resolve it.

This is classic midlife crisis! When we are lost and so regress to what last worked instead of groping our way forwards towards the new that is trying to emerge. We do this regressing in desperation to regain security, because we don't understand what is happening to us or understand what evolution and awakening feels like to endure. The old is dying away in preparation of the new being born, but we don't know what that looks like yet, so we can't help it. This is the butterfly emerging from the cocoon, but it looks nothing like a butterfly yet. Everything just looks like a mess, as the caterpillar turns into soup.

For me, this is all a sign of what happens to a society when we don't have a higher purpose or vision, when we reject the guidance that we were following because it has failed us and are left with nothing to keep us working towards a goal or moving in an understood direction. This is exactly where I was at for a couple of years before learning to trust the guidance that I slowly began to realise was actually helping me rather than out to get me. This was my moving from stage 2 to stage 3, victim to action. So I am not saying this is a bad thing; I am saying it is a good thing, as long as that new anchor and vision and understanding comes along fairly soon, before it all falls apart completely and goes backwards rather than forwards.

My World as a Psychospiritual Life Coach

But this is my world, the world of psychospiritual life coaching; this is where I come alive and am blessed to work every time that I sit with a client or a group that is in some disturbance (or not in disturbance, in some cases but usually not okay with something that is going on in their life) and not able to understand what is happening to them or see the solution. All they have to work with is how it was in the past, and that it isn't working anymore, much the same as our collective condition at the moment. Add to this situation the fact that there are very few people teaching them what they need to know to get to the other side, because there are very few who have done the journey, and we can see a microcosm of the macrocosm.

When I graduated from the Institute of Psychosynthesis in 2010, I was one of a handful of psychospiritual life coaches in Britain, and it isn't much better in 2016 either. I had to travel from Fife in Scotland to London for thirteen long weekends for five years, firstly to re-find my sanity and then to qualify as a psychospiritual life coach. I was in meltdown and crisis; trying to do a degree in London, run my own joinery business with several employees and sub contractors, be a dad and husband, and hide what was happening to me out of fear and shame, all at the same time. So if this book does only one thing, and that is to help people see there is a divine guidance at play in life and we have to help each other to follow it, then all that suffering and struggle will have been worth it. Not just my struggle and fear and suffering but also that of my family, as they were all caught up in it as well. So this is who I am and what I do. I don't coach business owners and CEOs to get rich; I help people to awaken and transform. I have tried getting large organisations like the NHS and Fife Council and Christianity to let me in and help facilitate change, but they are still too busy doing the same old, same old TOK and fighting the losing battle, just as the majority are. These great big institutions and organisations are like machines or monsters that are all too busy in the ego development level, trying to regress to when it worked before, and in most cases, they are also ignorant of the developmental dynamics of life, of how everything is always trying to evolve to be a purer version of itself through breakdown and reformation. To me, it is still the same base dynamics of gravity in tension with fusion, or the masculine inhibiting the feminine, instead of giving it a container in which to flourish.

Signs of Hope on the Horizon

There are signs of hope, as I mention above, where our more humanitarian self comes to the fore in times of deprivation and breakdown, but what we really need at this time is to understand what is really going on, to be helped to see that this breakdown is trying to serve breakthrough and reformation into something new and better. Then once we can see what is going on, we can move from being victim to being inspired and become motivated to do something to help, just as happened to myself in my breakdown. This is where we need a glimmer of light to help us see what direction to go in because otherwise, all we see is all the collapse and chaos of breakdown, and we lose hope and go further into the demise of fighting amongst our selves. At this point, we need to see the goal and the vision and the path so we have a direction to move in and a new womb to attach to. This is the emerging butterfly, unconsciously empowered by having seen the light and fighting its way out of the old form because it has a sense of purpose and direction.

I can also see that my own personal disturbance that initiated this book, is just a microcosm of the global situation we are in, and that my longing for peace and joy is the same collective calling. In Psychosynthesis and Heart Intelligence coaching, we work primarily from the concept that our disturbances ignite movement towards something else, something that is potentially better, if we work wisely and heart intelligently from the disturbance, finding our purer, more holistic want and working towards that, rather than be tricked by avoidant, regressive or lower level wants. This is why in Heart Intelligence coaching work, we work through those two initial questions: 'What's moving?' and then with that revealed, 'What do you want in relation to that?' The skill of the coach is then to listen for and discern the voice of their purest truth, rather than let them be influenced by all the other psychologically loaded voices. But given that the coach is always seeking to help the client move any amount forward, we often have to allow them to go with a less pure voice, because they aren't ready or available to hear or follow the purest one yet. The consequence of getting this right is that the unconscious is now conscious. From my Quaker attending days, I see this as being like when Quakers talk about holding something up to God or in the light, or source, as I am calling it, and waiting for the light to come in, but I think it works more effectively and efficiently through this small dialogue and coaching approach. From here, we can help others further by using three other questions: 'What's the fear if this stays as it is?' 'What's holding you back?' and then, 'So given all of that what do you need?' These want and fear questions arouse the emergent and energies for change, as we say in psychosynthesis, and the holding you back and need questions tease the unconscious psychological inhibitors to the surface. With this done and much realisations made, it is okay to stop, as some productive progress has been made, and the client may be exhausted, but it is even better if the client can be helped to do some physical act to evidence and embody the new reality, so the old mindset is no longer as true as it perhaps once was. Again for me, I can see within this the masculine inhibiting the feminine, the closed mindset or TOK energy inhibiting the alive TOL energy, but by bringing light or consciousness to something that was solidified, it becomes freed up and oxygenated and comes alive again.

From Too Hard a Masculine to Too Soft a Feminine

As I reflect and look back at some of what I have written, I seem to be spending a lot of time writing about an immature masculine abusing and suppressing the free expression of the feminine, rather than give it a safe place of containment and form so it can express itself. But despite spending so much time writing about the immature masculine, I also want to mention some of the changes I see happening in more recent times, now that we are seeing the result of having perhaps softened the masculine too much. We are seeing the consequences of a lack of good structure and boundaries in our homes, schools, and society. I think that it is due to this over softening, that we are now seeing more and more children and adults run amuck in society. I also think this may be affecting children's development, in that I seem to be seeing more and more children that are too fused with their mothers, too engulfed and embraced in the over loving feminine. Too much yes and not enough no. No is a very important word when it comes to development and separation individuation. Donald Winnicott taught us that it is the maternal failings that assist the process of separation from mother and the individuation process, allowing children to find their selfhood and individuality, gradually learning to cope and self-regulate and develop responsibility. But good parenting that includes the understanding of how important the word 'no' is, plays just as significant a role in my opinion. Over the past ten years, I seem to be seeing more and more mothers with sons that are just on the autistic spectrum, and to me these mothers usually seem to be overly fused with the child. I get that this is out of love but it's like they are running the child's emotions and life for them, unintentionally depriving the child of the ability to develop through these experiences, situations and finding of solutions. I am not talking about children that are very autistic here, but those that are just on the spectrum. If you are the mother of an slightly autistic son then just reading this will probably trigger your anger and have you raging at me by now, desperate to find out how you can give me a piece of your mind, due to my attacking your love object, into which you have placed your love so that you can protect it from everything that is out to harm it. Perhaps mothers are unconsciously doing this to shape their sons into the way they want their men to be, because they are not getting their love needs met by them.

I can also see the unconditional love that exists at this level of relationship and the intimacy between a mother and her baby, be it boy or girl, and can see that divine and sacred union that very few achieve with other adults. I am no specialist in this field and know that there are many factors involved, but nonetheless, in my ignorance and limited knowledge this is what I seem to be increasingly seeing.

Having been foster carers for over twenty years, we often see mothers producing a constant stream of babies that continually get removed from them due to their inability to care for them. Most women seem to be at their happiest when they can give their love unconditionally and have it be received, and so they will unconsciously create a world that allows them to do this. But babies become more difficult to unconditionally love as they begin to develop and this can be when it all starts to go wrong. But after my merging experience in Spain and from what I see going on in society, I can also see that this over loving and merging is just as harmful as an overly abusive or immature masculine; perhaps both being somewhat primitive. Our present-day society is in a mess due to a lack of structure and boundaries and no concern for the consequences of actions. We certainly needed to do something to correct the imbalance, but as we can see, we haven't got it quite right. Once again, I think this is partly due to not applying a more balanced and synthesising approach to resolving situations. Just like two thousand years ago, when Celtic Christianity was abandoned in favour of Roman Christianity, one being seen to be right and the other wrong, the TOK being at play again, society became forced to go with one to the exclusion of the other.

Today, we see the same dynamic at play in our putting an end to abusive parenting, because it was wrong and too damaging and destructive, physically, mentally, and emotionally and most of it being because the parent was angry with something else or wanting to be occupied with something else or had a mindset about something and the child was breaking it. This is all unconscious, self centred and immature behaviour of parents due to a lack of their own personal development and psychospiritual understanding before having children, and I will put my own hand up first. Of course this behaviour is also out of stress and preoccupation with success and survival and providing for the family, as well as materialism and status and all the other things that we become attached to and identified with. These are all things that we are conditioned to perceive as important and become caught up in as most of us seek first our own greater kingdom before becoming ready to seek that greater kingdom for others. Of course, we absolutely had to stop (and still need to do more to stop) abusive parenting, but not to the extent of losing all of our structure, boundaries, and guidance. But then I think we also need to be careful of what I see as the overly nurturing feminine that inhibits development in the child to get its own unconscious unmet needs fulfilled. I don't think this is the majority, but I certainly see it increasing. I see many parents being very loving and affectionate to their kids as well as giving them good containment in the form of firm structure and boundaries. But I still think we could gain a lot more from having a psychospiritual understanding of life and human development and by having a collective and conscious purpose and vision for the future. I believe we need adult education of this nature to help men and women mature for the sake of their own spiritual journey, but also so they can parent from the spirit of love and be assisted by having an attachment to a vision, rather than parent unconsciously and from the conditioning of their own childhood upbringing. This would then allow them to parent from being self-aware, proactive, and educated, rather than being unaware, reactive, and ignorant, mostly seeking to unconsciously meet their own developmental needs whenever the child triggers their unresolved issues.

For me, there are also lots of signs of where we are failing society as the creators of that society. The majority of children's cartoons these days are absolute mayhem and mania, and the governing bodies let this stuff go on the air. Surely this just evidences that we have the wrong people in these jobs. But then many parents are quite happy, as long as the kids are not bothering them. Kids are also hyper on sweets and junk food most of the time because once again it is an easy solution for the parents. More and more kids spend most of their time with their faces in laptops and mobile phones and iPad's. Our radio stations are full of immature DJs all being similarly manic and hyper. It took me weeks to find a decent radio station to wake up to in the morning, but eventually I found Smooth Radio, which is excellent and quite a contrast energetically.

As I said earlier the House of Commons is like watching a bunch of kids running a country and we are stupid enough to let them get away with it. It is absolutely ridiculous and for me all due to quite rightly abandoning a religion that wasn't understood or working, but leaving ourselves with no structure or beliefs or vision or purpose, as well as no understanding of how to follow the parental imago that does exists but that we don't even realise is there, leaving ourselves with nothing to steer ourselves by. I was chatting to someone the other evening, and he was talking about how academic qualifications are now all that matters, seeing newcomers coming into care and emergency work with no in the field practical experience. Once again, I see the TOK being given priority over the TOL. We need to know where we are trying to get too, or we will just continue to run ourselves round in circles in absolute chaos.

If we can get to a point where we can all see the same reality and see the same truth and way out, then hopefully we can align in the same direction, working towards the same goal. Because that is when the synthesis and nuclear fusion will happen, and we can begin to move together in the one direction with great energy, holding the same common vision and making manifest a more heavenly earth.

Schools and Social Settings

I also see something similar going on in some schools and social settings, where there is now a lack of mature masculine structure and boundaries, and the feminine energy is too soft and unstructured in its over-mothering, resulting in not meeting the containment needs of children. I feel that teachers are pandering to the whims of the children too much. Our school education system has come on amazingly in some areas, with teachers being like psychologists and psychotherapists half of the time. Add to that spending some of their remaining time doing the parenting that doesn't go on at home and in society, and they are left with little of the time to actually teach. I think they do an amazing job but are being limited once again by the powers at the top, even though it is those same powers that have got them doing the good work they are doing.

In other social situations, I see children being completely undisciplined by nearby parents, allowing them to run around and shout and climb all over people's furniture, leave their mess all over the place, leave clothes where they shouldn't, and wilfully damage property. It is ridiculous what is going on, and we the so-called adults of the society are letting it happen. Thankfully, we saw the harm in the abusive masculine energy and to some extent put a stop to it, but now we have gone too far the other way. We need to see the harm that we are now doing due to the lack of mature masculine authority and structure and boundaries.

This of course brings us back to my original situation and cause behind this book, the fact that existing paradigms get us to see new ones, but then the new ones see the limitations of the old, and we need to find a way to integrate and evolve. But what we really need to learn is that the old one isn't totally incorrect, because this is what we often do wrong. We see what seems better and abandon the old completely, making it outlawed when inclusive progression is what is being called for, integration and transcendence without suppression and exclusion, and that is what is trying to happen in my dilemma through writing this book. My other concern with the over softening of the masculine is that it will ultimately result in a rebalancing, one way or another. The chaos and disorder that is escalating will shortly lead to increasing disruption and probably war, setting us all back years instead of moving forwards. Despite this concern, I do however see this disruption as ultimately potentially healthy, because the current systems and parental imagos are too immature and they are not working, and this is creating breakdown in societies all over the world. We even have several mass exoduses going on. It is time for us to take some responsibility back upon ourselves and put the newly evolved collective conscious space to better use. We need to find a common enemy and common goal and come together, willing to fight for it.

I was at the remembrance service on Sunday past and reflected on the suffering and pain and the lives that were lost by all countries during these wars. Theirs was the time of physical fighting to get from where they were to somewhere better, but ours today is a time of doing it a different way before we end up dropping back to that level of dealing with it again. I find that energy tries to find equilibrium and harmony first at higher levels, but when it can't, it drops to the lower physical level to happen. This is why we need leaders with a psychospiritual understanding of life that are also heart intelligent and awake to the higher guidance that exists to serve and guide us.

Applying a Psychospiritual Coaching Approach to Humanity's Midlife Crisis

So if we then apply the 'What's moving?' and 'What do you want?' questions to this situation that humanity is going through, we get what I have already described above. And if we apply the 'What's the fear?' question, we would get answers like, *The fear is that if it doesn't change, we are all going to drive each other into poverty and starvation and more riotous behaviour; there will be even more fighting and killing and crime, eventually leading to total destruction of everything.*

'What do you need?'

I need help to see a way out, to see what has gone wrong so that we can try to fix it. I need a vision of how it can be, so that I have something to stand in and fight for if necessary.

'So what's holding you back?'

The lack of an environment that demonstrates a different way so that we can all begin to adapt to that environment, or even some insight or education that teaches us a new way, so that we can begin to be that environment for ourselves and for our children and grandchildren. We need something that will give us one common vision instead of all sorts of clashing beliefs, so that it can empower us to stand together and just move in that direction, because this one isn't working anymore. We need educated and help to escape being the way that we are.

And this is what things like Psychosynthesis, Heart Intelligence and Watchman Nee's Christianity can give us as well as bringing back more Celtic Christianity.

Avicii's song comes to mind as I end this chapter (*Avicii* in Buddhism means the lowest level of hell):

> Feeling my way through the darkness,
> guided by a beating heart.
> I can't tell where the journey will end,
> but I know where to start.
> They tell me I'm too young to understand.
> They say I'm caught up in a dream.
> Well life will pass me by if I don't open up my eyes.
> Well that's fine by me.

CHAPTER 5

The Urgent Need for Action

Is This The Holy Spirit, Hidden in Plain Sight

This chapter was never intended to exist; even after several weeks of writing and taking form, it wasn't on the cards until it was offered to me a second ago. But this same Holy Spirit that has always had a playful way of working with me is what we are actually talking about all the way through this book, as it shows how it works in its own mysterious and subtle, graceful ways. It is there to be seen in the everyday, ordinary world when we know that it truly exists and see it for what it is. I deliberately didn't say *believe* that it exists; I said *know* that it exists, because as I have been writing this book, I have seen it guiding me time and time again. As I increasingly acknowledge this to myself, I also recall the many times it has been there, blatantly revealing itself for me to see, and although I have seen it for the guidance that it is in the extreme moments, I have never actually considered it as possibly being the Holy Spirit, nor given it credit for the small everyday moments, even though its offering is always guiding, nurturing, and holistic in spirit. I can only think that this is probably because the Holy Spirit only ever gets talked about in the Bible and so gets painted as being something so above and beyond that I haven't looked for it outside of religion, nor to be what is guiding me.

However, for some time, I have been seeking some way to bring the spiritual down to earth, down from that high shelf that keeps it all untouchable and unusable. I am beginning to realise now that part of what is being shown by this book is that it is here amongst us, just as the Bible says, and in such an ordinary, everyday way that we don't even see it. Maybe we are too busy in the TOK all the time, or maybe we've been calling it intuition and instinct and even coincidence, instead of seeing it for what it really is, given that this guidance tends to be protective and nurturing in spirit. Perhaps the kingdom of heaven really is so at hand that we can't even see it.

So what makes me think that this could be the Holy Spirit and not just what we normally call thought or internal dialogue or tapping into my own unconscious? Well, for me, it is always out of the blue and revelatory, and there is always a substantial realisation from what it offers. It mostly happens when I am not that preoccupied about anything and in some mindless or thoughtless void or other. It is sometimes a bit abstract and playful and leaves me to do a little bit of thinking for myself, but that is always to my own amusement when I do get it. It is different from thinking because it comes in when my mind is empty but holding some question or other in the background, just as it probably does with you and everyone else. It is also always kind and loving, or helpful and guiding or playful and teasing. It is never nasty or immature or spiteful or hurtful.

As I write this, I am offered from somewhere the following to contemplate: *Surely a Jesus and Holy Spirit that is here on earth and interacting with us is a lot more useful to us than one that we can't interact with because there is too big a gap.* But just to help you learn the difference, this offering doesn't feel like that Holy Spirit voice or simply internal dialogue, it feels more like my higher Self. It felt like a higher part of me compared to what I am questioning as being the Holy Spirit. The offering that comes from that place does not feel like a part of me and is of a different energetic feel. It almost always instantly resolves something and is loving to experience. So what if this is an omnipresent guidance system that we unconsciously push out of reach because we are so caught up in our own beliefs, self-dependence, self-righteousness, mindsets, and opinions? What if we are busying our self so much out of our disconnect that I talk about, that we never give it a chance to get through? We walk around telling ourselves so many stories in our heads that we are constantly in the TOK, instead of being in the TOL, where it waits for us to return.

Watchman Nee talks about the different ways that the Holy Spirit works, with one of them being about how it facilitates our environment, bringing relevant things to our space and attention; things that usually seem a bit coincidental. It always amuses me how we project flukery onto the word *coincidental*, when it simply refers to two or more things coinciding. I have been having several of these as I write this book.

A Fuller Look at the Extent of the Crisis that We Are In

I believe that our physical, mental, psychological, and emotional health issues have a lot to do with this disconnect from source. Whether it is a connect through the nature-al and what is seen as soulical by Watchman Nee, or connect through that which is seen as spiritual, masculine and Christian. As soon as I reconnect to source by any means, I sense a vitality and vibrancy within myself that I can actually feel, making me feel healthier and happier and more joyful, all of which is about releasing healthy chemicals into my body. I feel reconnected to love, the ever abundant source, regardless of where or how I connect to it.

There are an increasing number of organisations and institutions such as the NHS, schools, employers, and prison services that are introducing things like meditation, mindfulness, yoga, and other holistic practices because we are beginning to realise the healthy difference that they make. The unfortunate thing in my opinion is that we have not quite realised what I am offering here: that the reason these things work is because we are coming out of the TOK and reconnecting to the TOL. We are reconnecting to the divine loving source to replenish ourselves not just taking a rest from the stressful and manic. Our NHS is on the brink of collapse and costing us an unbelievable amount of money per day, when so much of our health issues can be resolved by understanding properly what is wrong and addressing it. Adding to the NHS situation is overpopulation and more particularly an unhealthy overpopulation, where we are overeating and eating unhealthily to compensate for this same disconnect. Then there are drugs and alcohol and all the health issues and antisocial issues that come with that.

Having been a foster carer for over twenty years, I have also come to believe that women have babies to fill their unmet love needs, both to give the unconditional love that they essentially are and to receive it from their babies. No wonder some women just keep producing more babies when they are taken away from them. They are not getting their needs met by the men in their lives and so create their own love object. Also, once the child begins to get older and be less receptive and giving of that love, some women need to produce another baby all over again. We have mass exoduses going on in several parts of the world as well as several countries at war, and still we don't seem willing to reconsider that we may be getting the whole thing wrong.

Inferno: The Uncontained Feminine

As an example of the Holy Spirit's facilitating our environment, this afternoon, my wife and I went to see *Inferno*, Dan Brown's latest book set to screen by Ron Howard, and it reminded me of this urgency to change the way that we are living. The film emphasised the state of the world that we are living in today, as I have just mentioned, but it took it to a whole other level. I read the book a couple of years ago, but what a coincidence that it was released yesterday, just when I am writing this chapter. To me, the film is essentially about someone trying to redress the consequence of a humanity that has been functioning out of immature and suppressed levels of masculine and feminine energy. And even more particularly; the consequence of a lack of a mature and wise masculine containment and guidance on continuing generations of men and women, and the affect of that on humanity and the world. This film for me is about all that I am writing about, with someone desperately playing God to try to correct the situation before it is too late for everyone. The film for me, is speaking to an overpopulated out of control humanity due to an immature masculine not being able to provide the required container for the abundant feminine outpouring of love and beauty to express its self.

About three-quarters of the way through the film, the portrayed villain says to his girlfriend, something like, "I will create another way for you," and in that moment a penny dropped (or a revelation occurred). (This is another way in which we don't see the Holy Spirit due to our unconscious self righteousness in modern-day language and devaluing guiding experiences, the phrase *penny dropped* meaning a sudden revelation out of the blue). It is also interesting that the film should be released halfway through my writing this book and that I should see it exactly prior to starting writing about how Psychosynthesis and Heart Intelligence can help guide us out of this humanitarian situation; especially when we add it to the teachings of Watchman Nee and Jesus. Roberto Assagioli; the Italian doctor and psychiatrist behind Psychosynthesis, like many others, could see that we suffer separation from our divine source as well as separation from our earthly source, mother. This line, "I will create another way for you," just says it all: the masculine's longing for the feminine to flower and lead them both home to source so that they can be engulfed together into the awakened conscious realisation of being the blissful awe and wonder, in the expression of human form. These two energies having previously came out of the fused nonconscious oneness to separate into the two energies of masculine form and feminine outpouring.

At this moment in the film, I was suddenly pulled into the archetypal dimension then back again, so as to see the difference between our world of the immature, unawakened masculine suppressing the feminine, and the higher realm of divine union. Once again, something guiding and revealing had shown me a flash of what is going on at a higher level and giving me a momentary embodied, joyous experience of what we can achieve, giving me a boost and affirmation. The realisation that I am increasingly seeing is that something incredible is holding space for something beautiful to flower within, the masculine serving as a container for the feminine to reveal itself in, so that the source which is the essential union of both can be revealed in all its glory.

Michael Buble's song 'Lost' springs immediately to mind here, although it is there to be heard in most songs if you listen for it and if you know what to feel for:

> I can't believe it's over
> I watched the whole thing fall
> And I never saw the writing that was on the wall
> If I only knew
> The days were slipping past
> That the good things never last
> That you were crying.

At this point, I highly recommend you go and listen to the words of the whole song as I am not permitted to write them all out. But I especially invite you to listen from being in the spirit of what this book is offering you.

The Present and the Potential Future

This song helps us to see the archetypal masculine and feminine in the struggle and sacred dance of what they seek to make manifest. In contrast to this, I am showing our past state of unconscious and uninformed, immature masculine that was suppressing the feminine out of ignorance and fear and the pathology of childhood suffering. Fortunately, things have slowly been improving over the years, but there is still a lot of work to be done. The other thing we need to be careful of is that we don't just move to a wishy-washy, merged masculine and feminine with no clear roles, as can also be seen in society and which simply allows things to fall apart. In some areas of life, we have too strong a feminine energy, and things are not being given structure. For me, the feminine energy of abundance and outpouring needs to be wisely directed and contained or it can suffocate and over-nurture and not allow separation individuation to happen. Perhaps there needs to be the failing in the maternal care system to help facilitate individuality as well as that purpose aligned no.

What's Moving and What Do We need?

So what do we need to help us take the next progressive step?

Given my own journey and that of others that I have travelled with, I would say that we need exactly the same thing: a psychospiritual understanding of life to help us understand how human life is facilitated within the spiritual and psychological realms, and to help us to see what is and what could be. We also then need a heart intelligent environment to facilitate it to happen. The psychospiritual knowledge helping people to see and understand what is happening in relation to their own lives and the world they can witness, not some historical story they can't self-evidence. Most people have lost faith in everything other than what they can experience and witness for themselves, and are interested in what makes a difference to them and their world. The other reason for this TOK approach is because that is where we are functioning, and people's thoughts are often the first thing that is available when considering change. We think about things first because we are so used to living in the TOK and because it is safer to think first. If we allow our opinions and beliefs to become slightly changed and it all goes wrong, then we don't tend to lose a limb; we just get psychologically impacted. It is one of the safest parts for us to allow to move first. Once we begin to buy into something and see things differently, then other aspects of who we are will slowly begin to follow, as long as it remains safe.

This is also why we need to work with the whole environment at once, to increase the safety. We could alternatively go straight for Heart Intelligence and do it by example; safety and love will spontaneously provide the correct environment for people to awaken and flower. It is as simple as that. But most of us don't have that necessary safe enlightened environment, or capacity to allow ourselves to be more loving than normal because of our pathology, and this is why we need heart circles to help it happen. But the psychospiritual education can empower us by getting our resistant protective minds on board to assist us. For what would I push myself, and would I suffer taking this on, you ask? The answer is to be real, to feel alive, for your kids, your grandkids, your society, those who suffer and don't have, those who will suffer and die every day that we don't, humanity, ourselves, and the purpose of our existence: to play a part in the coming of a greater kingdom.

PART 2

Where We Are Trying to Get To

Part 2 starts with Watchman Nee's explanation of the Bible and spirit; his offering is quite profound and quite different from what I see being taught in our churches today. It is most specifically his work that has caused me to end up writing this book in an attempt to synthesise and transcend the disturbance that I find myself in. This disturbance being due to the polarity between his understanding and what I see going on in the world. Of course, it is actually the holistic guidance that I speak of that is more causal behind everything, but is part of that holistic guidance the Holy Spirit that Jesus said would come in His place, and that adds to The Old Testament, rather that replaces it, as He also said?

This is followed by the teachings of Jesus, which come partly from those writings and partly from my own perception and understanding, as well as from the Bible and other books that I have read,as well as training courses that I have completed. I find that Jesus offers us a way of living that can save us doing all sorts of trainings and personal development courses, searching to find the way. I find that when I focus directly on following His guidance, I don't need to do anything else. This chapter does not involve going into the Bible in general but is more specifically about understanding the teachings so that we can then follow them.

Part 2 concludes by introducing you to Celtic Christianity, which assists these other two chapters in helping us to see a different understanding of reality and how things can be, once we have the insight, knowledge, and wisdom, that has eluded us individually and collectively so far. For me, Celtic Christianity brings the religion back to life by bringing the feminine aspect of God back into the picture, balancing an otherwise too masculine comprehension.

CHAPTER 6

Watchman Nee, the Seer of Divine Revelation

B efore this chapter begins, I just want to emphasise that I am no expert on the teachings of Watchman Nee and have no chance of doing him justice. In fact, I am quite a novice and am sure that there are others far better informed than me to write this chapter. But it is from this limited contact that have I ended up sitting here writing this, so that the gifts from this seer of divine revelation can be more widely received. I also want to say before starting that I will continue to write as it arises in me and that my main aim is still to resolve my own situation rather than focus on giving a better account of Watchman Nee's teachings.

Ask and It Is Given

As I sit and think about it, this is probably the most important chapter in the book, given that this is what is rocking the boat for me. This rocking is because it was Watchman Nee's teachings that gave me a different insight Into Christianity and how we should be living in relation to source, ourselves, and everything else. It was his writings that showed me a different perspective of Christianity, compared to some of what we are doing. This left me with a disturbance that has caused this book to start happening.

Be careful what you ask for is suddenly and laughingly in my head, knowing that I have always been searching for that final thing that clicks it all into place for me. I am also wondering why I didn't write this chapter sooner, as it is Chapter 6 as I type, and almost two months of daily writing has gone before this. Surely it would have made more sense to give you an understanding of how Watchman Nee's work impacted me right from the start; anyway, better late than never.

You didn't ask for guidance, says the same playful voice. *You were too busy doing all that downloading and clearing your head. You were too busy enjoying yourself, and it was all holistic and productive anyway, so where was the need for me to intervene at that time?*

The heading for this section of the chapter is, 'Ask and It Is Given', yet I didn't seem to be asking, so why was it given? I reckon the reason is because I was asking without even realising it. The essential me at the core of my being, beyond consciousness, was asking (or at least seeking). My deeper truth is that I was subconsciously seeking or groping into space for something, even if I, the conscious awareness, wasn't doing it explicitly with my mind. I was genuinely seeking without other parts of me getting in the way, through their resistance or doubt or questioning of whether this 'Seek and ye shall find' works or not.

How Does the Holy Spirit Interact with Us?

So can this really be the voice of God, or the Holy Spirit? I ask myself. It is a guiding voice that is holistic in spirit and can be heard when we make ourselves available. This fairly ordinary, everyday, but nurturing voice comes into our minds from beyond our thoughts and generally feels like the response of another to our question. It is a response that seems to make a higher level of sense than what we are doing at the time and seems to resolve a dilemma. I suppose if I had ever thought to look for it, I would have expected the voice of the Holy Spirit to be a bit more booming or deep or godly or something, and I would have expected it to be telling me something that I should be doing; exposing my error in the process. Perhaps I would expect it to be telling me that I should be reading the Bible or asking why I wasn't in church or something. But this feels a bit too simple and a bit too everyday in its way of responding to whatever I am occupied with. Yet, if I were the Holy Spirit, I would try to connect with people where they were, so they could hear me and so we could develop a relationship that could progress from there. It seems obvious really, if we consider God to be a loving, nurturing source rather than wrathful or condemning.

What We Need Appears when We Need It; We Just Need to Have the Faith to Follow the Guidance

I am not really sure how I came across Watchman Nee; it was probably a book that Amazon flashed up due to knowing my interests. In Carl Jung's day, he spoke about the collective unconscious, but now we also have an incredible collective conscious due to the Internet and the World Wide Web, which allows everyone to be in touch with almost everyone else or anything else in seconds.

It was probably a couple of years ago when I happened upon – or was guided to – Watchman Nee, just like how The Institute of Psychosynthesis appeared through a Big Issue advert when I was in crisis and searching for something to save my sanity. Then the Heart Intelligence training appeared from somewhere, just as I was completing the Psychosynthesis training. Then the same thing happened again once the initial enthusiasm and big changes had taken place from feasting on Heart Intelligence for a couple of years, soaking up as much as I could and now starting to look for whatever else was out there. That was when Watchman Nee arrived. I wasn't necessarily looking for something Christian; it was perhaps just what was next on the path, or what I was now more ready for.

So as you can see, all of these things arrived out of the blue but were exactly what I needed at the time, and in the right order. I was — and still am — quite mind identified and needed answers for my sanity. Thankfully this was resolved through Psychosynthesis before being guided to Heart Intelligence, where I would use my new-found growth, solidity and understanding, to help me awaken to my own heart's intelligence, and wise guidance. Then came the move back towards untangling religion, and all that that involved. But this time, I was better prepared than I had been at the start of my journey; religion had been one of the first places I turned to when I started awakening and struggling with life.

The latest of these situations where something comes out of the blue happened after I had been reading Watchman Nee for a year or so and was struggling to integrate it with the present-day church. I saw an advert on Facebook about an upcoming talk in Edinburgh at the Augustine United Church. The event was being hosted by Edinburgh International Centre for Spirituality and Peace, with the talk about Celtic Christianity and the work of Thomas Merton being given by Matthew Fox. Once again, it was exactly the right next step for me, even though I had no idea of what it was about, but nonetheless leading me to this point right now.

What the Holy Spirit Does

Watchman Nee teaches us about the different ways that the Holy Spirit works. He teaches us how it facilitates our external environment in the way that I describe above in relation to our needs. But he also explains how its greater aim is to break our outer man, our self-righteousness, self-love, self-dependence, so we can return to functioning the correct way round: spirit led and following the guidance of something greater than ourselves instead of just being reactive and emotionally triggered all of the time due to disconnect from God, or source. I personally see our actions out of that emotional triggering as our attempt to get back to our own personal equilibrium and ultimately progress further towards being able to be more love.

So for me, he is teaching us how to be consciously proactive rather than unconsciously reactive, because the latter tends to just have us going round in circles hurting each other due to not working heart intelligently with the triggers. Yet if we can see it and work with it from the perspective I offer, we can see that it is holistically inspired either way. Even though one way comes out of consciousness and alignment with a higher guidance, and the other comes out of the religious or returning movement from our pathology of childhood suffering, in an attempt to return to love. They are still both seeking the same productive outcome: further awakening and enlightenment through self-realisation.

Watchman teaches us how the Holy Spirit is mostly about breaking our outer man through our sufferings so that our spirit may be released to be of use. He sees this breaking of the outer man as the dividing of the spirit and soul, and without this breaking, we can't work as cleanly for God and the coming of the greater kingdom because everything that comes forth from us will be contaminated by our psychological self with its psychological baggage.

The Power of Undeniable Knowing

Watchman Nee, as he later called himself, was named Nee-Shu-tsu by his parents; he had been promised to God by his mother before he was even born. He became a Christian in 1920 when he was seventeen and began writing straightaway, eventually writing something like 150 books. He was arrested in 1952 and imprisoned for his teachings, eventually dying a martyr in 1972. I believe he died whilst still in prison and after many years of physical ill health and breaking by the Holy Spirit.

I find it fascinating and reassuring how people like Watchman Nee, Roberto Assagioli, and many others in history, including Patrick Hamilton, whom I mentioned in Part 1 of the book, had such a strength of belief, knowing, and conviction in what they saw that it held them so strongly against all odds. I mentioned earlier how Hamilton was burned at the stake in 1528 in St Andrews for promoting Protestantism. Assagioli on the other hand was imprisoned by Benito Mussolini's Fascist government in 1940 for expressing his truth. Fortunately for Assagioli, his imprisonment was only for a month, but like Nee he still used his imprisonment productively.

In these historical stories, I usually tend to see the alive, active feminine energy, trying to break through the existing but inhibiting masculine fixed paradigm to realise a new perception of reality, then hold true and fast to it against the resistance of the old restricting masculine. What I now see as the alive and ever changing tree of life, and the tree of knowledge with its conditioned or fixed mindset nature of this is what is right and wrong.

The Alive and Vibrant within the Mundane

I actually watched it yesterday, 6 November, as I sat in a church that I haven't gone to before. My foster daughter and I had gone to support her friend, who was singing solo as part of an all-age choir. After the service had finished and we had returned home, I could still feel how mundane the service had felt within me. It had felt like the typical Sunday service, in that, we had done the same old routine that would have been going on all over the country. It was almost all tree of knowledge with very little tree of life, other than the little flickers that I saw in fleeting moments. These were moments like when the young girl sang solo, and I could feel her vitality through her singing, this connection bringing me into presence and feeling alive with her. I could also sense some people in the congregation subconsciously longing for something more without even saying a word; whilst others sat in what felt like numb, lifeless disconnect. We make all these films about zombies without seeing that half the time, we are the ones living like zombies.

Then there were the two moments of feeling real and alive during some meaningful conversation after the service. One with the minister and the other with the girl's mother, as real truth was exposed, touched, and felt in each other's presence. There was also the comforting feeling of being with of a bunch of complete strangers yet all having come together for a common higher purpose. And finally the hurt, discomfort, and love felt by us all when I told my foster daughter that she couldn't go to her friends to play, as we left.

These are the experiences and moments that are there with us so often and can bring us back to presence and life, but we often don't notice because we are not present or not willing to feel them. We are too busy in the tree of knowledge, thinking about this or that, or trying to find answers to the disturbances, usually trying not to feel them because they are disturbing and because we don't realise that they aim to serve us. Even the feeling of people simply coming together in a church, given what the church stands for, is something worth being present to. The hope, the longing, the worship, the faith, the love, and the friendship are all amazing to feel and watch the spirit of at play, if we take a moment to stop, get present, and actually be willing to feel and enjoy them. We don't see the kingdom of heaven because we don't know what it looks like or that it is right at hand, or because we have been taught that it is something for the future or something we don't deserve, or something we have to earn by good behaviour. We don't stay present by keeping oil in our lamps and staying awake for the bridegroom. We fall asleep in so many different ways and don't even know we have done it. For me, this speaks directly to the meaning of life: being awake and conscious to feeling life, because this is the building of the church, given that the church is to be built upon Christ revealed.

It is the spirit of Christ that we are talking about. Christianity is about the spirit of things, not the logical, or rational, or thought, or opinion, or emotion, or even about belief really, because that is all TOK and usually stops us from being alive, due to being in the fixed belief. For me it is particularly about being in the spirit of love in all that we do, this being the way and the truth and the life; actually being in love by being connected to source and abiding there, so that it is not us that acts but that. This is then the release of the spirit as it comes forth in us, if we can get our outer man out of the way and let that happen. In my experience, that is when I serve the world best; being present to the love that pervades everything and guides everything. Simply being present in the moment and empty is when I feel it come to me and I can then sometimes let it interact with others through me.

We Need to See the New before We Can Let Go of the Old

A few minutes ago, I got up to take a break, and in that break of not having my mind preoccupied with what I was writing, not being in the TOK, something had room to get in. It was a voice saying, *You need to move this chapter from the end of the book to the front, so that they can get a taste of the new, to feel and see and connect to, as they read the rest of the book, which will fill it all out for them.* This made complete sense in the instant of what most of us would normally call intuition, because I could relate to it from my midlife crisis of seeing the new before working towards understanding it more fully. This flash of information or insight was not a thought; it feels different from a thought once we learn to discern the difference. I know I wasn't thinking about anything at the time and had just been thinking about something completely different. It is also very poignant that this should happen when I am writing about it, as if it is offering this to self-evidence by demonstration rather than just by my limited explanation. This is the type of experience that confirms for me that there is a holistic guidance that is holy in spirit at play in our lives; call it what you will due to your own personal beliefs. For instance, my own personal preference for it is holistic guidance, a wording that feels to stand somewhere between higher Self and Holy Spirit and works best for me at this time, as I find myself caught between having a psychospiritual understanding of life and my struggles in awakening into Christianity. I can tell that this is just my own resistance from the past towards using Christian language, and can tell that this feels like a middle ground word as my resistance softens, but this is also where I believe a lot of our problem lies.

People are alienated by the old words and language that triggers them from their childhood, and so I use different language to manage that gap. What happens within you when I say Holy Spirit compared to holistic guidance? Take a moment to play with it, or say it out loud to someone in conversation, and see the difference. You can even do the same with the words God and source. But what I think we need most help with is seeing them for what they are and help to get them back down to earth. I reckon that this is where I resonate with Assagioli, Nee, and Hamilton in their ability to stand strong, because it is just as difficult to deny something once you have seen it, as it is to deny the everyday reality (even though it is difficult to deal with the rejection and disapproval of others). I am however also aware that we can all say the same thing due to our own individual perceptions at any given time; this is why relationship and change are difficult. We all stand firm in our own understandings and perceptions because they sustain us, and then suddenly, we are back in the TOK without even realising it.

Going back to my midlife crisis for a moment, it was because something was revealed to me and I could see another reality that I kept groping my way forward instead of regressing, as many others do in midlife crisis, desperate to find something to hold onto at a time of great disturbance.

As for moving this Watchman Nee chapter and all of Part 2 to the front of the book to become Part 1, so that you can see what life could be like, before discussing what I see as the difficulty of our current situation? I did; and it was there for a few months before I moved it all back during the editing and publishing process. I have just today, 19 April, moved it all back because another guidance within me was defiled by where it was every time I read through the book. This demonstrates how hard it is to discern the different guidance's and decide which one to follow. Having moved it however, I feel better and this is my signal to leave things this way around. This is following our joy over following our head, following the tree of life over following the tree of knowledge. This is spiritual discernment that is more in keeping with Heart Intelligence than with listening to the voices that we hear, and it is following this guidance over the other, that I have found tends to bear more fruit. So does that mean that the previous voice was not what I thought it was? Perhaps! But then again perhaps you would have taken more from the book if I had left it the other way around?

Seeing the Choice between Spirit-Led Living and Being Emotionally Triggered

Having just written these opening few passages, I feel for my own spirit and feel for where it is operating; is it caught up in the desire to teach you or convince you? Or wanting to lead or show you by present moment example and evidence? Perhaps it's the desire to share what I've found and how that helps me with life? All very well intended actions, yet I can still track myself looking for something better, something special or amazing, something that doesn't feel like it could come from me, so you will be completely convinced.

But then that same voice flashes across my mind again, saying, *What's wrong with what you've offered?* As I return to normal thinking consciousness, I realise that there is nothing wrong with what

I have offered. Upon reflection, they all feel holistic in spirit and intent, even though I was trying to find something better because they all felt a bit contaminated by me and any subconscious objective that I may have.

This is an example of where Watchman teaches us that the spirit moves through what he calls the outer man; it doesn't bypass us at the psychological, mental, emotional, or will levels of who and what we are; it works through us. Watchman Nee always quotes the Bible and teaches that the spirit is meant to guide the soul, which in turn guides the body. The soul comprising will, mind, and emotions working from top down. As per the Bible, he calls the spirit the inner man, the soul the outer man, and the body the outermost man. The correct way of functioning being that we use our self-aware consciousness and will to align with the guidance of the Holy Spirit, with this then directing the mind, emotions, and body.

The reality however, for most of us, due to being disconnected from source and not believing there is such a guidance available, is that we function the other way around. In our disconnected need to get our unconscious love needs met, we all go around unconsciously taking from each other and are therefore triggering each other all of the time. This is emotionally directed living and frequently leads to us trying to fill that spiritual void through things like; food, alcohol, drugs, sex, television or whatever else we can unconsciously do with the body to make that disconnect go away for a while.

As for the mind? Well; it's much the same there too, as we do all sorts of things and tell ourselves all sorts of stuff to manage that disconnect. This disconnect that I speak of being where most of us live in society nowadays, where we don't believe in a God or guidance due to the troubles that it causes in the world, and due to the wrongs that we see its leaders have done in the world. So we have quite rightly thrown it out, *and good for us!* But what we haven't realised is that we have done this due to following an inner knowing and truth that tells us that it simply isn't right. In other words, our true holistic guidance has guided us to throw the false one out, and we have done this whilst believing that there is no guidance at play in our lives. Quite funny and ironic, really, if it wasn't for the millions who have died and are dying every day due to our not getting it. I almost went off on a big rant there about the state of the world, but as I tracked myself doing it and read into the reader, I stopped, knowing that you already get it.

In fact, I have just realised in this instant, that this was a perfect example of my emotions taking over my mind, and then my will, and then running my fingers on the keyboard, just as Watchman Nee says. But I caught it due to having oil in my lamp and being trained to be present to myself. But then, I can also see that these emotions have been triggered because I am essentially love that is being compressed into feeling itself as suffering and pain due to my associating with the suffering of others. So it could be said that I was having a rant due to connecting to that suffering and so I was pushing to return to love, due to the safety of being at my desk and not really in any lack of safety. So if this were a real-life situation with myself and the other both pushing back and forth, out of both parties trying to not be compressed by the other, we would have exactly what we see going on in life and society. But if one of us wakes up and sees what is happening and chooses to be spirit led rather than emotionally triggered, then the whole scenario has the potential to change.

It is also amusing that once again, a live example of what I was trying to explain was offered into the space; fortunately, I was present enough to catch it and use it to demonstrate rather than just explain. This is the sort of thing that helps me have the strength to write a book like this; I know that what I am writing about exists. Science struggles with religion and faith because science likes repeatable outcomes from the same experiment, and it can't get that. But it is possible to demonstrate it when we operate at a level that can see it and understand it.

If You Live in Me I Will Live in You

Our spirit is always pure and clean but usually comes forth tainted or contaminated by our baggage getting triggered into the mix for healing: this is the movement of the spirit being tainted by the outer man as it comes forth. This always being in relation to what is happening in the moment, with the healing seldom happening, because we don't realise what is going on and therefore don't slow down to prioritise the healing. We just react back and forth at each other, passing the psychological parcel. It's not pass the parcel, it's pass the pathology, and this is where we unconsciously pass our damage onto our children. I sometimes refer to it as their true inheritance. This tainting happens because the spirit, or inner man, comes forth through the outer man, but with conscious awareness and will aligned towards seeking guidance, we can then track and catch our spirit feeling defiled and then chose how to respond in any moment in the way that best serves the other in relation to His coming kingdom, thus working towards a better world for us all. This positive development is increasing in our society as more and more people choose to transcend the impact that they just received from the other and respond more productively, turning the other cheek as it were, so as to not react from the one that has just been slapped.

This short explanation also demonstrates as Watchman Nee says, that the Holy Spirit is out to realign our will from being under the unconscious influence of our emotions and mind to being under its guidance. Psychosynthesis and Heart Intelligence also give much attention to the will and our being present to what controls it. We do this by tracking our self and watching where we are acting or reacting from, watching to see if we are responding from our highest altruistic values and truth in relation to who we aspire to be in the world and what we stand to align with. But even more important than this, is watching for the spirit of how our response comes forth, because we can still respond from resentment or anger or spite if we do not have oil in our lamp.

This for me is where the teachings of Jesus can help us because it is His teachings that we can use to discern our response. So when Jesus says, If you live in me I will live in you, he is saying that by always being Jesus-conscious, and always being present to seeking the kingdom of heaven, He lives in us and we can therefore respond as per His inner guidance within us. The kingdom is a better life on earth for all, rather than something that we will attain in an afterlife if we behave. But to be able to do this, we firstly have to buy into the vision and be more self-conscious; we have to be able to see that this is what can take us from the disturbed world that we are in to a better one, if we are willing to get on board and contribute. And this in turn is made easier if we get more people awake and onboard. This book can serve that purpose by helping to awaken and educate people into seeing what it is that is going on, see what happened in the past to have us end up here, and see what we need to do to get back out of it.

Seeing and Putting Watchman Nee's Teachings into Practice

I see more and more people these days being far more present, self-aware, and conscious of their behaviour and interactions with others than I did just a few years ago, and it isn't just an unconscious, self-protective behaviour out of fear of how the other will react. It is out of choice to behave differently. People are waking up and taking ownership of their self and their actions; it doesn't take that much work to get onboard with the shift. For instance, my most highly valued exercise; is watching for my words and actions to be clean spirited, rather than find my self reacting out of an emotional trigger. Whenever I am in the company of others and catch myself after being unpresent, I consciously realign to my purpose and feel to see if I have any subconscious opinions or mindsets running. I may simply have gone unpresent because I became engrossed in what the other was saying, or more likely because I was unconsciously in the TOK, checking to see if I agreed with them. I feel for any emotion that is tainting the spirit of my reply in such a way that I am likely to trigger the other into closing or defending or attacking, and try to act more productively so that they open.

At the moment, as I practice this way of being, most of this initial return from being unpresent to being present happens once I have already been triggered, because my inner body reacts to the other and I tend to notice my inner body change in some way or other. I notice my inner shift, as I did in the previous chapter. This ability is almost unconscious now, due to years of conscious practice through psychosynthesis and heart intelligence coaching work. So when my body does react and I do notice that I am with some attitude, emotion or defilement, I sometimes inwardly say, *Down dog*, to the energy arising within me that feels like a dog with its heckles up, ready to fight or defend something of value to me. Be that a sense of attack on my self or a loved one that I sense being attacked. To behave more cleanly of spirit; all that is required is the mindfulness of being present to our self and tracking what is going on within us. Our bodies usually inform us very well of any emotion that is present; we don't need to discern what that emotion is at the time. We just need to notice it and respond from a place of choice. This does not always mean being false or being all fake and nicey-nicey. It simply means being conscious of expressing yourself; if you are feeling angry or hurt, for instance, then that can still be expressed in clean spirit and owned, demonstrating to the other that you are mature and in control of yourself, proactively seeking to resolve something for both to gain from, whilst also being your truth. This is being awake and behaving consciously out of the desire to be your highest purest truth and self. Rather than be reactive in unconsciousness rebounding from an impact and then re-impacting the other in the process as we bat the hurt back and forth, trying to catch on and evolve to a higher level of being with a more productive way of interacting. This is what evolution is trying to get to happen and is partly what lies behind the reason why we trigger each other. In this way, you are more likely to come across as present, composed, and centred, yet willing to be vulnerable and humble rather than behave unconsciously neurotic, volatile, or destructive. Acting out of symptoms and pathology like a child does to avoid the pain of moving towards what feels annihilating.

But of course, we also need that education and purpose that I spoke of earlier. The *for what*, as I call it. This creates a new environment for the other into which they will naturally rise if they feel safe enough. However, if they don't feel safe enough, because you have awakened their vulnerability through your being vulnerable, for example, then they will leave or try to close you down from making them feel unsafe. Either way, you can still do your own bit for your own healing, awakening, and development (or personal religion, as I also call it). This is what I see the priority of life being about; everything outside of that is there simply as experiences to use towards that end. To me, this is what Watchman Nee calls the building of the church: being awake in the tree of life in the moment, feeling the life and vitality of what is going on, and then being spirit led in our response to that, working towards creating His kingdom: a better world, one conversation at a time.

So my offering to you is to practice the same thing; watch yourself and try to respond to the other heart intelligently rather than react from resentment or spite, angst or bitterness, contempt or jealousy. See if you can respond from the understanding and compassion that something has made the other person speak to you in the way they have because they are unconsciously trying to get back to a place of feeling better than they currently do. If we were all to do that one thing, then the world would change very quickly. Even if you can't respond heart intelligently because of being triggered, then simply avoid reacting from your trigger; this is a move in the right direction that is probably doable for you. I see many people avoiding hitting back nowadays and this is a big step in the right direction. This is, resist not evil.

When you do catch yourself having reacted in a way that you wish you hadn't, then don't beat yourself up; practice the same compassion and love with yourself. Have genuine forgiveness for your own limitations, and you will return to your true natural state of love. Jesus' saying, *Forgive them for they know not what they do*, has just been placed lovingly and poignantly in my mind; it is something we can also use on ourselves as much as on others who go unconscious in the moment or are less awake. Watchman Nee teaches us that those best suited to serve others are those who have been most broken by the Holy Spirit. He also teaches that mind touches mind and emotion touches emotion and spirit touches spirit, so we should always work from our spirit, not our mind or emotions, as best we can; saying that if we are not sensing the spirit of the other, then we should not shift to our mind to help them. Christianity is about the spirit, not knowledge and doctrine; Watchman claims that until we have discovered this way, we have not found true Christianity. Given that the Holy Spirit is selfless love, we also need to watch for feeling pleased with our self about how we are doing, because if we are feeling pleased with our self, then we are in our self-love and self-righteousness, not righteousness. We are esteeming the false idol of our self: not serving God and helping others to see His guidance at play.

Why Do We Refer to God as Masculine?

As I wrote the word *His* in that last sentence, I could sense, as I have just been explaining, a defilement or reaction in my body. I then immediately jumped to sensing (or perhaps just projecting) that some readers were disapproving of me referring to God as masculine. This is something I have struggled with all my life, but only until I started writing this book. After writing now for several weeks, much learning and change has actually happened, and one of those changes is that it now feels right in me because of the fatherly, guiding, correcting nature of the masculine. So now as I write that, I sense even more people being triggered and saying, Yes, but women can do all that stuff too, and even better sometimes. (If this is you, then this is the triggering stuff to watch for that I mentioned earlier; watch your reactions and return to peace: Peace be with you, as Jesus would say.) And anyway, I agree. Of course women can do it just as well as men (and in many cases, do it better), but this is often still the guiding masculine: the masculine within women, rather than men. This is because I now see the feminine as the formless, alive, TOL energy that moves everything, the abundant awe and wonder of life that just pours out of God or source, seeking to express itself in a myriad of colours, shapes, smells, sounds, and tastes, completely unharnessed and formless. I now see the feminine as the life force or active agent and the masculine as the multitude of form that it takes so as to have something to see, touch, taste, smell, and interact with. Perhaps the feminine is Albert Einstein's wave energy and the masculine is the form-giving particle, in his wave-particle duality, where he claimed that everything was wave and particle. So for me, it is no longer a sense of God being masculine to the exclusion of being feminine; it is just the masculine aspect of God that is being called to for its guidance and direction, with the feminine side of God or source being that abundant outpouring of love, simply seeking form and expression.

Summary

Even though we are making slow progress (both individually and collectively in our society) in the way we are interacting, I think that most adults are still working at the self-confidence, self-esteem level of development, in an effort to feel better about themselves. This is nonetheless productive and happens in an effort to transcend the lower level of feeling anxious or nervous or insecure in some way, etc. as a roll over from how we have been impacted in childhood and therefore function. However, there are also increasing numbers of people in our society that are beginning to function at the level that I have just described. I would say that some of this is due to these people doing personal development work and yoga and mindfulness and many other forms of holistic practices, whilst some of it is simply out of an inner pure goodness and wisdom of now seeing what is required to make things better. Those who escape childhood less distorted are more in touch with their pure goodness and don't need to re-esteem themselves. They still have the capacity to be the light of the world.

But now I can also see that this work of so called self-empowerment and self-esteeming is also due to disconnect from source and our not investing in any form of spiritual guidance, and not believing that there is a purpose and direction. I now see this behaviour as being due to disconnect, and that it happens to help us manage and develop an inner sense of solidity and sovereignty to help us survive in disconnect and eventually get us back to alignment. In my experience, I am now being invited to lay that self-sovereignty down again, or hand it over to something above my level of ability, that can do it better. This is moving from my will to Thine Will, as we say in psychosynthesis. The thing that I am now realising about my own progression is that it has not come from increasing self-esteem and building self-confide-ence, but from realising that there is a higher or holistic guidance, and confiding in that.

For me, Watchman Nee offers us an immediate solution to the present, with hope, vision, and a sense of purpose for the short- and long-term future. He sees a Christianity that completely follows scripture yet still manages to be both feminine and masculine in all their purity, beauty, and form; it is very alive, rather than heady and disconnected from source. He gives us the spirit of Christianity and a way to connect to its essential message instead of the usual heady scriptural teaching. All we have to do is give up our need to be in control of our self, and understand Christianity better than we have done in the past, and learn to follow the guidance that is there. Perhaps from this chapter, you can begin to see my problem and understand my struggle between what I expose here and what goes on in the name of Christianity out there.

CHAPTER 7

The Teachings of Jesus, as the Way to Live Our Life

Reframing Christianity and Bringing Jesus Back Down to Earth

I can't believe that I am actually about to start writing about the teachings of Jesus. A few years ago, I would have bet a small fortune that I would never ever be sat here doing this. That is because I have never been a religious or church going person; I've never made any real sense of the Bible or been convinced by any Bible-bashing tunnel-visioned Christian that there was anything worth considering. I didn't go to church as a child and so didn't end up turning away from it, as many have. In fact, as I have said already, I spent many hours arguing with others about it being a load of nonsense. The logical voice within me used to say. *How could God be God and human and some Holy Spirit thing, all at the same time? And how could God possibly be some invisible human type being that exists somewhere that we call heaven and watch over it all? Then there's Jesus: so God turns Himself into a man and comes down to earth, takes all that suffering for our sins and then dies, comes back to life, and floats back up to heaven again. It's a bit much and a bit infantile.* But that has now changed, and not because I have suddenly started to believe; it is because it has become reframed into a way that fits for me. Rather than be in the polarised TOK yes-or-no position that exists when I only have a closed mindset to work with, the mindset has become relaxed, and this has allowed it to differentiate, thus enabling it to take a different form.

The one thing I did buy into within Christianity was the wisdom in the teachings of Jesus. They never seemed religious to me in a Christian, Jewish, Muslim, Buddhist, or Hindu kind of context. They always seemed more like mentoring or coaching to me, more like being offered some ultimate high-level life guidance from the wisest person ever. And that is what I like about them: They actually feel wise and down to earth, like being given the answer book on how to live and treat others. The rest of the Bible tells variations of the historical story before and after Jesus. I can't feel or connect to that in the same way, but the specific teachings just seem to hit the mark in me, whereby I get them and just know that they are *the way and the truth and the life* of it. It is like when two things are simply made to fit together, they just do; it feels right.

I also think that Jesus and the Holy Spirit are of more use to us when they are also brought back down to earth; that is how they started working for me. So I guess what I am saying is that I have not gone from being a nonbeliever to being a believer. It is more that I can see a different Christianity through Jesus and Watchman Nee, that I can believe in, and that transcends and outgrows the old one, which doesn't work for me (or much of society), the one that we have been fed since childhood and see on television. For many of us, this becomes surpassed by another embodied guidance within us that feels alienated by the old one, and so we reject the one that is now a bit too Santa Claus and Tooth Fairy for us.

When I connect to the word God by saying it or reading it or taking my mind to it, I no longer unconsciously go into my mind with its old childhood sense of what I was taught God was like: something that feels threatening or over lording or condemning, like some unsatisfied father, a God that says I have to be good or I won't go to heaven when I die (the Tooth Fairy-type God). But then I also don't just go into a place of disbelief, as I did for most of my life, because I didn't buy into all that Tooth Fairy stuff. This is a place where I think most of society is, a place with no sense of understanding or greater purpose or direction in their broader life due to having nothing to believe in. A place in their psyche where there is nothing to guide them or believe in, other than living from day to day and trying to have something set aside for the future, being a good person as long as it is not at any great cost or burden. Then there is another sense of a God within my psyche that I no longer go into either, a God that could be there in some form or other but that I don't feel connected to because life wouldn't be like this if there was a God worth listening to.

So these are some of the God's and attitudes to God that seem to have been around for me in the past and I hear being around for others in my society.

So where do I go these days with the God word instead? Well, I tend to use the word source instead, or at least, I feel the word source when I see or hear the word God. The word source carries no baggage for me; there is no pathology with it. It feels like a living word rather than dead letter, and it always feels fresh and present in the moment, and alive and abundant in its nature. This creation-centred connection to source is more aligned with Celtic Christianity than our typical modern-day, scripture-centred Roman Christianity, where the word God feels lifeless compared to the word source, which feels alive and full of vitality; more TOL than TOK. That aliveness that I speak of always feels holistic and nurturing in its action as it seeks to guide us in the right direction, rather than chastise or punish us for going in the wrong direction. It feels loving and holistic or holy in the spirit of its action. So when I connect to God and the Holy Spirit of life in this way, I have something more tangible to relate to. And when I go to that place for guidance, it always coaxes me in the right direction, even if it is difficult for me at my lower level, or outer man level, to follow that guidance. It always offers me truth in a way that is doable, holistic, heart intelligent, and religious, if I am willing to pick up my cross and follow it. This is a more panentheistic God, where we perceive God at the essence of all things.

So what about Jesus? Well, other writings are interpreted as saying that Jesus was the first begotten Son of God, rather than the only begotten Son of God, and I see that we are all spiritually begotten of the same source, even if we are also created. I do, however, see someone who was able to hold a level of being and knowing that by far transcended the average human being, someone who was able to function nearer to the spirit of source than the nature of man. As for the historical truth about the crucifixion and resurrection; I still struggle with it, but for me the thing that matters most is that Jesus tells us to pick up our own metaphorical cross and follow Him, crucifying our old psychological self by following His teachings so that we can become resurrected in our true self. This for me is our religious transformation back to being our true self, from the psychological self that we had to become to get through childhood.

So what works for me now as far as God and the Holy Spirit is concerned is that I see us as the same divine loving source in our primary essence; and that we essentially seek to be and express that, defending and protecting it when impacted so that we can return more towards that pure state, never entirely managing to be pure love, because we cannot manage it. I sometimes see us as being like a small foam ball that has its default unstressed state of being, so whenever it gets squeezed and distorted, its natural tendency is to rebound and return to its neutral state again. In our case, we have the potential to remain in that relaxed and loving state by following Jesus' teachings and not be distorted by the impacts from others; therefore not needing to do something to get back to equilibrium. But because of our disconnect and disbelief in a higher guidance and loving replenishing source, we compensate by pushing and pulling against each other, offloading our disturbances onto each other in an effort to get back to a good place. If we can resist reacting to the other by holding our self in higher purpose, then we serve them also.

So what I really want to do with this chapter is show how Jesus' teachings help me in my life and can help you too, even if you don't believe in God or Christianity. And I want to show you how they help me to stop doing this immature, unconscious behaviour of offloading my bad feelings onto others because I have no other way of managing them. I want to show you the difference it has made to me by having a better understanding of His teachings, now that I have something to hold onto and have a sense of higher purpose, meaning, and value in my life. How they help me to stay on a more straight and narrow path most of the time, not hitting back at others when they offload at me out of their suffering because of their disconnect. In other words, when I live in Him, He lives in me, and I behave in a way that is more holy or holistic than I otherwise would, thus serving me, them, and the divine purpose of creating His kingdom, a better world for us all.

Being Available to Hear the Voice of Guidance and How to Discern It

Jesus says, Seek first the kingdom of heaven, but surely we need to have oil in our lamp first, because we need to be conscious and awake and watching for the bridegroom. The bridegroom to me being, life, where life to me has an aliveness feeling to it, it actually feels alive and vibrant. I can touch it and feel its vitality and tell that that doesn't feel like me, as I feel like the one feeling it. It is alive, and I can feel alive when I tap into it. I also feel less enlivened when I am not tapped into it. There is a me that I can feel myself being when I am not touching it, and a me that I can feel myself being when I am touching it. It is like feeling energised and stimulated and actually being a part of the awe and wonder of creation itself. It feels like that is all we have to do and be, and we will be doing everything that matters. It feels holy and sacred; I feel undeserving of its grace, of allowing me to experience its presence. I feel myself inside almost bow, humbled in its almighty presence, just like I feel when I say, Hallowed be thy name.

After writing the above, I took a break to go off and enjoy being in that place and suddenly heard a voice saying, *Abide in me; that is all you have to do.* So I thought about it for a second and quickly came to the conclusion that it is correct. It takes what I was contemplating and unites and transcends them both. The way that I was doing it was by switching our consciousness on, (the oil in our lamps) and then aligning ourselves with something, (seek first the kingdom of heaven) so as to keep us on the *narrow path,* but this offering that seems to come from out with me does both in one move. My effort felt like some mechanical TOK doing x y z to make it work, whilst the higher offering feels more like just being it, and feels more TOL. The first ones feeling like doing, and the second one simply being; even the voice's sound felt of that spirit. It didn't feel like a correcting or telling or advising voice. It was calling and loving and soft. *Inviting:* That's the word. It had a grace of inviting and welcoming me to be a different way that takes no effort or doing when it happens, but that takes effort to do when I try to do it in a TOK kind of way. It felt fatherly and lovingly sympathetic, smiling as we would when we try to help our children get something that isn't as hard as they are making it. The words that come now are *Just relax and it happens.* What way of being could be of more grace than that? *Seek and ye shall find* now comes to me, but in a congratulating, affirming spirit for the first time ever, rather than the usual instructional advisory way. It feels like having achieved something, and then the teacher lovingly saying, There you go, you've got it.

This voice that I speak of, by the way, isn't some profound voice that I hear from the sky or like someone standing next to me. It is much the same as the usual voice that most of us get in our head, but it has a different feel to it as I describe. There is a relationship that I have with it, as I am in one emotion, and it responds from a different spirit or energy or emotion. I will be in my own closed thoughts, and it comes from a place of responding to them rather than from within them. It is like I am seeking, and it comes in from somewhere outside of my psyche. So in contrast to what that voice feels like, explaining all of this to you was my own idea or thought that just popped up; it didn't come from this other place that I am speaking of. This came from within me.

It's still weird sitting doing this, because once again, it isn't going as I intended. I was going to do a list and explanations, but this is happening on its own, with me just enjoying watching and being with it. What a privilege to be in its presence, even though I end up feeling humble and unworthy.

Different Levels of Unworthiness

In Heart Intelligence, Christian Pankhurst talks about our core unworthiness: something that I have only felt a couple of times in my life but I can feel again here now. The last time was a couple of years ago on a Heart Intelligence retreat in the Spanish mountains where about thirty of us took over a retreat centre for a week. I took space for something or other; I don't actually remember what it was right now; Ah yes! It was to look at two different ways that I have of being in the world. The first being when I am my everyday me that does this or that as the dad, husband, joiner, coach, grump, clever clogs, annoying male; and the other is when I am able to be something less dense and caught up in everything, something that just feels like being loving and at ease with it all, knowing that it is all okay due to being present and consciously connected to the vitality of life. I don't mean all spaced out or hippy, tripping on life, because that would feel dissociated and unpresent; and that's not it. This is about being very present and embodied and connected to the awe and wonder of life as it is right in the moment.

Anyway, I tried a few things to express myself and couldn't get anywhere near it. Then eventually, Christian told me to stop listening to all that nonsense that I listen to in my head and suggested that I try receiving love, instead of giving it out all of the time; see if I could let in the love that I easily give out to others. He reminded us all about how giving can be a coping mechanism that keeps us from letting love in, or how it can be our passive aggressive way of being in control of getting our own love needs met, by being loving and giving to others. He invited me to surrender to receiving love from the women in the room. So without disclosing anything as I write, I was eventually able to let myself feel the love that these women had for me, and I was soon writhing on the floor, with my heart completely cramped up in resistance to letting it all in. I actually thought I was going to physically die right there in that moment on that floor. My heart stopped and my lungs stopped, and I fought with all my will to draw breath. There was no me and no room and no women, just will, in that moment, which felt like an eternity. I was nothing other than the will to live. I was also present at one moment to being terrified, believing that I was actually dying in that very moment. I even began spacing out of myself and into *This can't be it; this can't be how I die, all of my life, to die right here like this.*

Then I drew a breath, and it gradually calmed me down again. In that moment of fighting to live, I felt like I was a newborn baby learning how to draw its first breath. This was the result of letting in more love than I could manage and was perhaps my first conscious experience of core unworthiness. But this experience of core unworthiness was not a neurotic experience, as I believe others can feel in relation to not being good enough relative to others. It was not about not being clever enough or good looking enough or good at this or that. It was existential; it was about feeling undeserving of being given so much love.

So if I go back to what I was feeling before telling you that story, it is similar when I say what a privilege to be in its presence. I just remembered as I write that the moment before I broke down in tears, I asked, "What have I done to deserve so much love? I don't deserve this." It was due to that experience that I learned that the feminine simply wants to pour its love out and feel it being received. I am left feeling such gratitude, but not from my head or mind, from my embodied being. Who would not build their house upon this rock once they have come to know it?

The Value of Jesus Being Seen as the Most Incredible Man, rather than Just Being Seen as God

The Bible talks of Jesus being the only begotten Son of God and of being God made flesh, the human living aspect of a triune God, but I have heard that other gospels not in the Bible put it more like Jesus is the first begotten son; and that makes a massive difference to me. It makes Jesus more reachable and interesting, more worth attempting to understand and follow. I can feel myself move from seeing a Jesus I can never hope to understand or become like, to seeing a Jesus I can feel and relate to and invest in. It becomes more helpful to me to behold a Jesus who was a one of, but who also started out from the same place as the rest of us. I can then see Jesus as more of a mentor and life coach, offering advanced level life guidance of how to be and behave and how to perceive the world and everything in it. It's a bit like going from having a carrot dangling in front of you that you know you can never reach, and what it feels like to be in that situation; to a moment of feeling held and wanted and loved, feeling like you have found where you belong. It is like going from the feeling of not having to the feeling of having. But then once you have it, you can't deny it; you can't make it go away again, when you know you know. And this is what I was referring to in the Watchman Nee chapter about others in history who simply could not deny their truth, regardless of suffering to themselves. It's a bit like where Jesus says, Pick up your cross and follow me, or unless a seed dies when it falls to the ground it brings forth no fruit. We can't stop ourselves.

This is where life gets a bit crucifying for us at the level of self-righteousness for the sake of righteousness, or as Watchman Nee says, where the inner man is breaking through the outer man, and we consciously have to use our will to be willing to be the lamb amongst the wolves. This is where our spirit is seen in taking back our will from being at the mercy of our emotions due to disconnect from source and the spirit's guidance. This is what Jesus means to me when he says, Enter through the narrow gate. For wide is the gate and broad is the road that leads to destruction, and many enter through it. But small is the gate and narrow the road that leads to life, and only a few find it. But at the same time as saying all of this, I want to emphasise that what I am saying is that to me, we are all begotten of the same source, whether we call it God or not. It is not that Jesus is not God become man; it is that we are also the same in origin and haven't realised it yet.

Drinking the Malted Vinegar

For me, the parable of Jesus not drinking the malted vinegar when he was on the cross is about doing (or not doing) something to ease our psychological pain. We all do it and need to do it at times, but the skill is in spiritually discerning when it is wiser not to, just as I did in the Introduction when I chose to stay with something uncomfortable. We know that we should do or say the right thing, but it's hard; it's psychologically painful because we fear the consequences of our actions, just as I have concerns in writing much of this book and in particular this chapter. But psychological pain only gets felt by the ego as it tries to maintain control and self-worth; it doesn't want to feel weak or insecure or frightened or vulnerable. Our childhood neurological defence system is also a major player in this, as I will come to later. But this is also self-righteousness over righteousness as well as us worshiping false idols.

111

This is an opportunity for further spiritual progression relative to this particular area; we are in a moment of opportunity for growth if we are awake and can see it for what it is and take it. Being able to be our true self at the existential level of development, by being our heart's truth and being the way and the truth and the life, rather than be our neurotic egoic self, is the opportunity before us. But at the neurotic egoic level of development we don't want to feel foolish or silly or shameful or embarrassment or vulnerable, even though our heart's truth wants to be true and pure and to express itself in honesty. We have the choice to suffer for the gain of something worth suffering for, or suffer ignorantly in avoidance of awakening. This is us living in the tension space of self-survival and self-fulfilment.

Oil in Your Lamp

This is where I utilise the parable of making sure I have enough oil in my lamp. Because I see this parable as being about remaining present and conscious to the moment, feeling for the life of all that is in the moment, rather than be asleep to it or unconscious. It encourages me to stay attentive to the present moment, connected to the instant where life exists, sensing my environment, and feeling it without anything going on in my mind, no naming or analysing, just being with it. This is in contrast to just looking at what I see, as I am somewhere else in my mind and thoughts, not really there.

As I look out of my office window just now, I can shift between the two ways of being. Firstly I just look at the familiar country garden view in some numb, disconnected, heady way, seeing trees and grass and bushes and stuff. Oh yes, and there's the sky; fine, whatever, it's usually there anyway. Then I look again, and as I feel my way into connecting with what I see, I can feel a drop down out of my head and a drop down into my body. I feel alive and vitalised with what I see. I feel its substantiality of being through being in my own. I feel its existence, its interaction with its space and life; its aliveness. There are leaves on the wet grass and moss on the old concrete water pump building. The branches are gently swaying, and birds are crossing the bright blue cloudy sky. It all feels calm and serene with me, as leaves drift down to the ground and tumble across the grass. It could seem like I have gone unconscious and disappeared somewhere out of myself, but I am not. I am actually highly conscious and present of being me and my surroundings and speaking to you, all at the same time. But as I track myself, I become aware that I am seeing or sensing it all from my inner being, somewhere around my heart or solar plexus, and then I suddenly pop back into my head and notice it's gone, and I am back to the old familiar place that seems like the old me, just looking at the world again from a place inside my head. I have returned from the tree of life to the tree of knowledge.

I could however have easily become lost in there, daydreaming and disconnected, floating away, but then I wouldn't have been in relationship with it. I would have been merged with it in some autistic fusion that was undifferentiated, like the beginning of life or like someone fused in a dependent relationship, not functioning separately or independently. This floating away is also a coping mechanism at times that allows us to get a rest from the turmoil of daily life or dissociate from our body in traumatic, abusive situations.

Not having enough oil in my lamp to stay present and conscious could also mean that I am more susceptible to being in my preoccupations all the time, being in my mind, seeking to discern the right or wrong action relative to every situation rather than just the ones that need discernment. Again, it is partly about remaining in the tree of life, where life lives and is alive, rather than be in the tree of knowledge, always seeking to solve and be in control, to stay safe. I would also be more likely to be in my psychological self, running on autopilot and at the mercy of my projections, neuroses, and fears, rather than be the free me who is tapped into the source of life and replenishment. For those who don't know, projections in this situation, are ways of being that I unconsciously project onto the other as being what they are like or what is going on in them relative to me. Neuroses are then my concerns in relation to others perceptions of me, causing me to be inhibited for fear of what they will be thinking or saying about me, rather than be able to be my true self. This parable also refers to staying awake for when the bridegroom comes, and to me, this means that moment of connection to the spirit of life that I speak of.

The Tree of Life and the Tree of Knowledge

This being awake and feeling alive with life is the tree of life to me, TOL, rather than being unpresent and preoccupied with thoughts or all caught up in analysing and knowledge and information and explaining everything all the time. This is the tree of knowledge, TOK, to me. At the beginning of the Old Testament, God tells Adam that he may eat of any tree in the garden, but not of the tree of knowledge, for on that day he shall die. For me, God is telling Adam to stay in the tree of life and stay out of the tree of knowledge of good and evil, right and wrong. This is actually about every moment, not that on that day, he will literally die. He will die to being in the ever abundant living waters of life, in every moment that he is in the tree of knowledge.

He is telling Adam to stay conscious and connected to the awe and wonder and abundance of life rather than become unconscious and get caught up in his head all the time, trying to make decisions about this or that. He is telling Adam not to become lost in his mind with all its stuff and wanderings, preoccupied with this or that and not be awake to the moment or the fact that he is alive and living in the vitality of life. He is telling Adam to take in or 'feed on' life and not feed on drama and who is right or wrong. He is telling him to not get caught up in mindless conversation and mundane lifeless squabble. Trying to get one over on each other so we can gain some replenishment or sense of superiority, so that we can top up on each other at the expense and detriment of each other, causing resentment and retaliation, austerity and depletion for each other's momentary gain. He is telling Adam to replenish himself from the ever abundant source that some call God, so that he doesn't need to unconsciously take anything from others.

I reckon most people probably hear this quote several times in their life but just let it go, as it doesn't make easy understanding, but given that this instruction comes at the very beginning of the Bible, before Eve is on the scene, I see it as the most important piece of advice that we can get in our lives. It is telling us how we should live life, staying present and conscious to each moment, and sensing each moment from our being. Rather than just looking at it from somewhere inside our heads in relation to what is being discussed or what is happening so that we can see if we agree or not. Feeling the life or living waters in the moment rather than being not present because we have unconsciously slipped off into being preoccupied or identified within the content of discussion, seeking to be able to answer or respond or defend. In fairness, we have learned to do this to stay safe, because earlier in childhood, we were open and continually got hurt.

This is a bit like when we are somewhere special and aren't fully present; yes, we may be enjoying it, but we haven't stopped to really connect, appreciate, and recognise it for all the magnificence that it is. Then we just stop and take it in. TAKE IT IN. Feed on it; eat of the tree of life, become present in being with it, and feel ourselves being replenished by the momentary connection. The tree of knowledge has disappeared; there is no mental activity or processing, just conscious connection to and union with what is. If we also take our attention to our body in these moments, we feel our inner vitality and aliveness in a cellular way. It's like we actually feel our self being made whole again. This experience is also very healthy for us, as it causes the release of chemicals into the body that are good for us. This simple practice alone could reduce the extent of mental and physical health issues that we are now seeing in society due to disconnect from source.

115

Now, I am not saying that people have not had these experiences and even more importantly that we can't choose to have them several times a day, but what I am saying is that I don't hear anyone explaining them in this way, in relation to the teachings of the Bible and Jesus. I also don't hear people recognising them as spiritual. We are so full of ourselves in our modern-day psychological language that we simply don't see it in this context. To me, this is as spiritual as anything else out there that is going under the heading of spiritual, because it is holistic and realigning us with our holiness through realisation, healing, replenishing, even religious (where in my book, *religious* means realigning our awareness to and with source). This is in contrast to a religion, a formal following or system or belief or story or structure (TOK), that has the potential to help facilitate our religious journey if we don't get lost in the tree of knowledge again, analysing and fighting and arguing about what any respective religion is actually saying and whose is right or wrong. This once again would be where a religion in my opinion would not serve its intended purpose, as we would have fallen in the Garden of Eden once again, as most of us do all day long and as society and humanity are also doing.

I think that part of what I am being invited to show in these realisations is that the teachings of the Bible and Jesus are alive; that God, if we want to call the ever abundant source of life and replenishment that word, is alive just as the Bible says it is; and that its aliveness and movement is the Holy Spirit in motion, always moving in a holistic direction if we can get present enough to our heart's truth to watch, listen, discern, and follow.

I sometimes see the Holy Spirit as being a bit like spiritual gravity, where the primary core density is love, and it influences everything through the love that pervades the core of everything else. Resistance is then futile, as the Trekkies say. We can see earthly gravity at work by its effects on matter pulling all lighter matter towards its core, so to me the Holy Spirit does much the same thing, only with less dense matter and less visibly.

Shake the Dust from Your Feet

I suppose this is a bit like turning the other cheek or resist not evil. But what always matters most is the spirit in which our action is done. These actions are not being done spitefully, or with angst or resentment, or because you consider yourself to be better than the other and don't want to waste your time arguing with them. That would be self-righteousness.

This is one of my favourite parables. I think it is when Jesus is telling the disciples what to do after He has gone. He is telling them to spread His gospel. So to my understanding, He is telling them to travel from place to place, staying with people and sharing their learning and way of being with other people. If the people accept what you have to offer, then stay longer, as long as it is making a difference. But if they don't and can't allow this Christian way of being to become the centre that they operate from, and things just start to become disturbed or troubled, and turn into a battle of words, or a discussion of beliefs, then leave the house and shake the dust from your feet. In other words, let it go. Don't let it consume you; don't allow the situation to move you into angst or resentment or bitterness. Because if you do, then all that has happened is that you have then fallen in the Garden of Eden again and are no longer being guided or led by the spirit. You are being run by your emotions and your beliefs and are in the TOK. You are no longer present to who and how you are being and honouring your purpose of spreading the gospel. You no longer have oil in your lamp and have fallen asleep to the higher guidance within you. You are in your own self-righteousness, telling others that you are right and they are wrong. You are not being spiritually held in righteousness; you are in your self. You are not abiding in Him or seeking first the kingdom of heaven.

So if we jump back to the moment where someone begins to question the gospel or offer logical resistance from some perspective, then perhaps what is really going on is that their whole belief system is being questioned, something that has sustained them for fifty years and they can't just let that go without having something else in place. This is the rock they have built their house upon, and it is beginning to feel a bit like it is now on sand. Doubts are creeping in and washing away the foundations. Everything that they are is dependent on this standing firm so they can manage life, and someone else is offering something that is eroding the old structure. At this point, their neurological defence system is shutting down their availability to contemplate because resources are needed to re-stabilise.

Anyway, the thing I love about this parable is how it is real and alive in daily life, whether we see it or not, regardless of religion, belief, or other persuasion. Take any conversation that you may have during the day. You may be operating from an unconscious desire to coax someone into doing something for you or agreeing with you, so you feel better in your self about something that was bothering you. Essentially, we tend to operate from a want and so are not what I call *clean in spirit*; we are almost always up to something for our own satisfaction, even if it is slightly martyring so that we can feel good about our self having sacrificed for the other. All very noble, or is it, if it is really deep down about us wanting to feel better about our self by doing x or y or z? Perhaps it is still self-righteous, self-esteeming, self-affirming; ego development material. I am not saying that this is wrong, as this is still the divine reality of what is and is still Holy Spirit facilitated for our ongoing awakening. I am simply bringing it to view. At the core of behaviour, we want and need people to respect or admire or praise us. Ultimately, we are operating from a love-seeking agenda because we are not staying connected to the divine abundant loving source.

So what would life be like if we could feel that abundant love that is there all the time for us, if it didn't matter how we behaved or what we did, if it loved us even when we turned away from it and did all sorts of things? What if it is there staring us in the face and we go to sleep every night for no other reason than to reawaken to it every day, this loving abundance that exists purely for us to enjoy it and experience it? Spring, summer, autumn, winter, light, dark, hot, cold, moving, stationary, alive, dead, lost, found, and so on, an infinite, endless explosion of colour and form, smells and sights, sounds and tastes for us to embrace and indulge in whilst being conscious and appreciative for it, knowing that it is there in the name of love for us. We all connect to it and feel it now and again, but what if that is all we have to do, and everything else falls into place? What if this is God's kingdom? We could learn to see what happens when we remain embraced in the love that is essential, still working in daily life to earn our living, but from a place of fulfilment and abundance rather than a place of dependence on money to get this or that, so we can feel better by what we materialistically have or by what personal or public image sustains us as a poor and temporary substitute.

So as I now reflect back to the beginning of this chapter, I wonder if I have done what I set out to do. It was meant to show you what I think Jesus was teaching regarding helping others, to see a purer way of being and living, and at the same time being present to watching that we are actually doing it. I guess it's a bit like watching that we are walking the walk by being in the tree of life, rather than just talking the talk from being in the tree of knowledge, watching that in the exchange, we remain vigilant to being in our peace, as we have understanding, compassion, and love for the other so as to avoid falling in the Garden of Eden and doing the opposite. The level people operate at is never their fault. We all become the way we are due to our environment and survival needs, whilst continually seeking self-fulfilment by outgrowing the current level of operation. This shaking the dust from your feet as you leave, rather than getting pulled down to a lower functioning, can also be seen as resisting not evil, because when we are in resistance and forcefulness, we are not in purer spirit. There is a more demonstrative teaching in leaving the conversation (or house, as the metaphor goes) in grace than there is in reducing everyone to a squabble, depending on the spirit in which we do it.

Secondly, in shaking the dust from our feet, I believe we are being encouraged to not fester on what we have not managed to do, as that would also be detrimental and negative towards the divine way of being. The invitation here is that we abide in Him, be easy on our self with our limitations, and have forgiveness for our self, returning to peace and love by reconnecting to source again, and picking our self up again if we have fallen in the Garden of Eden.

Love Your God with All Your Heart, Soul, and Mind

Jesus gave us two commandments: to love the Lord God with all our heart, soul, and mind, and to love our neighbour as our self, going on to say that all else hangs on these commandments. Now if I go back to my earlier explanation of what the God word used to mean to me, then this isn't really doable, because there isn't really any relationship, never mind a loving one. But it actually happens all on its own now, when I simply connect to the awe and wonder of everything. I don't have to consider anything like heart, soul, or mind, or make any effort. All I have to do is remember to become present to the moment, regardless of where I am or what I am doing; even if I am upset or annoyed, it doesn't matter. Everything comes alive again as I come out of the tree of knowledge and go back in to the tree of life.

Unless You Become Like a Child You Shall Not Enter the Kingdom of Heaven

One day, I was driving my granddaughter back to our place after having collected her from nursery, when suddenly I found myself shouting at her to stop nipping my head because I was busy trying to think about something. The poor wee soul recoiled in shock, as I moved to guilt and self-disappointment. In that moment, I realised that I was being self-righteous and told her that I was sorry. She looked at me and smiled, and then with the grace of an angel, she said, "That's okay, Granddad." My heart almost burst. How many of us adults can forgive so quickly and easily? I had been completely unpresent and asleep somewhere in my thoughts or daydreams, and she had been pulling me back into the present moment. I had unconsciously wanted to stay in the amusement of my fantasy or thoughts, even though I should have been paying more attention to the road and her, but she forced me back by triggering me emotionally.

This example shows us how our emotions can serve our awakening as we are triggered back into the present moment and see the gift that it has to offer, rather than be emotionally triggered and react back at someone because we don't understand how spirit works and are not awake enough to see the difference. I should really have said thank you so that my spirit could amen hers. This is becoming like a child, and the kingdom of heaven was right there at hand in the car, but unfortunately, we don't usually have the eyes to see it, as I did then. On this occasion, it was because I could feel the defilement in my body and mind; I was alerted to my not behaving in a way that was Christian hearted and in keeping with the Jesus within. I was not being holy in the spirit of my actions and aligning with a higher guidance and purpose. I was in my ego, reacting psychologically to serve my own self-esteeming needs and sense of self-worth and self-importance; I was being self-righteous, and she was being righteous. This for me is an example of what Jesus means when he says that unless we become like a child, we shall not enter the kingdom of heaven. In other words, for us adults; if we do not do what feels crucifying to our ego self to transcend functioning at the ego level of development, then we will remain self-righteous and self-esteeming and never resurrect our true self.

Jesus' Second Commandment

As regards the second commandment, love your neighbour as yourself: Well, when we have a psychospiritual understanding of life, how it works, and why people do the things they do, then once again, it is quite easy to love everyone and have compassion and understanding for them in their own struggles and disconnection and lostness. So this loving your neighbour as yourself also just happens out of functioning at that level of development and awakeness. It is like being in the presence of a baby or small child; we automatically move to love without even trying. We just can't help but do it; they are the pure untainted manifestation of God or source, and they touch us at that level in our self. As Watchman Nee says, spirit touches spirit, and that is how we have the potential to be with each other as adults.

Being Clean or Contaminated in Spirit

Being clean of spirit is a phrase that I use to keep an eye on myself and my behaviour, watching to see what spirit I am in when I interact with others (the spirit I am in being similar to saying the energy behind my mood or the unconscious agenda that lies behind my actions, such as punishing or comforting). So maybe this is also a part of our problem with religion and understanding words from two thousand years ago. Maybe they are the same thing and nobody has realised it, just like when we say something's a coincidence or intuition or instinct. Simply watching and being conscious of our behaviour is the first step towards changing the way we behave and is more productive than being unconscious and reactive. Am I behaving out of annoyance or resentment or angst, rather than compassion, understanding, or forgiveness, for example? But then I also need to watch for being untrue to myself and the other when I act in a way I perceive to be more productive or positive? So in a situation that may cause me annoyance, for example, it is productive to notice it but untruthful if I don't express it and just override that annoyance, putting on a false appearance of sympathy or understanding, telling myself that I am being good or Christian by turning the other check; because this is not really being clean in spirit either. On another occasion, however, it may be exactly the most productive thing to do if I sense that it serves a more important purpose. But it is how I express my annoyance that can have a positive or negative effect on myself and others; that can heal or harm them; and it usually depends on whether I am acting proactively from spirit or reactively from hurt.

I Am the Way and the Truth and the Life. If You Live in Me, I Will Live in You. Learning to Use the Embodied Spirit

When I work with clients, I am using my truth detector all the time (or at least when I don't get caught up in the story, that is). But in every moment that I am present and awake, feeling the moment, I am feeling in myself for resonance with truth. Do I feel my heart amen what the other is saying? Do I feel unburdened or enlightened as I am with the spirit of their words, or do I feel contaminated and disturbed, not quite buying it? We all do this all the time; in my experience, women tend to be naturally better at it than men, as they are usually more in their feelings than in their minds, as men often are. So what if this is the Holy Spirit or advocate that Jesus said would come when He left, the holistic truth detector within us, and we simply aren't seeing it for what it is? Perhaps we don't see it because we are all caught up in modern words and disbelief and disconnect and simply not looking to find it; because we have put it so high and out of reach.

Seek First the Kingdom of Heaven

As I approach the end of this chapter, there are a few more sayings that I want to just quickly mention because they also play a large role in helping to guide me. Seek first the kingdom of heaven helps me to realign with my higher purpose. It is not about seeking something for the afterlife; it is about now in this present moment, again and again and again, always questioning if my thoughts and actions are serving in a way that is opening to others rather than closing to them. I know that it is all serving, but one way is easier. Then there is Repent, for the kingdom is at hand. This to me is not what most people think it is about: repenting for your sins, whatever they may be, like asking for forgiveness because you can now see where you went wrong and want to be a better person. No, for me this is about all of what I have been writing in this chapter: repent for being preoccupied with yourself and seeking to esteem and glorify and satisfy yourself. It is about self-righteousness, so repent putting your small wants before aligning with a greater purpose, because your lower self is in disconnect. In this way, we are being the light of the world.

The thing that makes all of this a bit easier, of course, is if a group of people come together to practice it; even two people is enough, given what Jesus said: Where two or more are gathered in my name, there I shall be. As we work at changing our self, it is like building a muscle; it gets a bit easier as we see the benefits for ourselves and others and see the change, but Jesus also said, to those who use their talents I shall give more and to those who don't I shall take away what they have. This again is something that I see and agree with.

So hopefully, you can now understand my dilemma more fully by seeing a contrast between what I offer here and what we see going on in the world. For me, there is quite a difference between what I offer in this chapter and what we have been taught. How do we synthesise this with what we have grown up with, or is it a case of growing into a new level of understanding and being?

CHAPTER 8

Celtic Christianity: Seeing the Divine in All of Creation

The Spirit of Celtic Christianity

I love the spirit of Celtic Christianity. I love how the words take me straight to a place of connection with everything and make me feel alive inside. In the beginning was the word, and this is what the word has the power to do: make us come alive. My being is brought straight into presence without even thinking about it or trying to do it; I go straight to feeling and sensing my environment and the aliveness and vibrancy that there is in that connection. This is God in Celtic Christianity: life itself, the ongoing explosion of creation eternally pouring out of source and the feeling of being awake and present to it all. Life is great if we stop to realise it and let it in. We tend to see the word *realise* as a mental process that we do, as if we are saying that we didn't understand but now we do. But to realise can also be to make real: now I realise, now I have made it become real. I have turned something from being not real to being real. I have realised it. I have moved from being in the TOK to being in the TOL with it.

Life is naturally holistic and self-governing, with some sense of self-regulation and order that just seems to take care of itself beyond our comprehension. When we cut our hand, it heals; when we don't understand, we naturally seek to understand; and when we become distorted in childhood, we become religious, in the sense that we seek to return to our former purity. Celtic Christianity is essentially about the goodness and abundance of life, the awe and wonder and grace of what we are, that we are essentially good, rather than sinful, and that we are simply out of touch with knowing the amazement of who and what we are: sparks of the same divinity as all the rest of creation.

But we also have the added gift of being able to awaken and become conscious to it. The more feel that I get for Celtic Christianity, the more it resonates with what feels right and true within me. I am the way and the truth and the life. Who doesn't love going out in nature, be it the woods or the beach or up a hill or mountain? Who isn't in awe and wonder at the universe and the stars and the abundance of life forms on our planet? The vastness of the seas and oceans, with their moods from glistening calm to wild destruction? Who doesn't soften and dissolve a little inside when they see a newborn baby, or isn't stunned by the smell of a fresh spring morning or the wondrous array of colours in the autumn?

This is us being present to life and reconnecting to it, our source, God, whatever you want to call it when we stop to see it and let it in. This is reconnecting to the vitality of life that is our source, and this is what replenishes us and keeps us healthy. What is that if not a Garden of Eden? To me, these are not experiences that we have because we believe in this religion or that religion or Darwinism or atheism or whatever else; because beliefs are all TOK anyway. These things simply are; regardless of opinion, understanding, or belief, they are truths unto themselves and each other; this is the TOL.

What is grace or falling in love; what is happiness, joy, spite, hate, or resentment, and where did they come from? Who ordered them, and how much do we have to pay for them? Can I get them on contract, or does it have to be pay-as-you-go? Can I trade them in if they begin to get worn out or if someone comes out with a better version tomorrow? Can you guarantee they will always feel fresh and new and shiny? Why can't we see what really matters? What is of real value? Is it because it is so freely given that we don't even notice it? What if living in presence to this is the way and the truth and the life and is what Jesus is pointing us to? What if being present to all of that and enjoying it is being like a child? What if being there is abiding and being single eyed and eating of the tree of life? What if that is the heavenly kingdom of earth, and the kingdom is so in our own hands that we can't see it? What if the *truths* of *life* simply are, and have their *way* of being, regardless of our persuasions, opinions, religions, or thoughts (all TOK)?

Practicing Being

So where does this leave you after having read the above paragraph? Please stop reading and feel into what is moving within you. Did it touch you? Did it bring you into life? Did it make you ponder? If it did, then how can a few words on a piece of paper change who we experience ourselves to be? Logical thought would say that they can't. They are just black squiggles on a piece of paper. But if the life within those words, the life that I put into them by being connected to source and feeling the life within them, gets past you and touches your spirit, because you can associate with them, then it has already changed you from what you were prior to reading them; it brought you back to life, the TOL. True love, beauty, truth, grace, tenderness, forgiveness, compassion, and several other states of being have a way of slipping right past the defences of our psychological self and touching our true or spiritual self because of their purity and because they are nonthreatening, holistic, or holy in spirit. It's the spirit of the words that make the difference; it's where they come out of, because of where the writer is connected as they write them. Jesus said that no branch can bear fruit by itself; it must remain in the vine. Spirit touches spirit touches spirit, as Watchman

Nee would say. That's why we feel certain people when they sing or dance and why we don't feel others; the former are connected to the spirit of what they are singing about or the spirit of the music they are dancing to; becoming one with the music; they are connected to the life of it. They are in the TOL. But the latter are preoccupied in the TOK and with trying to sing or dance well, even singing or dancing technically better in some cases, but it is still empty and disconnected and so doesn't touch us the same. The living water is not there.

Reunifying Celtic and Roman Christianity

To me, this is part of the narrow path that Jesus asks us to follow, but that few of us find or manage to stay on because no one is showing us the way and because of our psychological fears and insecurities. We don't come together to practice it with each other and in each other's company; this way and truth and life that we can live when we keep oil in our lamps and see the love in all creation and be in love with it, all without even trying. This is sacred and divine and full of grace and easily worshiped from the essence of our being, without any cognitive involvement. In fact, as soon as it becomes cognitive, TOK, it starts to go. It is about getting back to knowing and connecting through our essential being, the TOL, not about thinking, the TOK. It is about the spirit of who we are, not the rationality of what we should or shouldn't believe, say or do.

Young children can be very thoughtless with their words but are usually being truthful in that moment. This is righteousness rather than self-righteousness; despite the shock, we smile inside at the beauty and simplicity of their way of being. But don't go out and try to be like this because that is not the same thing; it would be impure and self-motivated and that would be more likely to be self-righteous. It would probably be about how you wanted to show up so that you could feel pleased about your self. Your TOK would probably be behind it.

How I Came upon Celtic Christianity

As I mentioned earlier, I came across Celtic Christianity very recently when I saw an advert about a talk at the Augustine United Church in Edinburgh. The event was being hosted by Edinburgh International Centre for Spirituality and peace, with Mathew Fox talking about Celtic Christianity and the work of Thomas Merton. I decided to go along for some unknown reason; perhaps I was just curious about some variation on Christianity and keen to see what the people involved with the EICSP were like. But then as I have said already, this is one of the ways that the Holy Spirit works in our lives, always facilitating our environment if we will simply follow it. Given the fact that this was just a couple of months ago, my knowledge of Celtic Christianity is even less than it is of Watchman Nee or Christianity, but this hasn't stopped me from being inspired to write about them due to the effect they have had on me. Most of what I am writing actually comes from where I am at in my own life; I have only recently learned how this resonates with Celtic Christianity. In addition to the talk that I attended by Fox, I have read a few things online and read a couple of books by J. Philip Newell and this seems to have given me enough to inspire me to write my own book, something I never thought I would actually do.

As soon as I felt what Celtic Christianity was, there was a resonance with it that touched a knowing and truth in me that I had experienced many times. This resonance and knowing is about how we can connect to God or source through creation and life by being fully present to it, embracing, worshiping, and enjoying it. This connection is eating from the tree of life and is what allows us to feed on our source and be replenished by it; and this Is a large part of what has gone wrong with humanity. We have spiritually cut ourselves off from our source and we are slowly dying; just like the branches that I pruned from my trees last autumn and watched dying away in the compost pile over the winter. The only difference is that we top up in small ways through food and nature and the moments when we do unconsciously reconnect, as I describe.

I had already had many peak experiences and moments of presence as well as experiences of realisation or revelation, and so this way of understanding God and Christianity fitted like a glove. It was more affirming than informing. I had only previously seen Druidic or shamanic-type associations with creation- or nature-based spirituality, never anything Christian. Up until now, I had only seen the word *Celtic* in a historical context, as tribal and more uncivilised, with people running about the woods in animal skins well before the times of Jesus. But it soon became apparent that Celtic Christianity, in contrast to early Celts, is not just about nature and creation; it is also closely connected with the Bible, most specifically St John, as he is associated with listening for the heartbeat of God: listening for the heartbeat of God within all creation and life, and all people, irrespective of cultural or religious persuasion. But that also begins to sound very similar to what we do in Heart Intelligence coaching, as we help people discern between all of the voices moving within them in relation to their dilemma, listening for the voice of purest truth; the voice that touches us differently; the voice that isn't avoidant, neurotic, self-esteeming, or pretentious. It is usually a voice that doesn't come from our mind or our personality, a place of excitement or a good idea, but more from our soul, a voice that knows truth and often comes forward tainted with the resignation of the outer man, as Watchman Nee would say, a voice with a surrendered spirit, accepting the reality of what is true.

This different Christianity just seemed to appear from nowhere when I was ready to see it, but already fitted with much of what I already saw, such as how I would quote to others in group that there is such an absolute purity in a newborn baby that even though it is entirely dependent upon us for everything in a literal context, it gives so much more back to us spiritually, simply in its radiant way of being (not that we tend to see it in that context). Then there is the admiration and upholding of the feminine in glory and equality, with women having been invited to read the scriptures, as well as seeing that God is in and for everyone, not exclusive to Christians and in some cases only the baptised. God is seen as all-pervading and inclusive, rather than excluding and condemning, more loving than judging. We don't have to try to be good to make up for being essentially bad and earn our way into heaven; we are essentially good and simply disconnected and unconscious, functioning in a way that serves our survival and fits with our tribe and environment.

For me, the religion of Celtic Christianity is similar to my concept of what religion really is: our returning to being able to be our truth rather than need to be our psychological self, our re - alignment with being able to be real, something that is not easy for us because we are so complex and are still being run by so many programs from childhood. This being real is in contrast to operating unconsciously out of our mindsets, beliefs, maintaining cycles, projections, transferences, defences, neuroses, spite, angst, resentment, bitterness, being good to get our needs met, being special and an example to others, being wise or clever or enlightened; on and on, the list goes. All of this has little to do with this or that religion and is more developmental and Psychospiritual. Perhaps you will see that for us to do this, we need to be willing to go deeper into ourselves to see who we really are rather than operate symptomatically and evasively out of not being willing to contemplate who and what we are. Once again, this fits with Celtic tradition in seeing that our truth is hidden deep within us.

I actually find it quite hard to write about because it takes me away from it. I keep wanting to stop writing and just enjoy being it, rather than try to describe or teach or work it out, so that I can write something. It is actually like jumping back and forwards between two worlds; it can be quite tiring.

Once again, I am going to follow this moment of higher guidance and stop working, TOK. Instead, I am just going to ramble for a bit, TOL, as that sometimes helps and feels better.

This now feels more like chatting with you, rather than writing something important that has to be fairly right. I can feel my energy drop back down into my body and come into peace again. Peace being with me, as Jesus would say.

I was chatting with a friend the other night about the amount of anxiety there is these days, when I spontaneously came up with the term *spiritual anxiety*, because much of the anxiety I sense people being with is not because they are concerned with a job interview tomorrow or something relative to their daily lives. It feels bigger and more general or overarching; it feels like it's because they have no sense of purpose or direction. Not career purpose or direction, and not even life purpose and direction, but more existential; more about their purpose of being, and existence. This type of anxiety is more of a *Why am I here?* or *What's the point of existing if it is for nothing more productive?* type of anxiety. But at least this feels healthier than when people are not in this place, because that is when I sense many people being in disconnect and avoidance and distraction, doing all the mundane stuff that we seem to endlessly preoccupy ourselves with these days, in our way of unconsciously coping.

As I ended that little ramble, I could see it in contrast to what I had written prior and realised that was maybe why I was subconsciously following some intuition or holistic guidance to just ramble for a moment. What a difference between these two ways of being in life; no wonder we are struggling.

This chapter is feeling a bit trickier to write than most of the other chapters. I can feel and discern within my spirit that I can't push it and shouldn't try. I need to allow it. In fact, as I feel that and write it, it feels like a message for life, not for a chapter. The fact that I want to get the book finished for a rest is immaterial; my job is to keep myself out of the way as much as possible. It is grace that guides us into our truth.

The Tree of Life and the Tree of Knowledge Are
Our Choice of Central Starting Points

As I have mentioned several times now, in Genesis, God tells Adam there are two trees at the centre of the garden, the TOL and the TOK, and that he may eat of any tree in the garden, but not the tree of knowledge, for on that day, he will die (die to being in the living waters of life, that is, not literally die). But I also want to emphasise that these trees, compared to any other trees, are central in the garden, and to me that means central in life. In other words, there are two options available to us at the centre of our daily life and life in general: one, to live in the TOL as I describe above, or two, to live in the TOK, where there is no living waters and everything feels a bit devoid of life. This is why the Garden of Eden is the starting point in every moment, our ground zero within ourselves, and why we can live as invited or fall before we do anything.

In moving towards closing this chapter, I ask myself what Celtic Christianity most essentially seems to be about. The answer that emerges immediately is that it is more connected to life than telling us what we should or shouldn't do to be living a God-worthy life. Immediately, I see the TOL and the TOK and feel the difference between Celtic and Roman Christianity; one being alive and living in life by following a way and truth and life that guides us from within and without, whilst the other feels old and dusty and disconnected from what it is about. Celtic Christianity invites us to celebrate the abundance of life and all its form, as well as enjoy the intimate depths of each other, rather than see intimacy as sinful and fallen. Once again, I think the main point here is the spirit in which we act and what we take from each understanding of Christianity, rather than accept one and exclude the other or take the Bible at the level of TOK. For me, there is a rich and grounded feel to Celtic Christianity that is missing from an aloof and disconnected Roman Christianity, whilst there is a divinity and guiding grace within Roman

Christianity that I don't feel in the Celtic; one feeling very feminine and sacred whilst the other feels very masculine and guiding.

Spirit or Soul

So what about psychic experiences and things like claircognizance, clairaudience, clairvoyance, and clairsentience?

One of my first claircognizance experiences happened when I was eight years old, and I remember it like yesterday. The house we lived in was built in 1796, and my father and grandfather bought it in 1961. In 1970, my grandfather was killed in a road accident going down to England to collect a residential caravan for my grandparents to move into, so that we could move into the house. On the day that he left, there came a point where I was standing outside the house beside the water well, saying to my mum that he wasn't coming back. From somewhere, I just knew we would never see him again.

"Of course he is coming back," my mum said, "Don't be silly; he's just away down south for a couple of days to get the caravan."

But I knew different, and said, "No, he's not coming back."

This was at about two o'clock in the afternoon, right when the accident happened on the A68. Another car had crested one of the blind summits on the wrong side of the road, causing the accident; my grandfather died as a consequence. We didn't get news of the accident until we were at home later that evening.

As I end this example, I am suddenly reminded of another story to tell you. About twelve years ago, my parents, my wife and I, and a couple of friends bought a piece of land to build a house on. I was the main contractor, and we were doing the site clearance, removing all the vegetation to mark out the foundations for digging. I was standing well back from the excavator as it stripped the ground with its ditching bucket; rotating through 90 degrees and depositing its diggings, ready to load when the lorry returned. The excavator was working at full reach, jibbing in and out as it rotated back and forth, so I stepped forward to pick something up. Suddenly, there was an ominous feeling, and I drew my head back a few inches in reaction and curiosity, then I woke up lying on the ground, spitting broken teeth and dirt out of my mouth. The excavator had clipped me on the head; blood was running down my face. I knew I was still alive but also knew that I had to be seriously injured, so before shock could set in and whilst the adrenalin of fear was active, I got up and shouted to the operator to get me to hospital. As it turns out, I am still here, albeit with neck and sleep issues, but thanks only to some strange intervention.

Okay, one more, but this is the last one. A couple of years ago, I was on a Heart Intelligence retreat in the mountains of Spain. There were about thirty of us who had taken over the retreat centre; we had it all to ourselves, other than some staff. We were about five days into the retreat, and things were beginning to feel a bit merged for me. We were all spending so much time together, with almost no interaction with the outside world, and working at such a depth with ourselves, that for me, we were becoming too merged in a regressive way. So anyway, on this day at lunchtime, I was walking across the dining area to get a spoon, and as I walked past someone, I heard them call out my name, as if they were calling to me from a distance. It was as real and clear as could be, yet I immediately knew that it could not really have happened because I was within touching distance of the woman concerned, and she just didn't do it. I collected the spoon in confusion and then checked it out with her, and we both just laughed. Anyway, twenty-four hours went past; she had asked me to meet her along with some others at the meditation building down behind the swimming pool. As I walked down the steps and turned the wrong way, I heard her calling, "Bill!" in the exact same way I had heard it the day before. As you can imagine, we had a good laugh about it. This is clairaudience, in that it is about hearing rather than knowing, but my reason for telling these stories is that this stuff really happens.

But is it spiritual, considering that it is otherworldly and guiding? Does it still fall within Celtic Christianity, given that it ties in with our more primal nature and is all part of the great creation? And what if we consider things like instinct and intuition and premonition, or go even further into other types of peculiar experiences such as visions or dreams, the voices I have mentioned hearing, hypnosis, breathing techniques, chanting, ritual, animal guides, symbology, mediumship, numerology, and astrology? Are these things spiritual, or are they psychic and of the soul, as Watchman Nee and the Bible suggest, or are they bits of both? Are these experiences spiritual in a Celtic Christianity context, if not Biblical and spiritual in a Roman Christianity context? Or are they more akin to paganism, shamanism, and Druidry and more about the primal soul and our deep connection to the earth, than to spirit, even though some would call this spiritual?

Well, I haven't seen any suggestion of this stuff being seen as Celtic Christianity in anything I have read. So perhaps this is more the nature of the things that were being rejected at the treaty of Nicaea by the Roman emperor and first Christian leader Constantine in AD 325. This was a decisive moment in history when Constantine gathered hundreds of bishops together in an attempt to put an overarching structure in place for people to live by, so as to stop the present clash of beliefs and end the chaos that was rife.

Watchman Nee, however, is saying explicitly that these things are not spiritual and are of the soul, as he offers us a way of discerning between the spiritual energies and powers, and those that come from the soul. Nee encourages us not to use our senses and feelings, as they are psychic energies, not spiritual. He teaches us that the power of the Holy Spirit is never affected by the outside environment and that the soul is alive but that only the spirit lives and can give life. So is this the difference between the unregenerated man, still of the earth and perceiving psychic powers to be spiritual, and the regenerated and born-again, aspiring to live in the spirit by abiding in Him, seeking the kingdom of heaven on earth?

So it seems as I close this chapter that I may have differentiated for myself a little between the Celts of earlier times and Celtic Christianity, as well as reminded myself of the teachings of Watchman Nee about spirit and soul energies and what is Christian and what is not. Or are these experiences still all spiritual, and Watchman Nee's particularly Christian? And is my theory about the words holistic guidance and Holy Spirit as similar as I thought? I am not so sure that I am not just creating more questions as I seek to find answers.

PART 3

What We Need to Complete the Journey

Reminder of Part 1 and Reframe of Book's Intent

Part 1 of the book was my attempt to show levels within levels of the same thing: that everything organic is always in a constant state of flux or psychosynthesis, as it is constantly guided to be the purest version of itself, whilst also being guided to take the form required for it to survive. This requires constant breakdown and reformation, dependent on the safety perceived in each moment, and over time this creates a personality of typical behaviour based on the ways that we have had to be most often. I showed this with my initial moment of starting to write this book and the moment-by-moment occurrences as I was writing. I also showed how the same thing can be seen in my midlife crisis and in the current breakdown of our church and society, as well as in the subcomponents of our society, such as the NHS, housing, banking, local councils, and education, as they all increasingly struggle.

I also believe that a large part of our society's breakdown is because our religions and guiding structures are flawed and outgrown and so the truth is beginning to transcend them, focussing particularly on the one that I have been searching within: Christianity. Within all of this, I have also exposed the masculine and feminine dynamics as I see them: the feminine energy of abundant love and outpouring, and the masculine energy of containing and giving form to that outpouring. But I have also shown how I believe that it is an immature masculine that is inhibiting this divine unity from working most purely, due to pathology and the lack of new wisdom, guidance, and light. But then we are now also seeing a lack of masculine structure and boundaries in schools and society, accompanied by an overly loving feminine, with the result being a wishy-washy facilitating environment that results in chaos everywhere. I didn't set out to show microcosms within macrocosms to do with breakdown and reformation; I simply realised what it was that I was doing about six weeks after starting the book, again demonstrating the guidance at play that I was following without fully understanding what was going on at first.

One morning at the six-week point, I suddenly got stuck again and was all horrible inside, trying to move forward but not being able to feel the context of where I was going or what the main purpose was. Subconsciously within this disturbance, I was actually calling out for a revelation, unknowingly calling out to my higher Self or source or God or whatever anyone wishes to call it for help. Not literally, but rather that my truth at the time was that I was in anguish and seeking to know, so that I could move again and feel free. It was then that I suddenly saw the common thread within all of what I had been writing: Seek and ye shall find, being evidenced within this.

I think it is also worth stating here that none of this happened because of my being of any particular religion or being atheist or anything else, for that matter; it is simply the reality of how it is, regardless of our beliefs. I simply know that there is a holistic guidance at play that acts in service of a higher purpose. It acts to serve our survival whilst also seeking to guide us to show up and be the purest we can be. I believe that ultimately, everything spiritual and natural also seeks to serve that purpose, be it sun, rain, the food of the earth, the higher guidance, disturbances, suffering, hope, faith, psychological conditions, animals, and so on, it is all one act of love seeking survival and full conscious expression of itself in form. We are self-healing in more ways than just when we cut ourselves.

So in summary, Part 1 of the book was about evidencing that there is a holistic guidance at play in our lives that constantly breaks us down and puts us back together all of the time, mostly prioritising survival but also seeking for us to be our purity in its fullest expression. And this dynamic also applies to families, businesses, politics, religions, societies, and humanity.

Part 3 of this book now moves towards telling you in more detail about the path I have been guided along so far; my initial need being to re-find my sanity and get to somewhere less disturbing than where I was, before continuing to untangle and awaken further through the other things that I was guided to become involved with. The main objective of this final part of the book is to show a way through the situation that we are currently in, with everything in breakdown, and show that it is something trying to go right if we can understand and work with it, rather than something going wrong. By showing the path that I was guided along and my understanding of why it took that form, I hope to convince others that all of what we see going on is holistic or holy in action and purpose, so that others may follow and then hopefully, we can all collectively take our societies, organisations, and institutions with us. The path I took was in the form of trying a Christianity that didn't help me, to Psychosynthesis, to Heart Intelligence and then to Watchman Nee, then Jesus, and finally Celtic Christianity. Arriving now at a place where I am writing this book in an attempt to synthesise them into a cohesive singularity that can be offered to others.

There were other events and courses involved, such as theta healing and quantum jumping, all of which add to the bigger outcome, but I don't believe all of that is necessary, only the thread woven within all of it. There is a loving source and holistic guidance at play in our lives, taking multiple forms so as to meet us at our varied levels of development and in relation to our varied interests and cultures. But I also want to stress that Jesus has given us a great teaching to follow, to help us with it. Psychosynthesis and Heart Intelligence then provide us with ways of understanding and working through the transition that lies ahead of us as we aspire to come out of humanity's breakdown in the more enlightened direction, eventually getting to a point where we are increasingly able to live more like Jesus, as seen by Watchman Nee.

We have tried to play God through the tree of knowledge, by breaking everything down to its smallest components and describing it all in different scientific ways. And we have expanded beyond the confines of our own earth visually and physically, but ultimately all of this effort and knowledge is still to no avail, as everything is starting to crumble away, including our more significant systems such as law, education, politics, and religion; we need to see that we are not meant to play God. There is a source and its guidance, and I believe that we will only ever find true joy and peace when we learn to accept our place in relation to it through following the teachings of its highest human example: Jesus.

CHAPTER 9

How Psychosynthesis Can Help Us

Evidencing the Higher Self at Work

It is amusing to watch my higher Self at play, as this is about the sixth time that I have returned to this chapter after the initial download that happened on 20 September and the few days after that. Every time I tried to untangle this chapter and the following one, or write anything fresh, I kept ending up back at the Introduction and first two chapters. The result of this was that I kept fiddling with those chapters until they felt structured and stable enough to hold my progressive development onto this chapter.

With hindsight, this makes complete sense when viewed alongside what evolution does and how childhood development progresses. The good thing about this is that for the moment, at least, I feel stable again and more able to progress forward, knowing that something more substantial is holding me as I begin to differentiate and expand this chapter. As I wrote the word *knowing* just there, I noticed something happen within myself. I realised that it was not a heady knowing but a real embodied sense of knowing, a knowing of truth rather than a heady knowing of knowledge. Some would call this claircognizance: a metaphysical knowing.

As Psychosynthesis sees it, it is our higher Self that guides us, and it was therefore my higher Self that guided me to differentiate, restructure and evolve all of what had been written, into more holding stable structures that could then sustain my further progress. It is actually quite amazing to watch something organic taking form at the same time as getting in its way. These are the moments when I end up back in the TOK, unconsciously following my own thoughts and opinions about what I should or should not be doing, compared to the more flowing TOL moments of watching what is being written and seeing what I learn or realise from it.

Psychosynthesis Psychotherapy and Psychosynthesis as the Constant Holistic Fluxing in Life

Roberto Assagioli was a pioneering Italian psychiatrist who lived from 1888 until 1974; he is remembered mostly for developing Psychosynthesis psychology to explain and teach the psychospiritual dynamics of life. He then used this in a therapeutic approach to aid others with their constant ongoing psychosynthesis (this means aiding us with our constant re-synthesising or constant instantaneous restructuring moment by moment, as we wrestle between the tensions of self-survival and self-fulfilment). He saw that all of our life was a constant spiritual awakening and that the cause of all our suffering was down to our higher Self trying to keep us pure and true. He could see that there was something spiritual and transcendent of our everyday sense of self and how that higher Self as our fullest potential, adapted us to cope with early life. Our higher Self achieving this by having us take on a psychological form, before guiding us back again, as we progressively need it less and gradually awaken to seeing our ego's behaviour as having been focussed on serving our survival; this self-survival needing to have been prioritised at that early development time. He saw how this adaptation process was constantly ongoing but was particularly observable in comparing childhood to adulthood. Psychosynthesis psychology therefore invites us to see that we are constantly in the flux of being re-synthesised within our psyche, moment by moment, and always with the purpose of being guided to be the purest us that we can be in any moment. Yet always relative to perceived threat from our environment.

Understanding Our Disturbances for
the Invitations that They Are

My Psychosynthesis training was a five-year training that saved my sanity when I was in mid life crisis. In Psychosynthesis, all of life's disturbances are seen as spiritually facilitated developmental crises. They are seen to be caused by our higher Self's consistent calling on us to awaken or develop towards being able to be our truest purest self. This pure self is also the way we were when we were born, pure but totally dependent and nonconscious: like a blank canvas ready to receive, or like a chameleon ready to take whatever form is required to survive. The reason that midlife, or anything else for that matter, becomes a crisis is because we are held back by the part of us that is resistant to the change; it is secured by the known and familiar. In addition to this resistance, the other factor can sometimes be a lack of guidance from something operating at the new level that we can attach to, feel reassured by, and learn from. It's a bit like separating from an old womb that we have outgrown and being in the birth canal towards a new one, but it doesn't seem to be there yet; hence the need for this book and more education about how life works relative to our development and awakening. This is why some people in midlife crisis escape their present place of disturbance by regressing and reattaching to an old familiar womb or way of being, whilst others advance by groping their way forward, as I did myself. The difference being that I was given several viewings of the next dimension, when most others are not. This was both a blessing and curse at the time because it made my life so difficult at times that I had to find a way to cope with it.

This insight into something new came in the form of having several peak experiences with animals and nature and love; the more I bought into it, the more I received. Seek and ye shall find is very true guidance. My psyche became very porous, and the more open I became, the more I began to feel the oneness with all of life, simply knowing a higher reality and truth by experiencing it. It was undeniable. This, however, was also accompanied by psychotic episodes of constant streaming of information going through my mind, flickering constantly like fast forwarding a television, as something within me searched for a solution, a way to make sense of what was happening to me and save me from the madness.

Roberto Assagioli spoke of four stages of spiritual awakening. The crises preceding, the crises caused by, the reactions to, and the phases of the process of transmutation. I had gone through the crises preceding and had been in good health and reasonable prosperity, but now there was a lack of inspiration in my life. This lack was something that invited curiosity and consideration of what else there was to life than what I had achieved. Add to this a couple of shocking emotional disturbances and some self-questioning of misalignment with my own morals and ethics, leading to guilt and shame, and I was in meltdown; the breakdown before the potential breakthrough. The peak experiences and psychotic episodes that I speak of are more related to the crises caused by a spiritual awakening, as I was in the flow of superconscious energies and unable to assimilate them within myself. Add to this the experience of oneness with all and overwhelming love, along with taking all of this on at the ego level, thinking that had an amazing gift, and you can see that I was in deep trouble. To some extent, I would say that I am still in the third and fourth phases, doing the work of undoing the old towards being able to stand more fully in the new, whilst also managing life and an environment that still functions in the old.

Fortunately, within all of this madness I was led to the Institute of Psychosynthesis, but many others don't find something to help them and often end up being diagnosed as schizophrenic, psychotic or depressed. Some are even institutionalised due to the lack of knowledge of where to go for help with this, and the lack of places to go.

Through the worst of this, I was still running my own joiner and builder business, with several employees and subcontractors to organise. I was in meltdown and hiding it from everyone; lying in bed at night crying in fear of losing my sanity, and hiding it all from my wife and kids out of shame and a cultural sense of male bravado and fatherly responsibility. This is where it is possible to see that our environment facilitates what we can and can't manage due to our dependence on it. Eventually, I learned to surrender (or perhaps had to surrender) and trust it, and it led me to finding Psychosynthesis via the *Big Issue* magazine. I then enrolled into what would end up being five years of travelling up and down to London to the Institute of Psychosynthesis. Five years of long weekends, thirteen times a year, taking myself to pieces whilst trying to remain stable enough to run a business, be a joiner, be a dad, and be a foster carer, as well as several other things, all at the same time.

Before finding psychosynthesis, however, I came to an almighty crash because my ego was becoming increasingly inflated with all this great stuff that I could do. This crash (or nemesis to my hubris) was because this stuff doesn't belong to the ego; it is of a higher realm, and so eventually I fell from a great height, smashing to pieces in the process. So whilst this was an incredibly beautiful and difficult time, I did nonetheless get to see a reality that exists behind the everyday one, and I believe this is what others need to experience in order to be able to make the transition. I didn't choose or want any of it; I was quite happy with life and being the most successful I had ever been. We were racing motorbikes in the Scottish and British Championships and holidaying on cruise ships; life had never been so easy, even though my wife and I were both working very hard to make it all happen. But unknown to me, I was ready to move to another level, a victim of my own success, having outgrown the level (or womb) that I was in. The difficulty for me, as I will go on to explain in this chapter, was that there was nobody else at this new level to help me, until I was guided to find psychosynthesis.

Even as I write all this, my insides are trembling in association with how disturbing and frightening some of this was twelve years ago. This experience that I went through, and my religious or realigning salvation through The Institute of Psychosynthesis, is why I do the work that I do; to spare others going through what I went through, as it is not necessary if we can avoid it becoming a crisis. I had to travel to London for five years, but others won't if we can get more psychospiritual education into mainstream society. Perhaps this is also something that is initiating this book. However, I sense that the point of all that forcing its way out of me was to let you see what is missing and needed to help others make it over that threshold. Something that can hold them and inform them of what is happening to them, as well as actually having experiences in the first place that reveal something transcendent of where society is living at the moment, experiences that left me with such a knowing that I can stand alone and wrestle with the rest of humanity.

Religion Seen as Our Return from Psychological Adaptation

This is what I personally see as the real religion, this realignment process of adulthood. I don't think it really matters whether it is facilitated by this or that religion, faith, or belief system. Psychosynthesis offers us that it is still really our higher Self at work using something as a vehicle to facilitate the growth, working through a religion or other vehicle of some sorts. Be it psychotherapy, counselling, coaching, mentoring, parenting, friendship, connecting with nature, sport, dancing, singing, work, rest, or play. All of these ultimately serve realignment or religious process in my opinion. In fact, psychological disturbances like abandonment, disappointment, feeling victimised, anxiety, lack of self-esteem etc. Also all serve this same higher purpose when worked with correctly and understood for what they seek to serve. They can all ultimately help us operate more purely and less psychologically, and be the grandest, fully blossomed version of our higher Self that we can attain in any moment, as well as developmentally attain in our lifetime. Sometimes when we feel like we are falling apart, or as we see our world falling apart, we are actually starting to be put back together properly again. As I see it, we all become religious in the first childhood moment that we psychologically adapt away from being our pure truth, in order to manage a life situation, so as to feel safe.

Hypnopompic Moments Seen as a Chance for Our Higher Self to Get Through

Wednesday, October 12, 8:00 a.m.

I woke up this morning, and in that hypnopompic state between the worlds, I received the usual morning torrent or download that I am having as I write this book. I would normally go to the relevant chapter and slot it in, but in keeping with describing psychosynthesis at work, I am displaying it more openly. I, (the conscious awareness) always tell myself, (the I or me that I sense myself being) that I will remember everything that comes to me in this state, but just like you probably do with dreams, I forget most of it. However, this is what was offered this morning, some of it feeling like material for chapters ahead, and some of it feeling like it was intended for padding out the previous chapters. This is just like in our development when we have established something fairly solidly but there continues to be little refinements to tweak that development more. That bit about filling out was actually one of the downloads. There was also a Jesus passage about Do not think that I have come to bring peace to earth. I did not come to bring peace but with a two edged sword, and it was offered for me to insert into the area where I was decrying ministers, to help show what my higher Self's intent is in getting me to stand fast in all that difficult stuff, the sword being about cleanly dividing and separating marrow from bone, spirit from soul, wheat from chaff, TOK and TOL, ministry and non-ministry. There was also something about the men who have been in my life in my Psychosynthesis training and Heart Intelligence training and how they had held something for me to introject or grow into; the local minister, Watchman Nee and Jesus are the current forms of that.

The minister has the ability to be very humble and show his heart and feelings as well as hold strong and be openly seen in his faith; he is one of the few ministers my inner truth detector believes when he communes with God and channels that to us. I think I am beginning to see that Jesus is being offered to us and held upon high as the ultimate symbol and personification of a way of being, a collective projection for us all to individually introject. There was yet another offering of a new title, *Religious Atheists*, probably in an attempt to help me have a single title to synthesise this situation that I am working through in writing this book. Yesterday, it changed to *It's All an Act of Love: The Return of the Divine Feminine*. But *Religious Atheists* feels closer to the overarching place that I feel myself going. My business sub-personality agrees by saying that this title would attract more buyers and return more money, as well as help more people. But I am not so sure that my business sub personality is really interested in helping people. I sense it is using that bit to con me. The new title feels very synthesising; feeling like a union of what previously felt polarised.

As I paused here to go and get some breakfast, I had a sudden moment of presence, even though I thought that I was present. And in that moment of disconnecting from what I was writing, I realised, I'm actually writing a book. Who'd've thought? And I am actually enjoying it.

Is this what my higher Self was up to all along? questions my observer.

Was it just tricking me into becoming a writer? Who cares! It is helping me to make sense and synthesise my polarity, and hopefully, it is helping you.

But is this the dawning of the newest stage of being me, becoming a writer? Is this the way that I get my message out, given that other ways have been very limited?

It's actually quite easy when I get out of the way and just follow what comes in without my TOK neurotically getting uptight about what I should or shouldn't write.

Anyway, the final couple of offerings from this morning were about hymns. I was lying there listening to Smooth Radio as our morning alarm, and was offered that this is what we should be singing in church: Robbie Williams' "Angels" and "Feel," Cyndi Lauper's "True Colours," Avicii's "Human" and "Wake Me Up," and so on. The type of songs we sing when heart intelligence practitioners come together at HIQ circles. Songs that lift the spirit and actually connect us to the awe and wonder of life, and connect us to source through actually being in communion with it. Honestly, if you had heard us trying to do the children's song on Sunday, you would have been shocked. It was actually like what Avicii is all about in Buddhism: ongoing hell.

Some of the usual hymns can lift us too, so what a relief it was when we sang Sydney Carter's "Lord of the Dance." Other hymns that come to mind are John Newton's "Amazing Grace," Carl Boberg's "How Great Thou Art," and Dan Schutte's "I the Lord of Sea and Sky" (what a beautiful hymn that is). I know other people have their favourites and they are not all meant to be uplifting, but this is also meant to be worship. What better way to worship the awe and wonder of our great source than to actually feel it and be replenished by it as we sing. Or maybe I'm just being too much of a Celtic Christian. Oops! That was just a little slip of sarcasm. Did you notice before I told you?

151

The Difficulty of Settling into a New Paradigm

As I was saying before all of that, the added difficulty with awakening and development into a new level is that this awakening or self-realisation process is always being held back by the fact that many of our needs are still being met by the old environment, at our former level of development. We have belonging needs that are still being met by something we are trying to outgrow. We have fears of change and the unknown, in contrast to the safety of the familiar, even though it is not entirely meeting all our needs anymore. We fear being different and being laughed at, or turned away from, because others don't get something the way we get it; they don't get what we are going through because they aren't ready to follow, so they have no need to face the same battle, and they are probably unconsciously busy with their own battle. In general, if there is not a new embracing and nurturing environment for us to attach to, then our current environment needs to move with us to make it more manageable. There are very few of us who have the ability to cut free from what sustains us and what we love and the everyday world we live in. Essentially, this is about our need to feel secure, and that takes the form of having things like money, self worth, respect, acceptance, inclusion, understanding, love, friendship, and belonging. These are a few of the things that add to the struggle of breaking free from the structure that has sustained us until now, and partly still sustains us. All of these and more sustain our need to survive and feel secure, and help us to get our unconscious needs met, so that we can feel better and return to a more relaxed state. So adult life, from a developmental perspective, is really about untangling ourselves from the childhood distortions and psychological forms that we took on to manage and survive childhood. We try to awaken or progress into newer mature levels of development whilst still finding some way of getting our survival and security needs met.

So that was a quick and very brief introduction to Psychosynthesis and its evidencable understanding of what goes on as we journey through life. We're always trying to self-realise, or become more of our true self, but we always have to take a psychological and less true form to feel safe, so that we can function and continually work towards reaching what I call self-fulfilment, in the future. We actually go through several levels of development in life, with most adults in our society functioning at the self-esteeming ego level, still building their sense of self solidity up and growing in self-confidence. This is actually about growing in ability to self-confide, rather than confide in others. But part of what I am showing here, is that there is another level again. A level where we don't just begin to transcend our ego to be more of our true self. We begin to see that there is an even higher Self above that. A universal Self which orchestrates everything, and is constantly juggling us, (the essential being that we are within all of that) between self-survival and self-fulfilment.

This is where we are then invited to give up confiding in our self and confide in something greater. In Psychosynthesis this is surrendering to Thine Will over our own will, just as is asked of us in scripture through faith, but for me it comes about through constantly evidencing it and seeing its higher holistic nurturance and leadership. This transition is the one that can be even more difficult than the previous ones as it is not so well supported. This is usually because there are few other people operating at this higher level, and this is why it is so difficult.

Yes, there are lots of people like myself who are in transition, but I don't know anyone who is there, from a development perspective. Perhaps Jesus was the only one and will be the only one. We don't ultimately get to become the transcendent higher Self in life, even though that is essentially who we are, because our function in life is to be the immanent embodied self. But we can reach a point where we can frequently surrender to it and allow it to guide us consciously.

So perhaps this explanation of how we are held back, and of how we often fall back, helps you to see how it is easier for me to fall back into the familiarity of my old ways as well as fall back into Psychosynthesis when I am struggling to integrate new learning's.

Psychosynthesis is the familiar that satisfies my minds need for answers and holds me in some feeling of stability; this is why it is easier for me to stay here than to struggle to make my way forward with a Christianity that isn't quite right. Of course it would be easier for me to move through this birth canal and into the Christianity womb on the other side, if that Christianity womb didn't feel so unsafe and insecure. Hence the reason for my higher Self helping me to assemble something out of all of my trainings that can allow me some movement. This insecurity is due to the contentious situation that I feel between everyday Christianity and my Watchman Nee Christianity. With the secure fallback to my Psychosynthesis feeling like a more secure place to remain.

It feels easier to return to the former womb of Psychosynthesis and be held in something that feels more stable. Seeing my higher Self as being the pure, trans-pathological, unadapted essential me that remains unchanged by the world. And facilitates my adaptation as required to firstly ensure survival, and then secondly reach maturity and self-fulfilment. This higher Self, that is ultimately the true me, can now be seen in comparison to my ever developing smaller every-day-in-the-world self, with its ego and psychological defence systems. These systems are things like neuroses, mindsets, coping mechanisms, maintaining cycles, projections, and transferences. All of which function in service of my survival, as do my fears and other limitations, yet they eventually also inhibit my ability to function at a higher and purer level.

So, in addition to our sense of having a small everyday self, what we refer to when we use the 'I' word and say something like 'I said this' or 'I did that.' There is this higher Self, but it isn't really anywhere higher or out there somewhere. It is simply the pure essential us at the core of who we are, unadapted to manage life and drawing us into being the fullest expression of our Self that we can be. And then this universal Self that is the union of everything, perhaps comparable to God or what I prefer to call source.

Understanding and Embodiment

However, when I do fall back into the former womb of Psychosynthesis and seek to align my words and actions with what I sense being asked of me by my higher Self. A peculiar thing happens: Despite Psychosynthesis being what I fall back on in my struggle, there is still a part of me that seems to need something more. I know that the falling back is partly about me defaulting back to the familiarity, safety, and comfort of my mind, but there is still a part of me that needs something in addition to this understanding of higher and lower selves, even though this training and understanding saved my sanity and is guiding this book. I feel myself needing something more than Psychosynthesis, because it sometimes leaves me feeling a bit like an assembly of psychological operating systems that are being operated by something that I can't quite feel and fully relate to. When I feel into *What would my higher Self do or say at this moment?* there seems to be something impersonal and psychological about it. Something that doesn't feel as relational as I would like. It's a bit like going to Dad when you are upset, and he talks to you about the dynamics of pain or says that you have the mental ability to not get upset, when what you really needed was a hug and to feel loved. Something you are more likely to get from mum.

I think there is a part of me that needs to feel felt and seen and loved a bit more than I sometimes feel that I get from Psychosynthesis psychology, even though I feel myself nurtured in Psychosynthesis and it has helped me several times in writing this book. Perhaps it is because Psychosynthesis is an academic training that It feels a bit more heady and objective and leaves me needing something that feels more loving and motherly than the teaching informing way that I often feel with Psychosynthesis. I think this may be part of why I abandoned writing my thesis and why Heart Intelligence came over the horizon; it is more about embodiment and feelings than knowledge, and so perhaps it met other needs that I was now ready to move towards, in a slightly different way.

Perhaps I was unconsciously sensing that I could get these needs met better by attaching to this new womb called Heart Intelligence, now that I had re-found my sanity and had a context, understanding, and container to move forward with. In fact, now that I think about it, it wasn't long before this that I moved from a male therapist to a female one. So it seems like the Psychosynthesis training met some of my needs, but I am beginning to realise that I must also have needed something more sensitive and more feminine, something I started getting from Heart Intelligence.

As I write all of that, I also realise that some of it is really just about words and language because my moment of being swept up when I reconnected to life by looking out of the window comes back to me. This reminder is perhaps being offered in this moment to help me see that my higher Self is holy or holistic in spirit, even if Psychosynthesis doesn't use that language. Perhaps whatever we use to satisfy our mind is immaterial, as long as it works. It could be this religion or that religion or this or that belief. It probably doesn't matter; all that probably matters is how it helps us feel as we return to a state of being that is easier to be and feel more secure.

What I am learning through my own journey and working with clients is that it's not about who or what way is right or wrong, TOK; it's about what works for each individual at each moment and what people need to help them feel safe enough to open and return to their awakening journey. This is in contrast to them closing to defend and protect, inhibiting that progress. This is where I see the value of the Bible again and God saying to Adam to live in the tree of life, not the tree of knowledge of good and evil and right and wrong.

Heart Intelligence feels more feminine and loving, more holding and human and relational to me. It always feels more subjective than objective, more embodied than heady. It feels to connect to the deeper me that lives inside my body and feels tangible and substantial. It feels cellular and communicative, and I can interact with it differently. I can touch it and feel it and sense it touching and feeling me. So having the combination of Psychosynthesis and Heart Intelligence training and personal development helps me understand and feel safe in the depth of deep transformational experiences.

When I turn my attention inwards to seek guidance from my inner movements and my inner truth, the guidance can always be felt and realised in body and mind, creating a deep cellular embodied experience that I can understand and hold through the Psychosynthesis more than through the Heart Intelligence. I suddenly recall Roger Evans, my main Psychosynthesis coaching trainer and co-founder of the institute, repeatedly saying, "Always love them to bits more than anything else." As I write this, I also recall the number of times I was in tears over these five years of training and how I was tenderly held in love and acceptance, sharing how I was feeling. Perhaps I was limiting the amount of love and feminine energy I was able to let in at that time. No doubt my higher Self facilitated me in the way that served my developmental needs best at the time and in the only way I was available, so as to save my sanity. When we are in crisis and fear, we tend to close and protect and so can only be as available as our defences will allow, even when that includes pushing away something that would actually help. With several years of practice, I am definitely more compassionate towards this now than I was back then.

Psychosynthesis and Heart Intelligence are very similar, but I tend to be in my head a little more when I am working through Psychosynthesis than I do when I am working through Heart Intelligence, where I go more to my body. In both Psychosynthesis and Heart Intelligence, we spend a lot of time holding the other in love, knowing they have all the resources at hand to reach what they are being guided towards. We try not to fix or judge or avoid or look after them, because that is probably more about us, not them. All that any of us need in order to untangle our self from our psychological adaptations is love and safety, and we will begin to open again.

Nonetheless, there was something that drew me to Heart Intelligence from Psychosynthesis at that time; perhaps it was a readiness to move into something more feminine to take me on the next part of my journey, just as we see in Dante's *Divine Comedy* as Dante moves from Virgil's guidance to Beatrice's.

As I bring this chapter to a close, I wonder if perhaps a big part of what the masculine is doing is analysing everything so as to keep us safe, and so in its purpose, it is always watching for problems and asking questions; putting structure and rules and explanations in place to create security and protection and satisfy the minds need. This then creates a safe space for the feminine within us to be able to be the awe and wonder that is the abundant outpouring of divine creation and love and joy; only, this is the part we have been suppressing for thousands of years due to our lack of understanding and wisdom and the immature masculine that comes from unmet developmental needs in childhood.

Another thing that has been emphasised in me again, is seeing that the returning part of our psychospiritual journey of awakening and development is the real religious process. The emphasis is on how we are always being guided by something holistic or holy in spirit, (be it what Christianity calls the Holy Spirit or what Psychosynthesis calls the higher Self) to adapt back towards being able to be our true self in every moment, but also progressively over life. At the same time, we see that it is the same protecting higher Self that gets us to behave as required to survive, adapting back and forwards like a chameleon between feeling safe enough to be our true self and feeling so unsafe that we go back into our coping self. Our environment, both moment by moment as well as generally and collectively, can then be seen to be what facilitates our ability to be one or the other.

This brings me back to why I see the need for our society to have a psychospiritual understanding of life and also demonstrates that we need a more heart intelligent environment for the next great evolutionary shift to happen.

With hindsight, and upon this moment of reflection, I think that at the start of this book, I was holding Psychosynthesis and Christianity as being quite different from each other. But in my struggle to find a Christianity in daily life that fits with my Watchman Nee understanding, I seem to have synthesised them somewhat. I was initially seeing one to be a bit too academic, masculine, and psychological and the other as divine and holy, even though it doesn't seem to be operating that way in our society at the moment. But as I end the chapter, I now see our higher Self as more holistic or holy in the spirit of its action, and when I take its loving nurturance within this chapter into consideration, I see it more motheringly than I perhaps had experienced before.

So something seems to have changed or synthesised from the start of this chapter to the end, as I started out saying that whilst psychosynthesis was my safety net in this struggle, I could also feel how it felt a bit too objective compared to Heart Intelligence, which feels more subjective to me. Suddenly, I can feel a change in myself as I allow in its feminine nurturance to add to the masculine knowledge and guidance that it has always given me.

I also think that this chapter has reminded me of how we see and personify and create what our mind needs in order to help us return to feeling more stable again. But I think it has mostly helped me to see the psychology behind the immature masculine that has suppressed the feminine from individual, collective, and cultural pathology due to loss of true connection to source and underdevelopment. When we have a psychospiritual understanding of life and begin to see our disturbances serving our route home, we learn to consciously choose working through these disturbances rather than pathologically reacting in avoidance, unconsciousness, and ignorance, as we did before understanding.

I wrote this following poem as it was actually happening. We were on our very last psychosynthesis training weekend in July 2010; the training was held at Debden House in London. The scene described at the start of the poem can be found beside the main house.

When Spirit Breaks through the Madness

I walked along a grassy track, contained on either side, by walls that held and guided me, towards my own way back.
I thought there was an opening, at the other end, that would take me to a garden, just around the bend.
I arrived to find no opening, just an old and disused gate, run down and capped with thorn bush; was this to be my fate?
I checked in desperation to see if I was right, and saw the thorns were placed there, to guard this threshold's rite.
Beyond it grew some brambles, both wild and uninviting, with a gap that I could manage, if I could take the fighting.
If I battled with the thorn bush, then headed for the gap, then maybe I could make it, to this other track.
Beyond this lay some barren land that hadn't seen much use; the road of little traffic offered no excuse.
This barren space of lostness reminded me of me; I looked around to find a seat, in the shelter of a tree.
No place of rest was offered, and I struggled what to do, to flee this place of awkwardness, or just invite a clue.
A seat appeared within a wall, it had been there all along; it called to me to rest a while, for it knew to leave was wrong.

When I reached this pause in writing, I reflected, "This was great"; these words would touch my colleagues, and they'd want to be my mate.
Then came the "No" to consciousness, with sudden lightning speed; I will not let this happen. Steal this beauty for your need.

This isn't of your making, and it isn't yours to take; if you tried, they'd see right through you. They'd see you for a fake.

"Ha ha," yelled out this voice inside, "I think I win again; you think that you're so big and smart; I know that you're just vain."

You think you're wise and wonderful, that you can change the world; "You clown," I sometimes laugh at you, your mind all warped and curled.

You had no chance to start with, for it was always me; you fool, you just don't get it, that you is really me.

But I could feel its panic and hear fear within its voice; its challenge almost over, its fight without a choice.

One tear sneaks up from in my heart and drips upon my arm; it primes the wick for others, though there seems like no alarm.

Then tears flood from my very soul, my heart now rives in pain, a soul that longs to know itself and feel alive again.

This pain that feels like more than mine: so old and without end, feels seen for just a moment, and then it's gone again.

It knows I can only take so much and regulates my pain, then with great big breath, it lets me go, to return to the world again.

CHAPTER 10

———————————————

The Need for Heart Intelligence

From Defence Focussed to Heart Led

Having been a Heart Intelligence practitioner now for several years, I would say that heart intelligence is about learning to consciously use our heart's knowing and wisdom to guide us through life, rather than continue to be run unconsciously by our childhood conditioning and our neurological defence system. When we get present to our inner embodied sense of self and truth, and then engage with the world from there, we interact differently compared to the normal going straight from our head and thoughts, feeling into and for the other, rather than one person gaining to the detriment of the other.

Me Spacers and We Spacers

I am what Christian calls a 'me spacer', what I would call a narcissist, because I am mostly preoccupied with myself and became that way in childhood to feel safe. So I don't naturally think about the other as much as I think about myself. So for me to be present to myself is not that hard, but to feel for the other is work. However, some people are what Christian calls 'we spacers,' or again what I would call borderlines, people who have become unconsciously dependant on the other in childhood so as to feel safe. So these people can initially spend more time in HIQ circles learning to differentiate what is theirs and what is the other's, because the other's moods and emotions can feel like theirs, and it isn't so easy for them to discern what is theirs and what is the other's. Life can be very tiring for we spacers because they are usually running the emotions of everyone around them.

Awakening the Self-Conscious Observer, so that We Can Be Real

So in both me and we spacers, we are looking to help people develop a consciously awake and self-aware central operating centre, the 'I,' as we say in Psychosynthesis. This is so they can consciously operate from there and go out into the world from that location, consciously feeling for what is going on and interacting heart intelligently with it. This sense of interacting heart intelligently with others and our environment comes from knowing that we are being our true self with them and knowing we are serving their development also. We do this not just for these reasons, but also because we know that without it, there is no us in the space with the other; we are just unconscious and functioning as an assemblance of psychological coping mechanisms, out to get our needs met. Or we are in unconscious fusion with the other, trying to feel safe. Once again, I want to reiterate that I am not suggesting that anything is wrong here; I am simply showing how things become, in an effort to manage and survive childhood and as facilitated by our higher guidance until we get to a point developmentally where we can begin to consciously do the work of taking our self off autopilot, much to its resistance. As we practice heart intelligence in this way with each other, we become real and substantial rather than superficial and empty. We begin to feel alive; we feel our vitality in each other's presence as we begin to be able to speak the truth as we experience it in the moment. We agree to not fix or protect or look after each other neurotically out of our own needs of avoiding discomfort, when we know that we actually serve each other more by operating more existentially. This does not mean avoiding something or not being there for each other; it means being even more there for each other and doing it consciously from our heart rather than from neuroses, knowing how we serve each other better, and knowing that is what the other is there for: not just there in the HIQ circle, but what they exist for.

Removing Our Self from Survival Autopilot

In childhood, we are like a planet with all of its space satellites turned outwards, so as to be on guard for threats to our survival. But as we begin to feel more secure, we can start turning a few of them inwards to see if our behaviour is meeting our expectations of our self, but also to see how well it is fitting in with our environment because that also keeps us safe. Our higher guidance, which generally lies outside of our everyday conscious awareness, facilitates all of this. But as we progress developmentally in life, we gradually increase in ability to remove our self from our self-survival program and gradually become more preoccupied with wanting to be our truth and live in the joy of full self-expression.

Freeing Trapped Traumas by Holding Them in the Light

As children, our unresolved and traumatic experiences get absorbed into our psyches and cellular bodies, awaiting a future, similar present moment experience through which to osmotically resolve themselves and become freed up again. This is why Heart Intelligence works so much with our embodied experience, using that awakened self-aware consciousness like a laser to connect directly to what is embodiedly moving when we are talking about something that is disturbing us. In my experience, this is similar to what Quakers do when they hold something in the light for transformation, but for me, this works better due to the focus, specificity, and human interaction, given that most of these traumas happened through human interaction.

Heart circles are also very mindful and meditative but in a more directly focussed and applied way; the skill of the coach or guide being to help the client to stay with their disturbance and let the light of conscious awareness do its work. Another skill for the coach at this time is to be able to discern the voices of all of the parts that become active, voices of parts that want to escape the difficult experience through deflection or by being too heady or by dissociating. Getting angry or tired or nauseous, needing to go to the toilet and so on. These are all avoidance tactics by the neurological defence system as it tries to do its job of protecting the client from suffering. The skill of the guide being to help the client not be derailed by them as best they can manage, given that this is very difficult for them. Initially, they are using a baby-sized present moment awareness to battle with a giant, well-developed self-protection system, with years of experience and operating under the extra impetus of fear. This is where the Heart Intelligence guide watches for conditioned answers that don't touch their own truth detector and also uses the group to assist this weeding out of the real truth through all the psychological material.

The Heart Intelligence guide therefore works frequently with what is moving in the client's body and with taking them to their heart's truth, seeking to see what its voice has to say in contrast to all these other voices. In childhood, many of us don't feel loved or understood or valued, we don't feel seen or felt or accepted. So hidden within many of our adult disturbing scenarios that we voice to each other are these experiences seeking resolution. Therefore, simply sitting in a circle feeling seen, felt, loved, valued, accepted, and understood is healing on its own. The problem in our everyday world when we go to this place of unconsciously seeking healing, is that we trigger similar unresolved experiences in others and then they are not able to be there for us. Not able to help us feel seen, felt, loved, valued, accepted, and understood because their neurological defence system shuts them down to protect them. They don't understand the healing and psychospiritual dynamics of what is going on. Add to that the fact that we are all busy trying to get work done, and we can see why we go around triggering each other all the time.

So we all go around unconsciously triggering each other to get something to the surface for healing and then closing it all down again, adding to the unresolved experience because we can't cope with it. Most people in the everyday world don't need psychotherapy or even counselling, in my opinion. They simply need help with seeing how we function, and seeing what life is about, so that they can have something to hold them. They need something that gives them understanding, strength, and purpose in life, as well as compassion, love, and forgiveness for themselves and others. The more of us that can see what's going on, the more of us there are to lead the way.

Listening, Following, Expressing, and Opening Our Heart

In Heart Intelligence circles, we practice listening for our heart's truth, following our heart's truth, expressing our heart's truth, and opening our heart to let in what comes from another's heart, as well as opening it to life. We spend most of our time in groups practicing and relearning how to be in relationship with each other in a different way that is from heart to heart. This work is not without its difficulties though, and also takes great skill and discernment, as there is often something additional sneaking into the space in terms of our unconscious needs, fears, aspirations, projections, and personality. We can get caught out by a mixture of our heart's truth and lust; our heart's truth and the emotions caught up in the situation that is active; our heart's truth and our unconscious resistant conditioning, that seeks to stop us from feeling vulnerable, as we try to speak our truth; or our heart's truth and our fear of feeling silly or embarrassed or shameful or guilty or anxious. We always have to be alert for hidden agendas like self-esteeming and self-diminishment and self-protection, both our own and those of the others in the group. So we are always feeling or sensing into the space within our self and the space with the other.

So this again is where the voice of my inner introjected Jesus returns and says, Yes, this is where it helps to be making sure you have enough oil in your lamp for when the bridegroom comes. In other words, in the present moment and being conscious, rather than be distracted or in your mind looking for answers or solutions so as to be clever or impressive. And my inner Watchman Nee says, If you are remaining present and conscious of being pure and clean of spirit in the moment, then you will sense within your body the defilement or contamination of your spirit as the other or your self are not being the way and the truth and the life. You will not be able to amen what comes forth from yourself or from them, as there are no living waters that come forth in the words.

The Need for Safety, Trust, Understanding, Awareness, Relaxation, Tenderness

From the above explanation, I imagine that you can see the need for our neurological defence system to be on low alert, so that you can do some of this personal untangling, or religion as I see it, by feeling safe to open something up. In heart intelligence, we talk about feeling that you are in a space of experiencing safety, trust, understanding, awareness, relaxation, and tenderness (S.T.U.A.R.T. for short), so this untangling can happen. When we feel safe, we naturally open and are more able to be our true self, but when we do not feel safe, we close to protect our essential core preciousness.

Practicing Heart Intelligence

To begin practicing heart intelligence right now, all you need to do is become more still within yourself. For most, this will also entail becoming more present to your embodiment than you probably are, and slowly settling down into yourself. As you will sense, this requires disengaging somewhat from your outer environment so that you can turn inwards, and this is something which requires a degree of trust and safety for it to happen. This simple practice of disengaging from the world and becoming still is enough to allow some change to begin happening naturally. Ultimately, you will develop the capacity to remain still when you are engaging with the world, but it is easier to start by dealing with your own inner activity first. For some of you, this will be very difficult, as you will have traumatic childhood experiences still caught up in your body, and your neurological defence system will be trying to stop you from going into your body to spare you feeling upset. Even in writing that, I can feel my body's reaction and feel my love for those of you in this situation. All I would suggest is that you do what you can and 'be gentle with yourself,' as Christian says. Don't be tempted to push through, as this just disturbs your S.T.U.A.R.T., and your neurological defence system will up its game to match. To begin taking a further conscious step from this place of stillness, you can begin using the four core skills of Heart Intelligence: listening for your heart's voice, following your heart's guidance, opening your heart when it feels safe to do so, and communicating what your heart has to say. This is where relationships can gain a lot from agreeing to adopt Heart Intelligence as their chosen way of being with each other, because practicing these skills really requires interacting with others. We can still do it on our own but the real change in our way of being in the world comes when we behave differently with others and so update our outdated systems. In doing this, we also give the other person's systems a different experience to add to their current files and thus feel safe enough in our presence to perhaps open more than usual.

So as you can see, we don't really need to change everyone else so it is safe for us to come out; we just need to risk being seen a little, and they will come out to meet us. These four skills take time to develop and can develop quicker in safer environments; that is why HIQ practitioners regularly come together to practice. If safety opens us and lack of safety closes us, then coming together with like-intended people increases the likelihood of success, compared to trying it in an environment that isn't awake or signed up for the challenge, and also closes as soon as vulnerability is experienced by its defence radar. Our heart is so much closer to love and our soul and our spirit than our head is, and we are wise to let it lead us, using our head to do the job of managing how we go about doing what our heart's guidance asks of us. In other words, allow our heart to lead and head to manage.

Practicing Tracking

Tracking is a core skill that we develop to get all of this to work, and it is actually because I was tracking myself that I realised I had not included it yet. I was sitting here typing the above and enjoying feeling the soft place I am in. I can feel it centred in my heart and spreading right across my chest, like a warm, loving glow. I now notice that my typing has slowed down as I remain focussed and present to it, appreciating that it is always lovingly there, waiting for me to return. I become aware of the joy and the smile that is going on inside my face, and I feel my eyes at the outer edges as this begins to spread further. My mind is telling me I am smiling because it is so simple and so beautiful and so graceful, so gentle and affirming that there is something loving that is always there and exists for no other reason than to be there for us. I feel the swelling in my heart that makes me want to cry at the beauty and sadness of it.

As all of that subsided for a moment, and in the space between returning fully to my head I heard that voice saying, *tell them that you have just demonstrated listening, following, opening and expressing, so they will have an example,* and as you can see, I have followed its advice. In practicing tracking so that we can develop our awareness, we tend to track our physicality, our emotions, our thoughts, the degree of vitality and aliveness that we can feel, and any judgements that pop up in relation to any of that. We also do this so that we are more sensitive and alert to picking up what is moving in the other when they talk to us, our radar becoming highly sensitive due to the practice and due to our being in a stiller place most of the time. The traditional spiritual practice of *Know thyself* has been around for thousands of years, as has been working with our heart's wisdom and intelligence, but for me, Christian Pankhurst makes it more current.

Heart Intelligence Coaching

Heart Intelligence work does not always involve coaching; if it did, then we would be doing the same thing I accused others of in previous chapters: *doing what we want, to the other,* in the belief that we are doing what they need. Sometimes, the other just wants to air out what is moving for them and not be guided or coached or get caught up in the coach's desire or need to practice. Perhaps they are not ready to give some control over to the other, due to insecurity. Perhaps it is the opposite, and they don't want responsibility, and so dump everything on the coach. There is an endless list of tactics that we all use and abuse; they all serve and don't serve us at certain times in certain ways, serving certain parts of us. We are incredibly complex beings. As coaches, we always have to be tracking our self to watch for our own agenda; do we prefer coaching to chatting because it allows us the position of feeling superior? Do we do it because it gives us structure to feel safer within? Do we want the other to take on our beliefs about life and how it works so we feel safer? All these things and many more are what we need to be watching for, or we will not be clean spirited in our service. This is why we need to do so much of our own therapy and development and learning before we can be of service to others. Otherwise, we will be passively taking more than we are giving.

Often, the coachee or client will naturally progress to a coaching space anyway, simply by being true to what is moving in the moment; it is a natural progression. Coaching is more about when the other has a sense of what they want, and they are struggling to attain it for some unknown reason. However, if and when we move to a more coaching space, we usually start by asking them what it is that is active or moving in them, what it is that is causing psychological disturbance. This allows them to start bringing into life whatever is emergent in them and being guided towards untangling, reparation, healing, or as I am saying, religion.

Once we do move to coaching through the Heart Intelligence approach, we use what Christian calls the four pillars of clarity. These four pillars are essentially the four questions that I have revealed and used a few times already in this book. They act as a core structure to guide the client or coachee through a space of realising what is bothering them, where they are trying to get to, and what is preventing that movement. Once we have a sense of what is going on, we may ask the pillar 1 question, 'What do you want, given all of that?' so as to get a sense of where they are trying to get. After listening to their answer for a bit and helping them with all those voices that I described, we will usually get to something that feels more existential and real rather than neurotic and contrived or heady, something that our knowing meter gets met by, something that sits at home in us and touches us in a deeper place and doesn't feel a bit impure or wishy-washy. After a minute or so of conversation and holding them in their true realisation, letting them get used to actually realising what it is they truly want, compared to what they thought they wanted, allowing them to really feel that, we will then usually move to pillar 2, asking, 'What is your fear if nothing changes?' (Be careful here though, as I see lots of people slip into what the fear is that is holding them back, and this is not where we are at yet). This pillar 2 question arouses whatever it is that is pushing them and adds to the newly discovered pulling from the want. Again, after some similar unconscious avoidance tactics, we will most likely get a real answer, which allows us to move on to what Christian calls the third and fourth pillar questions: 'What's holding you back?' and What do you need? Perhaps you can still see throughout all of this that we are actually still with seek and ye shall find. These four questions can also be mixed around as feels right at the time. For instance, I sometimes repeat 'so what's the fear if nothing changes' several times, to guide the coachee further down into finding the deeper fear.

This eventually helps clients to make conscious whatever is blocking their way, after working our way through the avoidance tactics if they arise. As you can see, coaching is mostly about gaining clarity around different aspects of what is going on so that people can make more informed choices and be more empowered by realising what their actual truth really is. I imagine you will also be able to see why we struggle to do this on our own, as we can't catch our own avoidance tactics as easily as others can (especially if these guides have done their own work as explained by Heart Intelligence, Psychosynthesis, or Watchman Nee). It's similar to when Jesus says, "Wherever two or more are gathered in my name, there I shall be". Real Christianity, as I am beginning to learn, is about being a *way* that is real and being our *truth* and living in the vibrancy of *life*, something we move closer to achieving through becoming more heart intelligent.

Heart Intelligence Coaching Demonstration, Using the Four Pillars of Clarity

Despite what I have just said about self coaching and given that I have something moving right now, I would like to see if I can give you a demonstration of this by coaching myself on something that arose earlier in chapter 6 around my not being as nice to ministers as I would like to be. I am sure it will be limited, as I won't catch all of my avoidance tactics.

By being present to the spirit of truth within myself, the spirit of truth that you will also be able to feel residing within you at times, I recall feeling uneasy about something when I was writing about how I can experience ministers as disconnected and too preoccupied with their own agendas. At the same time as this, I could also sense or track another aspect of myself that was wondering what it was that was disturbing me, and in the scriptural Seek and ye shall find kind of way, I felt it seeking for the truth of what it was that was causing this disturbance.

So as you can see, the truth of who I am being in this moment is that I am being a disturbance, a conscious aware observer, and a seeker of resolution from that disturbance. But knowing that there is a higher guidance at play in our lives, I also know what lies behind causing me this disturbance, as it facilitates me into something that serves my further awakening.

So what's moving? I ask into myself, to initiate the session.

I now sit with this for a moment, holding it in my body rather than going to my head for an answer, until I receive the pop-up, as we call it in Heart Intelligence. Then something gradually arises from within me, saying, *I don't feel good about how I have written about ministers and what happens in church. I think I've been a bit harsh and unfair, a bit unnecessary and nasty in the way I've said they're getting it wrong, and I don't feel particularly heart intelligent within myself doing that, never mind that I am not behaving or demonstrating heart intelligence. I don't feel clean in spirit, I feel defiled.*

What do you want, given that? (Pillar 1)

Well, there's a part of me that wants to go back and change it so that I am being kinder, because it feels cruel and a bit unnecessary. I don't want to be that way. I want to be the more loving and compassionate understanding me that I can be when I am not so caught up in something, just because I'm not getting my own needs met.

What's the fear if nothing changes, if you don't change it? (Pillar 2)

I suppose the fear is that ministers and people I know from the church won't like me after they read this. They will see me as two-faced; going to church appearing one way but in reality feeling like this. They'll be looking at me with distaste and behaving disapprovingly towards me, withdrawing from me and being withholding in their conversations with me. I can just see them feeling uncomfortable around me and being apprehensive and false with me, or avoiding me altogether, or maybe even getting angry with me because I have upset them, perhaps even having a go at me.

So I summarise this as being a fear of the withdrawal of love and being left feeling unloved and abandoned, or even worse, rejected and cast out of the tribe, unwanted, unwelcome, and despised for betrayal. So if anyone did behave this way, then they would probably be behaving out of retaliation for my attacking their love object; they would feel like they were defending and protecting it as a part of themselves that they are dependent on for stability, because their sense of self and goodness is caught up in it all.

Then there are those who may read this and take pity on me, from feeling me struggle to be my truth and admire me for daring to speak up, but I don't want their pity or admiration or smothering love all over me either, from feeling sorry for me. They can keep it. That's their stuff.

So here we can also see a pushing away of a smothering, suffocating love. This is actually early childhood development behaviour still at play in me. So I don't want to lose love, but I don't want to be suffocated in it either, especially when it feels infantilising and diminishing; they feel like they are unconsciously in their need to give love rather than be more awake and conscious to themselves and express how it makes them feel. I can actually feel my body squirming around, wanting to get out of all this sickly, sweet love.

What's holding you back from just changing it to what feels right? (Pillar 3)

Because if I change it, then I know that I'm no longer being my truth, and I'm just changing it out of fear. Because I know that what I wrote is my truth and how I see it now after learning what I have learned. I believe that what I am saying needs to be said and seen, and shown for what it is, so that everyone else can see it in contrast with how I am saying it could and should be. I have seen a different way, and that is why I am no longer satisfied with the old way, but unless I help others to see it, then they won't know any better, just as I didn't. I also know that the part of me that fears the reaction of others is being neurotic compared to this being my existential truth. This can make a difference if I have the courage to stick with it, and if I don't do it, then I am just a fraud and can't respect myself for not practicing what I preach. I would be as well to stop coaching and all of the work I do right now.

So this is where our discernment is vitally important. Which idol am I going to worship, the original one that felt like the truth that just poured out of me like living water, as I originally wrote what I wrote back in chapter 6, writing without questioning myself and out of the TOL? Or the false idol of neurotic fear that comes from my neurological defence system seeking to protect me from anticipated suffering, but at this moment is based purely on my own projections? And bear in mind that these people who I am projecting onto would probably only be upset with me because I am hitting at something they are unconsciously dependant on for stability and security, something they value highly and are attached to because it helps to sustain them, but doesn't mean I am wrong. In fact, what I am offering them would give them even more once they can see it. It is actually what they are going to church for, if they can see it. Do I go with the egoic, self-protective, neurotic psychological part of me or the existential, ego sacrificing part whose longing is more about being its purity and truth rather than being the neurotic fear of what may be suffered from others. The deeper, more embodied existential is more willing to bear that suffering for a higher purpose, crucifying though it can feel to us at our egoic level of experience.

But isn't it amazing what our neurological defence system does to protect us? As I wrote that last sentence I felt grateful and instantaneously received the following to contemplate: *Maybe we should consider our neurological defence system as another aspect of our holistic guidance or Holy Spirit.*

What do you need? (Pillar 4)

As I stay in this still place that I am in, just feeling it, I suddenly feel an inner drop, or actually more like a plummet right down to below my stomach, like falling out of my mind and deeper into my embodied truth to receive no voice but simply a knowing that I have to leave alone what I have written, regardless of the outcome, even if I am just deluding myself in all this madness.

If I go back and adjust everything to be all nice and sweet, then not only have I been run by my immature neurological defence system, neurotically trying to protect me out of past evidence from my pathology, I will have deprived thousands of people of the opportunity to contemplate things for themselves and perhaps begin to make a change that desperately needs to happen.

Then suddenly, I drop even further and hit the bottom, where I hear the following, and everything just stops completely still: *I will not be able to live with myself. Betraying myself will be just as bad, if not worse than suffering whatever comes my way from others.*

So the response to the question 'What do you need?' was that I needed some extra impetus to tip the scales; rather than initially coming from a part with a voice, it came from dropping deeper into myself to a place of knowing. Then came the voice showing up the difference between the neurotic, ego-focussed level of development and the deeper existential that can sacrifice its shallower self for something greater and to honour being its truer self. But as I write that, I can also see that it could be said that the greater fear won the battle, not love; either way, the existential is still winning over the neurotic. But what lies behind that fear of experiencing being my core unworthiness and not being my existential truth? Is it existential dread from the mind's judgement; or the movement towards feeling annihilation, respect for self, self-worth, the need to be my truth, love? Or the feeling of contentment and peace once it has been done? Perhaps it is the greater sense of worth from aligning with a higher purpose?

The Benefit of Working in Groups to Assist Broader and Deeper Healing

So that was quite a limited example of self-coaching to let you see it in action; I know I could go in there again and get a different result, as there is actually lots of stuff in there. I also know it would probably have gone differently with someone else coaching and using a group to help me discern truth from conditioned answer, by the coach and group members using their own truth metre to feel for when I felt as if I was in my truth or not. This gets used when clients express what they want and the coach takes a reading from the group, asking them if it felt juicy and alive, full of living waters, as I would say in a Christian context, or if it felt a bit flat and lifeless, dead letter. So when I said I want to go back and change it, the groups read would probably be that they could feel something true but not my ultimate truth.

The coach may also ask at this point, Does it feel better being me when I feel into having changed what I wrote?

And as you can probably feel as you read this, the answer would be no. This tells the coach that I am not on the money, because my want is not true or because it is true but too out of reach. The coach also has to discern if my want was too much for the group to manage, as they may say no because of their own stuff that is being triggered. So this searching for the true want goes on until something deeper is felt, something that is felt in a more embodied way; something that feels enlightening and life giving even though it feels scary.

The Use of the Amplified Field, Mirroring, and Medicine

So now we all feel it and know this is what is really moving; we are in an amplified field because everyone is in touch with what is moving, as they hold the main participant. This all being in an amplified field doesn't just serve the client; it serves everyone in the group because everyone in the group will have something in their life that resonates with the client's situation. This is where the mirroring and medicine concepts come in, mirroring because the others may have a similar situation going on in their life that they are being helped with, by someone taking space for something similar. And medicine because they will probably get something healing from being in their own similar issue, at the same time as being in the amplified field with the client as they gradually get their healing. *Feel it to heal it* is what is going on, and by one person taking space for something and being guided by the others into the depth of what it is truly about, then everyone feels it and gets the medicine.

This extended explanation of how things may have gone in a group is intended to help you see why heart intelligence is almost always done in a group setting because it serves so many people at the same time and helps us learn that it is safe to be vulnerable in the right place with the right people, thus moving the whole community forward.

We Are Always Being Invited to Update Our Software

This inner battle that we are always having is the battle between our need to survive and what I see as our true religious draw, pulling us back into being able to be more of our pure true self. As you can see from my struggle, a big part of the difficulty is that our defence system is always projecting probable, undesirable outcome experiences into our unconscious to protect us from doing something that will cause us suffering. Now that in itself seems like a desirable system to have looking after us, but the difficulty is that it is mostly running on experiences from childhood, when we had to behave differently because we were children.

It's like having a defence system that is running on windows 93 or the original MS DOS (which some of you won't even remember). So this system is always being updated, but only when we do something that causes it to update, only when we evidence to it that it needs a reframe of mindset; the alive feminine energy forcing the set masculine energy to move. This software update has to be going on constantly out of our disturbing experiences, if we are to continue awakening in life towards full self-realisation and being of service to others and the world, as well as fulfilling our purpose for being. This is why in Heart Intelligence circles, we also get the client to actually do something literal and physical at the end of their space taking, to self evidence into their own system something that the old program said would not be safe to do. In my case, I will leave the church chapter as written.

Short-Term Suffering for Gain or Long-Term Suffering in Avoidance

This to me is the real heaven and hell, the light and the dark: our ignorance of the fact that our suffering serves to awaken us and is facilitated by a holistic or Holy Spirit or energy. We can make better use of our suffering when we learn to understand that that is its purpose and learn to work with it, rather than run away from it to escape suffering or medicate against it. It is often crucifying, but at least the suffering is in gain of something rather than suffering in an endless hell of the same torturous life scenarios coming around and around again in search of resolution and freedom. Heaven and hell are both right here on earth, and the kingdom of heaven is at hand. It is literally in your hands to have by eating from the tree of life instead of the tree of knowledge, but the alabaster box has to be broken open. The seed falling to the ground has to suffer and be broken open so that something new may grow.

This escaping from suffering comes in many forms and always serves to escape consciousness of what is distressing. Roberto Assagioli came up with a beautiful diagram to show this, called the egg diagram. It shows us functioning as the everyday self within consciousness and the different levels of unconsciousness out with that, as well as our higher Self that guides us. In our ignorance of the healing that is trying to happen through the disturbance, we can seek medication from the doctor to suppress what is trying to heal, we can become workaholics to stay preoccupied, we can use drugs or alcohol, we can dissociate and just not be present, we can bury ourselves in television and books. There are all sorts of coping mechanisms, and they all function to spare us from suffering and moving towards experiencing feeling unloved, unwanted, unvalued, unimportant, and ultimately feeling unworthy or annihilated. But as I explained earlier, this defensive protective part of us is not conscious to the pull from our higher Self to fully bloom in full self-realisation. This is the tension that we live in that makes life difficult and exciting.

How to Instantly Replenish Yourself on the Ever-Present Source

Having reached the end of another chapter and 'feeling complete' as we say in Heart Intelligence (or at least complete enough), considering this is just a quick and brief introduction to Heart Intelligence. I relax for a moment into the great void of emptiness, and gazing out of the window at the late autumn breakdown, I reconnect once more to the abundant awe and wonder of what is unfolding in every moment. Then from that space comes another offering, saying, *tell them to try it right now. Tell the readers to disidentify from reading this and get up and go outside for themselves and into life, step into the living life that is you and all around you. Feel its vitality and aliveness and be it, sensing it without thinking or naming anything. Just watch and enjoy being it.* I have chosen to write this in the script font to represent that external feeling voice, but I am not entirely convinced that it wasn't just a thought.

This eating or feeding on the tree of life and getting out of the tree of knowledge, out of hell and into the kingdom of heaven, is the meaning of life. Life means to be consciously present and feel alive in the moment by being connected to source through any means that facilitates it, rather than be disconnected and unpresent to life and the moment, by being away somewhere in our minds or dissociated. If you can't go outside, it can still be done anywhere, anytime; just stop right now and become present to whatever is. Stop and feel.

Changing My Diet to a Different Source of Replenishment

As I let go of feeling into what Heart Intelligence is all about and connect back to what seems to be the primary context for this book happening: me trying to reconcile what I have learned from Watchman Nee with what I see going on in the churches and society and humanity. A part of me sees that it is all beautiful and perfect just the way it is. Everything is just taking its individual survival form before coming into flowering in its own way, just as it does in the garden, so the difficulty is actually more mine than about anything being wrong out there. Perhaps this is just how it is to be nearer the leading edge, and all I need to do is stop looking in the old places for support and affirmation. Perhaps I should just keep reconnecting to what does sustain me, the awe and wonder that never fails me and always fills me with vitality, love, and joy again so I can manage the world and help others, simply by not falling in the Garden of Eden again. Because when I do slip back into my old familiar patterns by become Identified in my psychological needs and go unconscious to that omnipresent source, it seems like I end up serving no one: not me, not the other, and not the grander purpose of the coming of a greater kingdom.

Hopefully, from this brief introduction to Heart Intelligence, you can get a feel for how beautiful a place Heart Intelligence circles are and how wonderful it feels to serve each other's awakening, from coming together in this way for this purpose. I keep going to hit the Save button and exit this chapter, telling myself it is complete. But that inner knowing and truth within me stops me because it knows I haven't transferred to you something more vital and important about heart intelligence than the basic mechanics of what it is and how it works. It wants me to convey to you the joy of simply being in your heart's intelligence and wisdom in the presence of others. It wants me to find some way of getting over to you how incredible it feels to be safe enough in the presence of thirty other people to open your heart and be the love that you most essentially are.

I always find it fascinating to watch all of this as the dance of life, watching the masculine and feminine struggle at our current level of awakening and functioning, whilst at the same time see it all guide itself from the archetypal level.

The words of the following song by the 1970s soul group the Real Thing (written by Ken Gold and Michael Denne) offer us an insight into the divine and sacred interplay between the archetypal masculine and feminine, as they do their thing beyond levels of our everyday perception:

Oh, I would take the stars out of the sky for you
Stop the rain from falling if you ask me to
I'd do anything for you, your wish is my command
I could move a mountain when your hand is in my hand

Oh, words cannot express how much you mean to me
There must be some other way to make you see
If it takes my heart and soul, you know I'll pay the price
Everything that I possess I'd gladly sacrifice

PART 4

∙━◆━◆━◆━◆━∙

Conclusion

The first thing I want to reiterate here is that I don't claim to be correct about anything I have written or speak for any of the organisations I have discussed. The main thing happening in this book is that I am trying to work something out so I can return to a more peaceful and joyful place in my self.

So how on earth do I try to reach a conclusion from all of that? Some of it has been questioning by me, some of it has been demonstrating by me, some of it has been demonstrating by something more than me. Some of it has been told, and some of it was ranting. Some of it was kind and gentle, some attacking and challenging, and all of it unintended in the first instance. The message I receive as I write that is, *Just write and see what comes out, trusting that whatever does come out, will not be wrong and will serve in some way.* I suppose this is called having faith.

So is Holistic Guidance the Holy Spirit?

It is now 6 December, and I have learned quite a lot from writing this book. I think one of the biggest things I have learned is the extent to which guidance is available in such a variety of ways. I have probably only revealed about half of what went on, as my intuition was that the reader would get fed up with it, and it distracts from getting the actual content over. There were so many times that I had one idea, and the holistic guidance had me do something else, because I paid enough attention to it and followed what was moving within me, even going back to the point where I had no intention of writing a book. I just wanted to escape the kitchen for twenty minutes. *I suddenly find that quite funny at this moment.* Is that not a prime example of how it is our disturbances that initiate our progression, especially when we understand their purpose and do something constructive with it. I think that one of my biggest takeaways; is the amount of times that some form of holistic guidance simply spoke to me in a conversational stream; the fact that it felt so absolutely real and interactive and holistic and will meet me wherever I am, if I get my mind out of the way and am available to it. There's a lot to be said for taking a tea break. Even that can be seen to be following our true holistic guidance.

Over the past twelve years, I have had many similar experiences prior to writing the book, but not in such a continuous, conversational way; and not in this matter-of-fact way about small things. Previously, I have only really noticed it in more significant situations or when I have been in real disturbance or on retreat. I had also never seen how many different ways that we receive guidance, such as intuition, instinct, dreams, visions, interactions with nature or animals or people, premonition, claircognizance, clairsentience, clairaudience, and clairvision, divination, astrology etc, and how they could all potentially be seen as holistic guidance. I had never thought that these types of experiences could actually be the Holy Spirit at work going unseen because we use our modern day self-righteous psychological language. If I had given it any thought in the past, then I would probably have thought that the Holy Spirit is something that only communicated (communed) with people who were very devout Christians, and even then, only if they were very special or very awake or enlightened. In fact, I had never really used the word holistic guidance before: a wording that seems to bridge that gap between the two worlds of psychology and religion, the psycho-logic-al and the psycho-spirit-ual. Therefore, prior to starting the book, I had never actually called it holistic guidance, or seen that wording as a possible variation of Holy Spirit, or even that the Holy Spirit could be a part of our holistic guidance. The words Holy Spirit seem fitting because that feels like the spirit of the holistic guidance. I suppose now that I think about it, we have all been far too self-righteous to stop and think about it; too clever with all of our psychological words to see it. I even see that same self-righteousness in us, when I see high-rise buildings towering over that built to honour the greatness of God.

Is God the Same as Source?

This is also something new for me. I don't think I actually used the term *source* as a variation for the word *God* until I started writing. I probably used it verbally and subconsciously in relation to the awe and wonder, but I don't think I actually considered it as an alternative for the word God.

The Value of an Imminent and Transcendent Jesus

One of the things I speak about in the book is the value of bringing Jesus and the Holy Spirit down to earth a bit, to make them more accessible and useable. But as the book has gone on, I have sensed that I had made the same mistake as those at Nicaea and Whitby in excluding one thing in favour of other. I had brought Jesus too far down to earth and had also done this to the exclusion of also continuing to see Him in the transcendent. This is especially relevant when I become present to the spirit and depth of knowing and understanding in His teachings and also when I feel into and follow those teachings; the way that I feel when I actually catch my self and apply them, and when I see the effect on the other. They create an almost whole new existence hidden within this one that we all live. Everything changes when I abide in Him and repent myself, limited though those moments are, or when I stop functioning in the TOK and function in the TOL; when I manage to be righteous rather than self-righteous. Or when I manage to stay on that narrow path, or see the righteousness of others through the innocence, purity, humility, and grace of their words and actions, and I just dissolve inside so that there is no me or them; just beauty.

I was just looking back at what I wrote a minute ago, saying that everything changes when I abide in Him and repent myself. And as I felt back into it, I realised that I was slightly wrong; I don't repent my self when I abide in Him, because there is no me to repent when I am in Him. So now I would change it to; I only need to repent when I am not abiding in Him. Even writing this paragraph changes the me that I feel myself being as I experience myself become love and joy and lighter. All I have to do is keep that oil in my lamp and be single eyed, seeing God at the heart of all His creations and therefore loving God and loving my neighbour. If I seek this before doing anything else, then I seek first the kingdom of heaven and have it in my hand; abiding in Him also being to abide in love.

But then I also have to be vigilant for being triggered by others so that I don't resist evil, or forget to be at peace, or shake the dust from my feet. I sense that this is what Jesus means when he says that He has overcome the world. But how on earth can we hope to do all that in the present world? I suppose we just keep trying and forget that it is about anyone or anything else but our self and Him; that the stuff going on in the world is just the material to work with. So it seems that I have put Jesus back up a bit from where I had brought Him down to, seeing Him now more clearly as useful and serving to us in both His immanent and transcendent forms, rather than as I used to see Him: as untouchable. This for me is the second coming of Jesus, a fresh reconnection to the spirit of what Jesus is about. I don't believe there will be any individual person who will be born and be a returned Jesus. I think the second coming of Jesus is a collective reawakening by humanity to the wisdom, teaching, and spirit of Jesus, resulting in a new body of movement that moves in His way. This being what the church is meant to be doing.

Can We Synthesise Watchman Nee and Today's Church?

Perhaps this is why I haven't synthesised my main polarisation: the contrast between Watchman Nee's teachings and what I see going on in today's churches as Christianity. One is TOL, and the other is mostly TOK.

Having just typed that, I suddenly feel some shift. I suddenly feel able to see them as the duality they are. I am no longer at the same level as them, trying to get them to merge. I am above them, seeing them for what they are. So I haven't synthesised them as I set out to do; I have transcended them and can now accept them as they are. The message *You don't try to integrate masculine and feminine* has just been offered to me as an example, and it feels like it is being offered to confirm my realisation. I also then heard, *You can't synthesise them, they are two separate trees at the centre of the garden;* both messages have that amused parental feel to them, like when your parent sees that you've got it, and just lovingly smiles. This voice feels to have personality and so I am leaving it in this font, whereas sometimes the voice that I hear doesn't feel to have personality. This doesn't mean that it is the Holy Spirit of course; it just means that it has a loving nurturing feel to it. But I sense that there is something more to it than just being an internal sub-part of my self. Isn't it amazing how we can go from not getting it to suddenly getting it in an instant? *It's a shame that the instant didn't arrive a few months ago,* flashes across my mind. *Ah, but then you wouldn't have written the book, would you? It isn't about polarisation here, seeking synthesis or transcendence. It's about awakening and realisation, leading to growth; it's about development and progression, through inclusion instead of exclusion.*

Is Celtic Christianity in Conflict with Watchman Nee?
Our Pure Nature and Our Impure Behaviour

With that said, there is still a bit of a clash between Celtic Christianity and Watchman Nee's teachings (or at least as I understand them both in my limited and brief encounter with them). This is because Watchman Nee teaches us we are being guided and invited by the Holy Spirit's working in and on us, to transcend and move away from the soul energies of nature and move back to being guided by spirit. Celtic Christianity on the other hand seems to be essentially about finding God right at the raw heart of creation and nature in our soul, fully connected to the earthy energies.

But through the differentiation process that is coming with the writing of this book, I seem to be able to integrate or synthesise them somehow, by seeing that they are perhaps not actually saying opposing things at all. Watchman certainly urges the need for us to break the outer man, the psychological us, and release the inhibited spirit. But it now feels like he is talking more about our pathological self; the tainted, thwarted us that is behaving reactively in situations, due to conditioning and not knowing or being able to do it a better way, and because we are out of connection with the Holy Spirit, our higher guidance. And so this thwarted pathological self that we seem to become acts out in search of healing and in an effort to return from being forced into the discomfort of being in a defiled and impure, untrue state. In other words, it is the same *pure* spirit trapped within the pathological distorted self, that is trying to break free of being trapped in a distorted state within the outer man. So it is not the *pure* soulical, physical, emotional or mental us that I sense Watchman Nee opposing now; or the Bible opposing for that matter. But the damaged reactive distorted us that does whatever it can through our bodies, emotions and minds, and through the pleasures of the flesh; due to its disconnect, and in an effort to find relief and pleasure, stimulation and intimate connection, in the only way that it can. I now see that this is what is being perceived to act sinfully as the spirit within it actually acts in an effort to free its self.

I actually feel better now that I seem to have synthesised this inner conflict to some extent and can once again feel that joy within myself; a joy that sometimes feels like a magnet pulling on me from the other side of the disturbance, guiding me through the disturbance towards it. I think; NO; sense that it feels better because there has always been a part of me that gets the shamanic or druidic type guidance, especially given the amount of holistic guiding experiences that I have had of this nature. This psychosynthesis at play is always fascinating to watch and evidence when we are able to see it and understand it for what it is. It has been difficult to experience holistic guidance from what I am told are two conflicting beliefs, whilst the knowing truth within me that transcends them both evidences that they are both real, productive and wholesome.

Spiritual and Soulical Powers

For me, the space between these two tensions feels similar to the tensions between self-survival and self-fulfilment; self-survival being about independence, self-belief, self-sovereignty, self-confidence, and self-righteousness. Compared to acceptance of and surrender to the Will of something wiser and greater than ourselves, and accepting dependence on that; going forward then to act in service of that. The former of these feels self-empowering, in an effort to escape the egoic way of being, that feels less than what we truly are. Whereas the latter then feels self-sacrificing to that second level, and suffering once again to attain something more than just development to the self glorified level. This is suffering to attain the self transcended level of functioning more in keeping with our higher spiritual nature, the way of Jesus. But this is not to the disdain and rejection of the lower levels, it is to love and embrace them in their disconnect, thus helping them to return to their purer divine nature. Jesus does not curse those who are disconnected, he comes to suffer enlightening them, and this tells me that it is all spiritually facilitated as God allows us to fall before guiding us back again. As parents we don't reject our children and tell them that they are sinners because they don't understand or don't know better, we endure teaching them the way. The Bible tells us what God says to Adam and Eve after the fall in the Garden of Eden, about how much more difficult life will be for us. But for me this just tells me that we have fallen and will have to work to get back up again. As I write this, I also recollect that part of Watchman's teaching is that the power of the Holy Spirit is not something for us to feel and that feelings are of the soul, not the spirit. Having gone back and reread the Watchman Nee chapter, I can now see quite a difference between the guidance that was going on in that chapter compared to the Introduction. The Introduction was more about being guided by what was going on in my body and then gaining some insight or revelation. In the Watchman Nee chapter, however, there were no senses involved and no embodied relationship, just a voice that interacted and guided. So now, I can see the guidance within the Introduction, as being mostly soulical and embodied with some spiritual, whereas in the Watchman Nee chapter, it would seem to be pretty much all of the more spiritual form, if I am discerning correctly as per Watchman Nee's teachings. *But surely this can't be right, that this is actually the Holy Spirit?* I can accept higher Self and holistic guidance, but to think that this is the Holy Spirit of the Bible is a bit hard to accept, and I can sense that I am quite sceptical and doubtful. I notice the undeserving, self-diminishing part of me play it down and say, *It's just a higher wisdom superego type voice that is guiding me in the right direction.* But what if that is pretty much the same thing, and this is simply us once again being in separation from it due to being in our own self-righteous psycho-logical language?

The love that I can re-harmonise with through the soulical or spiritual dimensions is the same love. Whether I am sensing my connection through the spiritual awe and wonder or the natural earthly awe and wonder I am still in love with two different aspects of my God.

Love your God with all your heart soul and mind being Jesus' first commandment. I have the capacity to touch and experience it directly, yet I can also connect to it in the other and with the other and see or sense it in and through the other, like perceiving their divinity and purity regardless of who they are or without even knowing them at all. It's a bit like that looking at the newborn baby, when they have no character or personality or culture yet; no blemishes or hair style or clothing preference, and are just pure and fresh, untainted by life and the need to take form to survive and manage the world. It is like being the pure spirit and the pure soul that hasn't had to fall in the garden yet, that hasn't fallen into adaptation and survival mode yet, choosing the TOK so as to manage the world. Jesus' second commandment being, love your neighbour as your self.

So once again, I come back to seeing us at spirit and soul levels as pure and good, and see that the latent powers within the soul seem to be there as a reserve or emergency system to facilitate our survival, if the environment that we are born into is not as pure as we are at birth and essentially always will be. Watchman Nee may then be seen as guiding us to awaken to aligning with the purer ways of the spirit rather than utilise the lower powers of the soul, because we only have to do that when we are disconnected from source.

Synthesising it all with Heart Intelligence

This now brings me to how this all synthesises with Heart Intelligence. For me, Heart Intelligence is very much about the body and utilising our spiritual embodiment. Feeling into our embodiment so as to spiritually discern what is right and true in contrast to what defiles us, (to use a Watchman Nee term) allowing our self to be led by the amening and defilement. So Heart Intelligence like Psychosynthesis sits in the middle ground, purging the soul upwards from functioning in the psychologically conditioned self; the level that is functioning in its coping mechanisms due to disconnect.

Yes, but are we glorifying our self or Him? asks that familiar voice within. *Do you take the time to recognise that the glory and credit of discerning the truth belongs to something other than yourselves?* My answer being that we certainly don't do it to the extent that we should, and that would serve us and the coming kingdom better.

Perhaps I am only now seeing that we are working with both the soulical and spiritual powers in practicing Heart Intelligence and that by learning to discern and utilise the combination of them serves to move us from where we formerly were: unconscious, psycho-logically functioning, and disconnected, to conscious, psycho-spiritually functioning, and connected. I said in an earlier chapter that I see we can connect to spirit from where we are, or we can fall due to disconnect or not getting it, and come around to it in the longer direction. I am reminded again that *Christianity is about faith over feeling.* Do we stand for our self or Him? What is the spirit of our action? We are usually controlled by how we feel in our environment, but when we are led by the Holy Spirit acting through our spirit and give up the self, then the Holy Spirit facilitates our environment differently. *Passivity of will is not Christian* is offered to me now, and I think I am being invited to take this to mean that we need to keep ourselves spirit conscious through the application of our will, rather than allow passivity of will to cause us to be unconscious and abiding in our lower self. This reminds me of how much Roberto Assagioli and Psychosynthesis is about the will.

So Did Constantine and the Bishops Get It Right at the Treaty of Nicaea in 325?

I still think that they probably didn't. I think they should have included and transcended, rather than excluded. Excluding doesn't feel loving and understanding, compassionate, or Christian. This may then have allowed the disbelievers, the resistant, and the unawakened to progressively come to the realisations that I have done in writing this book. And then aspire to align with the higher spiritual guidance once they could see its value for themselves; but without making the lower guidance wrong. Perhaps they could have seen that some people are functioning at a level that is served by one type of holistic guidance and some people are functioning at a level that is ready for another.

Seeing the Psychosynthesis

This is beginning to feel more summarising and psychosynthetic, seeing it all as guiding and holistic and simply having been misunderstood and not seen for its true function, purpose, and service. So if I then go back to Nicaea, I can see that both Celtic and Roman Christianity, as well as paganism could have been accepted as holistic and guiding, serving different levels of development and functioning. This is similar to how we accept and work with the lower and higher unconscious in Psychosynthesis. Perhaps it's a bit like synthesising the work of Sigmund Freud, Carl Jung, Abraham Maslow, and Roberto Assagioli with Christianity and paganism, understanding that different levels of development function and interact with holistic guidance in different forms and in different ways. I now see the understanding of Watchman Nee and the teachings of Jesus being at the most developed level and Psychosynthesis and Heart Intelligence being the bridge between where we are, and where we are moving to next. The present-day church can then be seen to be where Christianity is at in its own organic religious journey. This being the same psychospiritual journey of awakening unto itself that we and anything else organic goes through. Journeying from its own pure start into becoming psycho-logically functioning and then awakening through its own religious self-realisation process back towards full self-realisation and functioning psycho-spiritually.

So Where Am I at the End of Twelve Weeks of Writing?

Exhausted, is the first answer that gets voiced in my mind.

I am mostly a bit more at ease about it; I don't feel as disturbed as I was or as desperate to find what I may not be seeing, searching for something to integrate all of these teachings, trainings, and realisations. I simply feel a bit more at ease about it all, seeing that for the moment, my new perception seems to re-stabilise me, and that what is required now, is to offer this new insight into the space of the existing misperception, just as this book is doing. It feels like I have moved from being in my disturbed TOK about it all, searching for a way to resolve it, to being in my body with it, holding it, carrying it, accepting it, embodying the reality that this seems to be the situation. But now I have to be careful of wanting to tell everybody that they are doing it wrong because of what I have seen. I need to help them to see it for themselves. I suppose it's the difference between causing people to rise up in resistance when they are told they are doing something wrong, to being able to persuade people when they see something for themselves and consider it in their own way and in their own time. *Perhaps this is what was trying to happen at Nicaea and Whitby*, teases that loving voice. As I wrote the above, I could see how over the recent years I have been telling others out of my own psychological self's need to feel safer and more secure by having others agree with what I see, whereas now I feel that I need that a bit less as I am more invested elsewhere.

The Potential that Comes out of Consciousness

I think the book offers us a chance to see what has formerly been an unconscious incompetence on all of our parts. In other words, we have been living the only way that we have been able to see, and through writing this book, we are now in conscious incompetence. So we can now see our incompetence. The third move is then to conscious competence, where we begin to get it right but with a struggle and lots of effort, and with time, hopefully we can get to unconscious competence, where it becomes like jumping in the car and driving to work; we don't even think about it. This model that I describe was developed in the 1970s by Noel Burch and helps us to see an incompetence that we are unconscious of, taking us gradually to such competence that we can become unconscious and not have to work at it.

Accepting Our Place in Life

One of the things that I think I have learned from writing this book is that it doesn't matter what we call God, or what we think about it, or what it is, or how we analyse it, whether we see it as energy or accident or personified, or even if we believe in such a thing or not. And it doesn't really matter what religion we are or if we are atheist or whatever else. We are all getting it equally wrong when we get caught up in a belief and treat others nastily for being of a different belief. It is not about who is right and who is wrong about the source and meaning of life; the only thing that really matters is how we get life to work best for all of us and bring us all back to being in the abundant joy of life.

In looking at Genesis the other day, I noticed that God actually says, at the centre of the garden there are two trees. I had not realised that it said *centre* before, because this emphasises the importance of this TOK and TOL thing even more, because we are being told that this is central to everything else. We can't put God or source or creation into the box that works for us, just so we can feel safe, and that is why we can't get it to work; we keep wanting to overlord it. Those who believe or operate from faith get it to work because they are not trying to be above it. They are not trying to get it all sorted out nice and neat so that they can cope. If we stay out of the TOK, it works. We are not meant to be able to transcend it. All we have to do is stay in the TOL, and it will allow us to see it as we are able and ready. Of course, we need to be in the TOK to deal with life, but that is from us downwards, not upwards. It is a bit like wanting to know all your employer's business, instead of just doing your job. You need to know your bit, and they deal with their bit. I heard a saying a while back that was attributed to Mother Teresa. Someone asked her about this and that, and she answered what was hers to answer and said that the rest of it was none of her business, it was God's business.

From Psychosynthesis, I can see that in the early part of our life, we operate as a chaotic assemblance of individual parts, all jumping to the fore, dependant on the present moment situation. And that gradually these subparts come under the control of the central self-conscious awareness that eventually takes control: what we mean when we say 'I' this or 'I' that. This I or self is that central self-aware consciousness, and Psychosynthesis also sees that that I or self is in fact also a subpart of something greater, as well as being an imminent embodied awakening version and expression of its own greater form, as we can come to realise and surrender to.

As I was writing the earlier part of this chapter and subconsciously asking my holistic guidance to help me to get it to come together. I had a sense of where I was meant to be going with it all, but something essential was missing to make the point and pull it all together. A moment or so later, I received a message that I am familiar with, but this time it was quite amusing. The voice said, *Nothing unites better than a common enemy;* that common enemy being ignorance of the fact that we are all operating from the TOK. We are all getting it wrong, and perhaps that is what needs to be seen to cause us to unite because we all suffer as a consequence. It is not that these people are right, or those people are wrong; we are all getting it wrong. The common enemy is our own self-righteousness, ignorance, and tendency to eat from the tree of knowledge.

This entire book is psychosynthesis happening right here; clashing mindsets, understandings or beliefs causing disturbance and breakdown, before being synthesised or transcended to bring a new reformation. Suddenly for me, they all lose their individual power and the energy of their argument, as they, like parts in a nuclear fusion process, get fused together into something greater than themselves and now seek to function at this level and find a new way forward again. This time, however, they are all together in the same common vision and understanding; they are re-energised with the release of a new fresh impetus and energy.

Can you feel the effect of that within you, the disempowerment and deflation in realising that we have all been getting it wrong? But for me there is also humility and hope as I see we are all in the same boat getting it wrong and how that releases potential and hope for the future, now that I can see it and see that we have a common ground to move forward from.

I think it is clear to see here that the solution and revelation came from my following the guidance that urged me to move from trying to do it all myself in the TOK, to seeking the holistic guidance of the Holy Spirit. And the thing that I always find so beautiful in these moments is the grace with which it moves. As I said earlier, science looks for evidence and a repeatable outcome, so what is this, if it is not that? If we are genuinely seeking a more heavenly kingdom on earth and genuinely accepting that there is a holistic guidance, then when we seek, we shall find, and we shall receive our daily bread.

If I now go back to Psychosynthesis, these parts are simply not seeing where they are actually subparts of a greater singular thing. Watchman Nee gives us a deeper insight into the true spirit and understanding of Christianity and shows us how to live a spirit-led life in relationship with the Holy Spirit. Roman Christianity holds fast to the value of scripture and story and glorifies the transcendent Jesus as it continually offers us His teachings. Celtic Christianity reawakens us to the awe and wonder and abundance of life in the name of God or source, resurrecting the feminine and nature-al back to where it belongs. Add to all of this how Psychosynthesis shows us the psychospiritual dynamics of how life works and what religion in our life really is, and we finally have a chance to be heart intelligent with each other. We don't even have to try to love God or love our neighbour; we automatically have understanding and compassion for each other's struggles and common journey. This is the building of the church and the coming of His kingdom, and all we need to do is check that we act out of love and the TOL, as best we can, regardless of what our TOK is telling us inside our head.

Our Society Going Forward from Here

I suppose the first thing that I would say in summary for society going forward from here is that it is already changing very slowly. The church isn't as condemning as it used to be, and the atmosphere is becoming more friendly and relaxed, something that is necessary for growth and awakening to happen. But I would say that we really do need to get beyond trying to psychoanalyse the Bible or teach the messages within it through metaphors, and we need to get ministers to stop droning on in dead letter and TOK. We need to start walking the walk a bit more, rather than keep talking the talk. And we can do this by helping each other to better understand and align with Jesus' teachings and come together to see how we are doing. Actually spend time together in groups seeing how we are doing, rather than sit in house groups discussing chapter and verse; in other words, moving from TOK to TOL. We need to stop talking about it all and be trying to get it with our head, and actually start doing something. To be Christian is to endure and surrender to something greater, not to esteem the self into a sense of its own greatness; but then being self-serving is our only way back if nothing in our environment is teaching us this other way. It is really just our need to feel like God in our absence of God, and feel self-secure. Unless we are enduring our cross for others and the coming of a greater kingdom, we are not yet being Christian, but we are always on a progressive path, one direction or the other, towards realising that we serve our soul best by living the Christian way.

I also think that we need to start seeing our love for fun, play, dance, walking the dog, singing, sport, meaningful conversation, nature, even work, when we are alive and present to the joy of doing something meaningful, as spiritual. Because that is what it is: It is spiritual and religious, and it is God's great creation, and we are loving it in these moments without seeing it as love your God and love your neighbour. This is how near the kingdom of heaven actually is; it is literally in our hands if we just choose to see it. This is something that I see happening every day unconsciously, but it has so much more to give us when we see it for what it is and take in all that it wants to give us. I also see many special moments of people simply being the way and the truth and the life, when they are actually just being their plain simple truth, untainted by agenda or need or want, and it is simply beautiful and replenishing to enjoy and see for what it is. It is also there when people feel alive and are in their vitality, appreciating the awe and wonder of all that we are and have, and taking the moment to be truly thankful with all their heart. Surely that is abiding in God or source when we are awake and present and enjoying it. Surely that is what is meant in the Lord's prayer by 'give us this day our daily bread,' the replenishment and food that we are really seeking, instead of becoming obese by trying to mistakenly fill that void or re-find that stimulation with all the unhealthy food that we eat to compensate for being in disconnect. No wonder there is increasing physical, emotional and mental health issues.

That connection to source is also there to be seen when we come together at Christmas and celebrate in joy and abundance feeling the spirit of Christmas. Yes, there are failings here as we become increasingly materialistic, but some of this joy is also there as we are abiding in Him, for this is the TOL. In these moments, we are not caught up in who is right or wrong; we are simply in the living waters. It is the same with people enjoying walking or running in the park or embracing the outdoors in some way, appreciating great buildings and wondrous achievements that come from our creativity. This is Celtic Christianity, and it is about being connected to source, where we replenish ourselves, rather than remain disconnected. The only thing absent in these moments is that we don't see them for what they are. We don't see them as religious and spiritual, even though they are some of our most healing and spiritual moments. We need to be conscious and see it for what it is: the joy of life as created and sustained by what some call God. To see love, truth, and beauty in these moments as sacred and as source enjoying its self. Our essential nature is good, not bad and sinful; it is when we get caught up in the TOK about right and wrong and argue about this or that, that we do wrong and harm to each other and compress each other into ways that are then damaging and destructive and lead to disease.

So we are getting there by being our truth and following our joy, but we could be amplifying it by seeing it for what it is, in a better understanding of religion and spirituality than we presently have and by making an effort to show it to those who don't see it yet. When we fell in the Garden of Eden, it didn't go anywhere; it is still here. We just haven't picked ourselves up yet, and this is what I want to help us all see.

Does This New Learning Change How I Coach?

With the hindsight of writing this book, does it change the way I will interact or coach or guide anyone, now that I have a more integrated sense of how all of these parts come together? I worked one way after my Psychosynthesis training and then slightly differently after my Heart Intelligence training, and this feels like realising that they were both progressive and developmental, as well as temporary and transitional. And this feels like a metaphor for what humanity should have been doing all along: attaining growth from including and transcending rather than by excluding and oppressing. Psychosynthesis at the time that I was lost was perhaps mostly helping me through will and mind and intuition, with some love and sensory interaction. Heart Intelligence then took me more into embodiment and feeling for our truth through it. But now this third way of working is more a synthesis of both with extra added to the mix. This new way of working seems to ask me not to use my faculties and what I have learned, having learned them simply so as to be able to note their presence being active in me, so that I can then see it and step out of them. It's a bit like learning more of what is, so as to be able to avoid it. It's a bit like having no emotional driver unconsciously active behind my actions and no mental opinion informing me of how best to interact with the other. It just feels clean and pure in spirit, with the only alive connection being love and intention of goodness, abiding in the will to good whilst feeling and understanding the other, but abiding in Him rather do x, y, or z from any teaching. It's being able to feel the defilement in the soul of the other as their spirit, mind, and emotion touch mine but remaining undefiled in the soul and spirit of myself and my response. It's almost absorbing and washing the energy of what comes from them as it passes through me and is returned from a cleaner energy or spirit that can remain detached whilst still feeling the other.

Amusing as this sounds, it feels a bit like being an air filter or purifier for people's souls. Taking in their despair, struggle, disconnect, hurt, longing, hate, resentment, angst, or bitterness as contaminated energy and responding back from love by allowing myself to feel it but not be affected by it. Not because I am in fear or want to spare them from suffering or because I am clever and have the solution. But because I understand their journey and purpose for being and can hold fast to my higher purpose and vision and abide in that, knowing that I don't actually need to do anything other than feel them and love them just as they are. So this is not to avoid emotions or thoughts but to help the other purge themselves, as is trying to happen by these things coming forth from them.

As I got up to take a break, I heard that familiar voice say, *Be the light of the world, just as the children are,* and I could feel my heart knot up in recognition of the gift that they purely are. Then, as I came back to write it down, I heard *Love them to bits,* as was always the offering from Roger, my Coaching Psychosynthesis trainer. The difference that these messages make at this moment is that I realise that by abiding in them, I am not unidentified or untethered and therefore available to be caught by something else.

The answer to, will this change the way that I coach, is that I am not sure, because it always depends on the client and where they are and what way of working they are available to. But given that they now all feel holistic and guiding, then there doesn't seem to be such a concern for me, I can just love them more easily from all this revelation.

Taking Ownership and Responsibility for Our Self and What We Stand For

So here I am, 23 December, seeking to write a final closing statement about all this and suddenly with a publisher waiting to receive something from me. How did all that happen, and what was the point? And where am I at the end of it all?

Perhaps the suppressed teacher in me could be suppressed no longer. When I ran my joiner and builder business for twenty-one years, I always found teachers difficult to work for and have always had a resistance to them. In fact, the only person I took to court in those twenty-one years was a teacher. I remember being in the second year of my psychosynthesis training when this thing about teachers came to light, and I worked some of it through. But then I realised that it was still there, as I covertly taught others in Heart Intelligence circles, always teaching rather than doing what I was being asked to do. Always seeking to lead and be the teacher, never comfortable being the pupil. Even when I look back at my career, I always progressed to a leadership position. In my last place of employment prior to starting my own business, my boss committed suicide, and there I was once again, asked to run the show. But then as I look back, I have always covertly taught without owning it. Whether it was carpentry, motorbike riding, gymnastics, trampolining, or whatever else, there has always seemed to be a teacher screaming to get out and be owned. But in resistance to that teacher and keeping it suppressed was the mindset of being a smarty-pants and being too big for my boots, being arrogant and too full of my own cleverness, and the price I have paid in childhood for being good at things. I was bullied and rejected because I was good at sports and metalwork and woodwork and could turn my hand to almost anything and do okay. But then perhaps there is also the fear of responsibility that comes with taking ownership for standing up and being seen for what I stand for and being held accountable for it. The opposition and challenge from others of a different view make me want to just keep quiet and keep my head down, keeping my learning, knowledge, and wisdom to myself and staying safe. In circle, we occasionally work with our shadows and our gifts. Our shadows are the ways that we don't want to be seen to show up in the world, and they can always be seen by looking for the opposite of the way that we do show up in the world, such as arrogant, obnoxious, childish, fake, nasty, anything that we judge to be negative. But our gifts are often hidden within our shadows when we turn down the volume and have the courage to own them. So perhaps that is what I am being squeezed to do by the infinite intelligence, as Deepak Chopra sometimes calls it. No longer able to avoid the inevitable, the truth will always out, and in the process set you free.

Affirmation

Once again, I can see the breakdown, breakthrough, and reformation with regards to where I was at in myself when the book started happening, in contrast to the reformation of where I am now. I am also in an easier place with it all now that I can see all the different perspectives mixed up in the one soup bowl. I can see that there is a very diverse and complex holistic guidance pervading everything and that all perceptions of reality serve the level of development that perceives them in that way, as it all seeks to move us forward without rejecting former levels as we advance. I can see how we tend to accept one thing and reject the other when we are in the TOK, always discerning what is right and wrong, compared to enjoying the awe and wonder of life when we are connected to source and present to experiencing life, including and transcending in the way that natural growth works, rather than excluding and exiling and oppressing. I can see how it is our insecurity that causes us to do this due to disconnect, which in turn is due to the wanting to know, so that we can feel safe. In other words, it is back to having faith in what created and sustains us, rather than seeking security from knowing. Having learned from writing this book that there is holistic guidance at play, operating in a multitude of ways at all levels of perception and development, I can feel myself relax a bit more, knowing that it has got my back.

I am not suggesting I have figured it all out or I won't continue to spend most of my time in the TOK, but rather I now have an even greater solidity of understanding that it is all the one thing moving in the one direction from different comprehensions and levels of development, rather than a battle between good and evil. As for the main issue of Watchman Nee and the present functioning of the church, the disturbance that caused me to write the book: that just seems to have settled within me as the reality of how it is and what needs to be brought to light. I don't see lower levels as sin or wrong and never have; maybe that has been the essential rock at the core of me that causes me to synthesise in the way I have.

Whatever disturbance or behaviour is happening is always about growth and development and our seeking to experience being in a better feeling place, the problem being that our lower levels of development and perception cause less constructive behaviours, and we often regress to feel better, rather than work to feel better. It sometimes feels like the soul wicking its way spiritually forward, like the hard wax of a candle groping its way to the light through the flame.

In development work, there always comes a point where the session is about affirmation, as clients look back at their journey and can see where they have travelled. This helps us to see and solidify the new ground in reference to the old and helps us to own who we are now and how we perceive the world. Quite often, what comes out of our own mouths is meant for our own ears (or in this case, my words are probably for my own eyes).

Closing Offering

So as has been the case for most of the book, my final offering comes when I come out of my TOK, searching for what to write next, and empty my mind whilst waiting on the kettle to boil; simply looking out of the window in connection to God's great kingdom via the TOL in all its vitality, beauty and awe.

I think the main revelation that helps me with my current dilemma is that as Watchman Nee says, some of our guidance is soulical and some of it is spiritual. But then this progressed towards allowing me to see that it was still, all an act of love, and all holistically guided in seeking to direct us in one direction rather than be a battle between good and evil. It also allowed me to see how throughout the book, I have been following both sets of guidance without realising it, stopping when my embodied self felt defiled and then receiving the revelation that could then get through.

I would say that the second most important revelation is that we are all getting religion wrong. This is such a unifying revelation, to suddenly be able to see that we are all in the TOK when we are arguing about which religion or belief system is correct; this is so disempowering of our self-righteousness that we all end up knocked back to a common starting point, a starting point where we are all on a level playing field, seeking to move forward with the same common realisation, vision, and purpose. I think these two revelations have helped me integrate and understand so much; they offer us the way out of humanity's current situation. I think it is fascinating how I only managed to fully differentiate the two different types of guidance at the end, after questioning if they were the one thing most of the way through the book.

I think these two revelations, along with their self-evidencing within the book, are enough to convince me they are real and alive and active in our lives, seeking to show us the way, just as the Bible says. All we need to do, along with believing in them, is get present in the way we do in Heart Intelligence, and work with them so we can properly discern their offering within the chaos of other active voices within us. And I think we need to do it in group to get it to work best.

So my advice for us all is to realise this holistic guidance that is active in our lives; call it what you will, and realise that it is the active energy of our source. And then seek to follow its guidance by gaining a fuller psychospiritual understanding of life and by coming together with others in the Heart Intelligence circles that are now happening all over the world. In this way, we are all realigning with one vision, purpose, and holistic guidance and then collectively progressing from our self-esteeming level of development to self-transcendence, where we can put our self second in service of something greater than our self. The wondrous and ever abundant Source that Celtic Christians see essentially pervading everything. I also think that one of the things that can help us discern the voice of that holistic guidance is the teachings of Jesus, whether you are Christian or otherwise or 'religious' or not, and even if such a person never even existed; these scriptural teachings from Christianity are what we need to follow. Then ultimately we will be living more out of the guidance of spirit as understood by Watchman Nee; rather than out of the lower levels of individual survival instinct as a last resort to maintain self-survival, rather than live in His kingdom in self- fulfilment.

After completing the book today, 29 December, I have been fiddling with titles, as I have done all the way through the book, watching them organically evolve in keeping with the spirit of where I am identified. Then one final time, I paused and stopped trying, and the title came to me, instead of me trying to go get it. This is the grace of the spirit that guides us, if we can just let it. The words that came were *A Christian Heart: The Wisdom that Guides Humanity.* This for me combines the mature guiding masculine energy of Jesus, with the soft and loving ever abundant energies of the feminine and acts as a summary statement to hold me where I want to function. But whether or not I go on to use this title will also depend on how it sits within my embodiment, because one of the things that I have relearned in writing the book, is that I need to be careful of listening to my head too much. Sometimes I can discern its guidance wisely and sometimes not; but ultimately it is my embodied spirits contentment that discerns what sits at rest within me, and allows me to be at peace. Perhaps the Holy Spirit is our embodied spirit of knowing and truth, and guides us through our embodiment rather than through our minds and the voices that we hear. Nevertheless, I can already sense that the rest won't last long, as a part of me has already started pondering; how would a second book go about demonstrating what living from a Christian heart may look like?

Call to Action

If you only do one thing after reading this book, then I suggest you access Heart Intelligence and Psychosynthesis online and get involved. Neither of them promote any religion in the normal sense of the word or get into any religious conversation, as I do here. I would now say that Heart Intelligence is about learning to access and follow the truth of your heart's deeper embodied wisdom and guidance, with some connection to your higher guidance. On the other hand, although psychosynthesis is more of an academic training for psychotherapists, counsellors, and coaches, it will help you learn and understand how we work and are affected by the higher and lower energies in our lives. You will learn to see that whatever disturbs you in daily life, it is about your higher Self serving your souls spiritual awakening journey through life; Psychosynthesis facilitating that journey just as well as Heart Intelligence does.

For those who are more religiously inclined or those who are anti Christian, I would suggest adding Watchman Nee to the list because his work will give you the pure understanding of what Christianity is. But I honestly believe that you will take more from Watchman Nee by having some insight into these other two first.

In the Psychosynthesis chapter, I explained how we gradually grow, develop, and awaken to consciously function at the self or I level of self-conscious awareness. This is the level where we begin to manage our lower parts with their individual agendas. Hopefully the time has come for us to collectively realise there is a higher Self level, and that at the self or 'I' level we need to surrender to it, in realisation that we are similarly sub self's of that even greater Self. The problem we have had so far with trying to live by the guidance of the infinite intelligence, is that it is very difficult, and that much of it has been misinterpreted and corrupted by individuals functioning at a lower level than required, who have then controlled the rest without seeing the error of their ways. *Let's hope I am not doing the same here,* flashes through my mind.

I am also amused as always by the psychosynthesis that is evident right here in the development of this book. This comes from the fact that I didn't just integrate several conflicting perspectives of life on their current level of perception, so that they don't conflict with each other any more. But that I have been guided to find the new transcended level above them all, that comes from synthesising them. In other words the book is not just an amalgamation of all we have looked at. The new integrated perception transcends them in what it offers us as an understanding of what is going on, how it went astray and how to get back.

Final statement

In conclusion of all that is in this book, and all of the teachings and ways of being in the world; I think that the teachings of Jesus show us the way to live and the way to life. If we can interpret His teachings correctly and abide in Him, (irrespective of what we believe or don't believe about the Jesus story), spiritually discerning truth and right action through the defilement or amening of the spirit within our embodiment. Then we will be living within the guidance of the Holy Spirit and the other holistic guidance's that exist to serve us. In this way we can act from being present to our own embodied spiritual discernment, understanding that even when life is difficult, it is the Holy Spirit that is bringing us what we need to awaked further out of our childhood conditioned way of being. This way of living then inviting us to stay present and conscious within our embodiment, to the awe and wonder of all of life, trusting that the Holy Spirit brings us what we need to stay fresh, replenished and vitalised.

So more simply put with regards to where we place our attention. I think my final conclusion and book synthesis, is that we stay present to our embodied soul and enjoy all of what life is when we follow the amening or defilement within our embodied spirit. Allowing this truth to guide us in our relationship to ourselves and others, by apply the teachings of Jesus as best we can; but always being gentle with ourselves and others in acceptance of our humble limitations. Because surely this is living in the awe and wonder of all of what life and God is, as it gracefully guides us using a variety of holistic guidance's relative to our respective cultures and our respective levels of developmentally, at any given time.

As is often the case at the end of a chapter, my spirit lifts me to a simpler way of experiencing and expressing what I am trying to say; in this case through the following Hymns.

How Great Thou Art, by Carl Boberg

Then sings my soul, My Saviour God, to Thee.
How great Thou art, How great Thou art.
Then sings my soul, My Saviour God, to Thee.
How great Thou art, How great Thou art!

When Christ shall come, with shout of acclamation.
And take me home, what joy shall fill my heart.
Then I shall bow, in humble adoration.
And then proclaim: "My God, how great Thou art!"

And also with; "Here I am Lord" by James Kilbane.

I, the Lord of sea and sky, I have heard My people cry.
All who dwell in dark and sin, My hand will save.
I who made the stars of night, I will make their darkness bright.
Who will bear My light to them?
Whom shall I send?

Here I am Lord, Is it I, Lord?
I have heard You calling in the night.
I will go Lord, if You lead me.
I will hold Your people in my heart.

Epilogue

When we abide in what connects us to love.
The will of love then guide us.

It is now the end of April and several months have passed since I finished writing in December. Since then life has returned to the usual duties and tending to things around the house, as well as doing some life coaching. But I am also enjoying springtime and being present to the re-emergence of life; when I remember to get out of my head and reconnect to it that is, or when I don't get caught up in all my self-righteous frustration when life doesn't go the way I want. I did however, initially find my self trying to re-find that wonderful connected place that I was in when I wrote most of the book, so that I could continue writing from where I left of last year. But then, just as always; that vital connection was waiting for me when I stopped trying and took a break. When I came out of preoccupation and became present again; that was when I came back to life, plugging my self back into the living existence that is omnipresent and omniscient, and that Jesus was teaching us about. This is the way and the truth and the life that He invites us to live, and that He points us to and tells us that we can have, by abiding in Him and His wisdom. This is what pervaded Him; divine loving wisdom that is all around us in all of creation and in all the forms of guidance that I have discussed in this book. Our Garden of Eden world that is ever abundantly providing and replenishing, in a vast array of

211

form and a multitude of guidance's; with Jesus at the top, teaching us how to see it all, as well as literally teaching us how to live together. This is living in the knowledge and embrace of the divine love and wisdom that nurtures and guides us and is the union of both Celtic and Roman Christianity. This in my opinion is what was lost at Nicaea and Whitby in favour of Roman Christianity only. Add to this the further loss of leaders that can abide in Christ consciousness, psycho-spiritually functioning from His divine love and wisdom, and we can see why we are in the state that we are in today. Psycho-logically trying to do it on our own with our souls caught up in our minds.

Prior to going to print, I have received the book back for one final check, and in doing this I have realised that the only thing that feels a little unfinished. Is the way that I now see Jesus; the one who physically walked amongst us, and is spiritually still alive and living through us when we follow His guidance, in addition to embracing all of that around us. But as I sit here I realise that it's not the conscious me in my head that moves towards answering this question. It's not the me that wrote the last sentence, but the love that has arisen within me, the love that I most essentially am when life feels safe enough for me to be it. It is that which moves towards offering an answer as I witness this experience and feel the grace of its presence within me, and know that in this moment, I am blessed to be love seeing its self as love in everything else. But I can also feel it when I gaze and connect to the life in other things as well; not just looking in the usual mentally busy way, but gazing as we do at children, or nature, or the mountains, or birds, or the sky, or stars; safe in their sacred presence just long enough to unconsciously slip into awe and wonder for a second or two. *How can we not see it?* I notice that longing voice within me ask. *Because we don't abide in Him* comes that loving parental voice with its answer. *That is where life is, and nobody comes to the father but by Him.* But as I also sit with that the revelation unfolds, that this abiding, is abiding in what I have just described, because this was what He abided in. Abiding in Him is a means to abiding in the loving guiding omniscience of God, and the kingdom of heaven that is everything within and around us. Jesus was abiding in the loving creative wisdom and guiding energy of God, rather than be preoccupied with earthly affairs, as we are, in our disconnect. In the book of John He tells us. 'I have told you these things, so that in me you may have peace. In this world you will have trouble. But take heart! I have overcome the world.' It is the wise and loving way that Jesus lived, that we should follow, and worship and abide in, rather than get caught up in what is right or wrong about the Jesus story. He is the way and the truth and the life that guides us when we consciously abide in Him. But we are not always able to do that, because our neurological defence system switches us to survival mode; and because we don't believe, and have not experienced, and don't understand, and are too busy, and value other things, and are unconscious, and get preoccupied with other things, and meet our needs in other ways, and on and on it goes. But we do unknowingly do it without realising, when we enjoy life in all the healthy revitalising ways that we do, or fall back into love in all the ways and moments that we do. But we can also have the kingdom and find that higher purpose and meaning as well as spiritual belonging and comfort by abiding in Him, and by following His teachings of how we should live with one another.

Reading List

Below is a reading list of some of the books that
have influenced me over the past twelve years.

Basic Elements of the Christian Life, Volumes 1, 2, 3. Watchman Nee and Witness Lee. Living Stream Ministry.

The Latent Power of the Soul. Watchman Nee. Christian Fellowship Publishers, Inc. New York.

The Communion of the Holy Spirit. Watchman Nee Christian Fellowship Publishers, Inc. New York.

How to Study the Bible. Watchman Nee. Living Stream Ministry.

Spiritual Discernment. Watchman Nee and Witness Lee. Living Stream Ministry.

Release of the Spirit: The Breaking of the Outward Man. Watchman Nee. New Wine Press.

The Maturational Processes and the Facilitating Environment. D. W. Winnicott.

How to Be Used by God. Philip Rich. Ekklisia Prophetic Apostolic Ministries, Inc.

King, warrior, Magician, Lover. Robert Moore and Douglas Gillette. Harper Collins Publishers.

Listening for the Heartbeat of God. A Celtic Spirituality. J. Philip Newell. S.P.C.K.

Christ of the Celts. The Healing of Creation. J. Philip Newell. Wild Goose Publications.

The Divine Comedy. Dante Alighieri. Oxford University Press.

The Twenty-Nine Pages. A. E. Affifi. Beshara Publications.

The Power of Kabbalah. Technology for the Soul. Yehuda Berg. Kabbalah Publishing.

The Drama of Being a Child. The Search for the True Self. Alice Miller. Virago Press.

The Holy Quran. Abdullah Yusuf Ali. Wordsworth Editions Limited.

Psychosynthesis in Education. A Guide to the Joy of Learning. Diana Whitmore. Turnstone Press Limited.

What We May Be. Techniques for Psychological and Spiritual Growth through Psychosynthesis. Piero Feruchi. Tarcher Penguin.

The Integral Vision. Ken Wilber. Shambhala Publications Inc.

Discover Your Subpersonalities. Our Inner World and the People in It. John Rowan. Routledge.

The Geeta. The Gospel of the Lord Shri Krishna Put into English, by Shri Purohit Swami. Faber and Faber Ltd.

Zen Buddhism and Psychoanalysis. Eric Fromm, D. T. Suzuki, Richard De Martino. Souvenir Press Ltd.

The Door Is Open. The 7 Steps of Spiritual Awakening that Western Scripture and Mythology Have Been Trying to Tell Us All Along. Andrew Cort. Geo. Canon Books.

How to Know God. The Soul's Journey into the Mystery of Mysteries. Deepak Chopra. Rider Books.

The Act of Will. A Guide to Self-Actualisation and Self-Realisation. Roberto Assagioli, M.D. The Psychosynthesis and Education Trust. David Platts Publishing Company.

Feel the Fear and Do It Anyway. Dynamic Techniques for Turning Fear and Indecision into Confidence and Action. Susan Jeffers. Century Hutchinson Ltd.

Eyes Wide Open. Cultivating Discernment on the Spiritual Path. Mariana Caplan, Ph.D. Sounds True Inc.

The Primal Wound. A Transpersonal View of Trauma, Addiction, and Growth. John Forman and Ann Gila. State University of New York Press.

The Power of Now. A Guide to Spiritual Enlightenment. Eckhart Tolle. Hodder and Stoughton Ltd.

A New Earth. Create a Better Life. Eckhart Tolle. Penguin Books.

Synchro Destiny. Harnessing the Finite Powers of Coincidence to Create Miracles. Deepak Chopra. Rider Books.

Psychosynthesis. A Manual of Principles and Techniques. Roberto Assagioli, M.D. Mandala, Harper Collins.

Transpersonal Development. The Dimension Beyond Psychosynthesis. Roberto Assagioli, M.D. Smiling Wisdom, Inner Way Productions.

Working More Creatively with Groups. Jarlath F. Benson. Routledge, Taylor and Francis Group.

Ask and It Is Given. Learning to Manifest Your Desires. Esther and Jerry Hicks. Hay House.

Conversations with God. Neale Donald Walsch.

Understanding the I Ching. The Wilhelm Lectures on the Book of Changes. Hellmut Wilhelm, Richard Wilhelm. Princeton University Press.

The Essential Ken Wilber. An Introductory Reader. Shambhala Publications Inc.

Teach Yourself Jung. Ruth Snowden. Teach Yourself, Hodder Headline.

The Kernel of the Kernel. By Muhyiddin Ibn Arabi. Ismail Hakki Bursevi's Translation. Beshara Publications.

The Search for the Beloved. Journeys in Mythology and Sacred Psychology. Jean Houston, PhD. Tarcher Penguin.

Courses and Trainings List

Below are listed some of the courses and trainings that I have done over the years, all of which have influenced me, and had some influence on this book.

Nine Day Intensive Esoteric Retreat. Beshara. 2005

Diploma in Psychosynthesis Life Coaching. Institute of Psychosynthesis. Hendon, London. 2005 to 2010.

Quantum Jumping online course. Burt Goldman. 2010.

The Astonishing Power of Emotions. CD set. Esther and Jerry Hicks. The Teachings of Abraham. 2009.

Theta Healing Basic DNA. Certification Course. Jennifer Main. Edinburgh. Theta Healing Institute of Knowledge.

Heart Intelligence Practitioner. 1 to 1 and small groups. C P Network Ltd. 2013.

Reiki Practitioner levels 1 and 2. Local college evening classes. 2005.

Love or Above online course. Christie Marie Sheldon. Mindvalley. 2012.

Alpha Course. Local church. 2011.

Weaving Worship Certificate. Church of Scotland. 2016.

Lightning Source UK Ltd.
Milton Keynes UK
UKOW01n0739240817
307824UK00002B/40/P